More Advance Praise for
Castle of Concrete

"Through vivid description and crisp dialogue, Katia Raina portrays a crumbling Soviet Union and a people uncertain of what comes next. Readers won't easily forget spunky Sonya Solovay, struggling to understand her Jewish roots amid rising anti-Semitism, her activist mother's secrets, and her attraction to two boys, each of them dangerous in his own way."
—Lyn Miller-Lachmann, author of *Gringolandia*

"A tour de force about the Russian people and their first, tentative steps toward what had been denied for generations—a private life in all its imperfect glory. And then comes the ending."
—Lynda Durrant, author of *My Last Skirt*

Castle of Concrete

A NOVEL

Castle of Concrete

A NOVEL

KATIA RAINA

Young Europe Books

Williamstown, Massachusetts

Published by Young Europe Books, an imprint of
New Europe Books, 2019
Williamstown, Massachusetts
www.NewEuropeBooks.com
Copyright © by Katia Raina
Cover design by Kurt Stengel

ISBN: 978-0-9995416-3-0

Cataloging-in-Publication data is available from the Library
of Congress.

First edition, 2019

10 9 8 7 6 5 4 3 2 1

In memory of my grandmother, who raised me with books. Even though she always did worry I was reading "too young." I still do, Babushka. I miss you and wish you had gotten to hold this book in your hands.

This book is also dedicated to my mama, who taught me to be brave and free.

Finally, this book is dedicated to my husband, Romain Raina. You are my guiding star. You make everything possible.

Part I
New Life

1

Summertime or the Moscow Blues

I shouldn't be here.

Under the city of my dreams, during rush hour. Inside the blue train, rushing me toward New Life. Next to my mama whom I adore, whom I haven't seen in how many centuries?

I shouldn't be anywhere.

Mama—my dear *mamochka*—was on her way to an abortion clinic—when she saw a baby. Just a regular little baby. And then, the story goes, Mama's head spun, and her heart squeezed, or something, and she patted her still-skinny stomach and whispered—whispered to *me*—"Everything will be all right, little one," or something of that sort.

Here I stand, fifteen years later, squeezed between passengers' hips and elbows. I wonder if that baby Mama saw had a runny nose. Probably not. Because if she did, maybe Mama would have thought babies were too much trouble, and I wouldn't be here, under the vaulted roofs of the Moscow Metro, zipping through shiny marble stations, breathing in wind, the sweat of strangers, and Mama's spicy perfume. Just another sardine in this Soviet can of sardines, pressed tight, body to body.

At each chandeliered stop more feet shuffle in: unfeminine pumps step over someone's sandaled toes; sharp-nosed half-boots trip over my suitcase. Almost suspended in midair, held by the crowd over the dusty linoleum, I shouldn't be here.

Unsettling thoughts of this sort settle over me. Maybe they're gifts from my comrades pressing from all sides. A worry from a retiree's face. A scowl from a young woman with fake blond hair. The anger of a poking elbow. It's like all our feelings mash and grind together. Like our thoughts soften, losing their freshness as they simmer in the heat of summer bodies, turning into one angry-tired mass coated in salty sweat.

In between luxurious, palacelike stations, swift underground blackness flashes in rectangular windows. Mama tries to talk to me over the train's thunderous *ta-da, ta-da, ta-da, ta-da.*

"Tired, Sonya?" she asks. I listen to the jazzy notes in her voice. Her back is straight, her eyes just as reckless and carefree as I always remembered them. No one could ever turn *her* thoughts into Soviet mush.

I grip a railing that is moist with the last days of summer. How I've missed her. In the Ural Mountains, in limitless Siberia, on the bank of the Volga River. In this sanatorium cafeteria, in that small, wallpapered kitchen, I have kept her under the pillow of every bed that has ever been mine.

"Hungry, *da?*" she asks me. My dissident poetess moneyless famous jobless mama, hiding moving seeking floating in and out of my life in a cloud of smoke, suddenly on this train so real—too real for words. "A Friday rush hour," she says, sighing. "Sorry we couldn't take the taxi. Andrei and I, we spent everything on furniture. Oy, but you'll love it so, Sonya, ah, Sonya?"

I nod. Of course I'll love it. I already do.

Some woman's bag is leaking something juicy—or bloody, I don't know. But when that woman points her plain, beige-tired face at Mama, venom leaks from the woman's gaze. Is it what Mama just said about the taxi and the new furniture, or Mama's long hair the color of a crow's feather and her proud Jewish nose that irks the woman so? I know that stare, from a store long ago, from a neighbor's twisted mouth, from a crowded bakery somewhere in my childhood, the whispers, "*Jid*," which taught me early that to the world, being a Jew was something dirty.

I don't remember ever meeting my father, but imagine I look more like him. Green eyes, thin nose, light chestnut hair on my shoulders in disobedient waves. A Russian-looking shortie, Jewish blood simmering under my skin, so no strangers can see.

Mama, having noticed the woman's leer, no doubt, decides to join me in the squad of the mute.

I shut my eyes, trying to contain an urgency inside me, a wanting exploding in the silence of the train's roar and clatter. Andrei: a new father. New apartment. New furniture. New Life, a true life, it has already started. And I haven't made anything happen yet.

To soothe the nervous jingling within me I play soft sounds inside my head. Maybe they're the sounds of my childhood that finished five days ago, when I packed my suitcase and kissed my babushka goodbye. The sounds of my fingers stroking the piano, the sounds of my voice dreaming, stretching "*Summerti-i-i*-ime."

Now the soft melody swells inside me. My fingers start crawling up and down the railing, as if it were a keyboard. I don't even know who sang it first or who wrote it. All I know is it's famous and American, and right now, I am grateful for its cool shine on this stuffy train. My mind rocks to the train's beat. A voice bursts out, puncturing a quiet inside me, *my* voice singing about summer heat and stretching your wings—oh!

Mama is pulling on me, trying to hush me and laughing at the same time. But an old man with bushy eyebrows seated in front of me is already applauding. The others just stare. Except the woman with the leaking bag, the one who doesn't like Mama. She glares.

The quiet comes back, crashing over me.

God. How loudly was I singing?

"A fine little performer we got here," the man booms. "What a pretty *devochka* you are, too."

I cringe and cross my arms over my chest, trying to get used to the idea of some man calling me "pretty." To my relief, the man leaves us at the next stop, along with a whole horde of other passengers fighting their way out with their elbows. The rest of us push at each other in a mad jostle for the emptied seats.

The leaking-bag woman almost makes it to the bench, but gets stuck in between the metal railing and someone's impressive butt.

"The first rule," Mama whispers, pushing me forward, "move swiftly in Moscow."

She and I snag the last two seats. The woman sends us both a look of loathing.

I plop down onto the beat-up brown leather, mounting my suitcase over my lap, trying to hide behind it. But the venomous woman drags her leaking bag in my direction. Before my little debut she probably didn't even see me. Now she stands over me, glaring, as she positions her bag right above my feet. The train picks up speed. She shifts her gaze from Mama to my suitcase and back, her face contorted, mumbling.

"They keep on coming, keep on coming," the woman says to no one in particular, but not too quietly, either.

Mama rolls her cat-eyes, letting me know that she doesn't care and neither should I. The woman keeps on mumbling. I watch with fascination the woman's yellow teeth.

". . . As if we need more people in our lines, scooping up the last sausage. . . . One thing's for sure—we don't have a *Jid* shortage here in Moscow. "

That word—the color of tobacco-stained teeth—that word—jagged like bared fangs—here it is again, following me all the way to New Life—it is—a word—that changes everything.

Mama's eyes are no longer laughing.

People stare at Mama and me. I stare right back—my face heated up to *borscht* temperature. They look away, when Mama stands up and releases her words, slow and hoarse.

"One. Thing." She aims her words straight at the woman. "One thing Moscow doesn't need—surely—is another filthy anti-Semite, oozing spite."

The woman looks perplexed. Even her bag stops leaking for a second—I swear—perhaps insulted at the "oozing" reference. She shakes her head. She shifts her eyes.

The train shifts to another stop. Mama grabs my suitcase and me. I squeeze Mama's hand.

"Screw this," she says. "*Poshli.* Let's go spend some of our Jew money on a relaxing taxi ride."

The Moscow sky greets us with light rain and fresh exhaust smells—wonderful, bewildering big city smells that make me giddy. A giant tower of a building evokes the grandeur and the terror of Stalin's times. Its top looks needle-thin from the distance, its shoulders broad. Its concrete façade is massive and real. Other buildings, older ones, show off their long fancy balconies and tall narrow windows, their ancient yellowish paint tinged with noble dust.

People smoke, cars cough. I know I'm not dreaming, because dreams don't have such smells.

"That toad reminded me of something, something good," Mama says. "I have a present for you back in the apartment."

Traffic roars and rushes past us along a boulevard that's as wide as a sea. New Life, loud and stinky, throws possibilities in my face. I make a promise. To Mama, to myself, to heaps of future friends I will be making in my new school on Monday.

A smoky Siberian city. A quiet classroom. The gossiping neighbors on a bench, suddenly quiet at my approach. Me always quiet, too quiet, with too many feelings and things to say. It's all behind me now, or it should be.

I promise that Sonya the Shadow has stayed behind, like the latest nothing city she inhabited, like the self-suffocating crowd she left on that train. Look out, Moscow Region, for the new Sonya Solovay! This isn't wishing like before, not some childish dream. This is a promise.

For all my faults—you know, the cowardice and unremarkableness and such—at least I always keep my promises.

2

Demons Live in the Quiet Pond

"Where to?" asks the driver, giant and solid as an armoire. "Moscow Region, the city of Lubertsy," Mama says.

My heart does a flip. That's my new address. *Our* new address.

Mama doesn't have much cash on her, but apparently a pack of imported cigarettes counts for a lot around here. The giant invites us into his Volga sedan with neither a taxi sign nor a speedometer.

A Volga! I marvel. The very best kind of a car ever produced in my lovely Motherland.

Mama squeezes my hand. "Let the adventure begin!" she whispers. Like I am still ten years old, and she's visiting me in Siberia.

I smile back at her. I'm not much of a talker.

The luxurious car races us toward the setting sun. Past the Moscow River contained in its concrete bath, past the castle-like towers of churches, we ride in the once favorite vehicle of communist chiefs. I have the entire backseat to myself, like I am some kind of a princess.

My muscles still throb from a three-day cross-country train journey. But I am a princess, or that's the way it feels, behind me a pair of swan wings from an old Russian fairytale.

I lean this way and that, angling for a better view of thin gold crosses that pierce the sky atop the churches' onion-shaped heads.

"Haven't had myself a decent smoke in a hundred years." The man lights up his newly acquired Marlboro, sharing the light with Mama.

"Just look at this!" the driver says.

Outside the Volga's window two women Mama's age walk by, wearily swaying their miniskirted thighs. A beggar babushka makes the sign of the cross.

I turn my face away from the begging grandma. The driver's lively little eyes find mine in the rearview mirror.

"How old are you?" he asks.

"Fifteen," I say, reddening.

"Just turned last week," Mama adds, and I redden more.

"So?" the driver asks. "You like democracy?" He spits out the word

"I like it," I manage. My voice comes out all squeaky and rusty-sounding, like a door that hasn't opened for centuries.

"Sure you do." The man nods. "You can say anything, say this country is a pile of stinking shit, and no one will start a case on you. Pardon my rudeness." He sounds so stiff and unnatural that my blush deepens. "Before it was 'religion is the opiate of the masses'? Now, it's: 'Believe in Buddha if you like!' Before we were building communism. Now we've got *perestroika,* now we are *restructuring*. But what good is it? Isn't it like rebuilding a house using the same rotten wood it was built with in the first place?"

I don't want to listen to him. I am a swan princess. But his question gnaws at me.

Can we change, rebuild ourselves, grow free from the inside?

Outside the window, the grand buildings from the city's center give way to ordinary blue kiosks that sell vodka and newspapers, the kind I used to walk by in Siberia. I peer hard through the glass foggy from my breath, trying to find *Moscow* in the chipped, scrappy façades that might have been white once.

"The old, hardline communists sure don't like it, though." The man keeps poking the air with a thick finger. "I hear they're getting ready to take back power. I hear it's, 'goodbye, Gorbachev' soon. Goodbye, perestroika."

Mama turns around and gives me a quick look, a roll of the eye, as if to say, *Don't you pay attention to this goat.* The man's words go on spewing like diesel fumes. As he talks, he keeps glancing at me. I really wish he wouldn't. "Perestroika! Young girls selling themselves on the streets! Retirees, invalids begging right out in the open! All sorts of nationalists rousing! Anti-Semites popping out of nowhere. . . ." He turns around and steals a look at Mama, raising a thick eyebrow.

"They aren't *popping*," Mama says quietly, her eyes fixed on an invisible spot just ahead. "They've been there all along."

"Besides," Mama adds at a red light, "it's because of your tiresome perestroika that my daughter and I can finally be together again."

The driver turns his head and stares at her so long I fear the car will crash into the back of a giant truck spewing gray diesel all over his Volga's front window.

"Prison?" he asks in an awed whisper, examining her still. "Exile?"

Mama takes a long drag of her cigarette.

"I wasn't an important enough fish for any of that, I guess," she says. "Still, I irked them enough." She turns her head back to me. "Didn't I, Sonya?"

As if I would know.

"They trailed me," she says to the driver. "Called once a week. They made sure I didn't get accepted into a single university I applied to." She coughs, before continuing. "I didn't want that for my daughter. The farther she was from me, the better off she would be. "

"How long has it been?" the driver asks after a long, smoky pause. Mama doesn't answer.

"Eleven years." My voice cuts in, hoarse from all the smoke filling the Volga.

"Eleven years!?" The driver whirls around to face Mama. The car swerves, throwing me against the side of the door. "For eleven years, you haven't seen your little girl?"

"We saw each other." Mama's voice is suddenly flat, quiet. "When we could. Didn't we, Sonya?"

She turns to the driver, and even in her profile there is no mistaking the savage sadness flashing in her eyes, her expression daring him to say another word.

At first I think it's Mama's stare that makes the driver look away. But then the car halts with a screech, and immediately I become aware of a low rumble spreading outside, making the windows jingle.

I see it in the front window of the car. A line of tanks, crossing the intersection. A bunch of boys, men, what do you call them? I am practically sitting in the front with them now, my head in between Mama and the driver, my knees almost hitting the ashtray bin where they both had put out their cigarettes. In puffy vests, with sharp haircuts, and guns by their sides, guys that could practically be my classmates are sitting atop death machines, as if on tractors.

Suddenly, my back is all sweaty and free of wings.

"It's nothing, Sonya," Mama soothes me. "Go back to your seat—don't start trembling so. Nobody is shooting. There is no war."

"I'm not—trembling," I say, as I settle in once again. My back sticks to the seat and my cheeks are burning.

"It's just the army in training," the driver adds, though his voice is shaking a little.

Training for what? Anyway, I *wasn't* trembling.

I push the image of the dusty machines out of my mind. They won't be my bad omen.

The window grows foggy from my breath, as I look hard for it, so hard my eyes tear up—New Life. Tanks or not, I know it's out there somewhere. Waiting for me past the streetlights with missing light bulbs, beyond the *Producty* shops, general food stores with empty shelves gleaming dully.

"Your school is across the street," Mama says.

I strain my eyes against the thickening darkness. It's hard to believe we are just an hour away from the bustling, noisy capital. A stray dog scampers into an alley.

The car jolts onto a dirt road by a concrete fence. I let my breath out in a jerky motion, thinking of Monday, the first day of school. The day I make my first appearance in New Life. I wonder if I'll have the courage to tell my future classmates about the tanks I saw today. I wonder if I'll be bold enough to even say *hi* to them without drowning in a wave of hot scarlet.

Privet. I'm Sonya Solovay. A new girl. A brand new Sonya.

I must be wearing an odd expression, because the driver's eyes fix on me in the mirror again. I pull my shoulders down and raise my chin at him.

"Watch out for this one," he says to Mama.

"Don't you worry about her." Mama laughs out in a tense burst. "My Sonya is nothing to worry about, *nothing*." She throws her head back and smiles at me. Her arm extends backward, her fingers reach for me, her ever patient, always reliable little *devochka*—daughter. I squeeze her small soft fingers in my hand, just the way she expects it. But I don't return her smile. The car slows down before a construction site that in the dark resembles the ghostly ruins of a castle. The man shakes his head, examining me still, with eyes small and thoughtful. I brace myself for the final offering of the man's gruff wisdom.

"I know her type," he says as he brings the car to a halt. "Too perfect. Too quiet. Demons live in the quiet pond, as they say. She's going to let you have it, this one. You'll see."

3

Sleeping on a Star

"Is something wrong? The tanks? What time is it?"

"It's only ten-thirty, and no, nothing's wrong, sleepyhead," Mama says. "I just almost forgot your homecoming present."

Mama thrusts something jagged into my palm. The light from the foyer shines on the thing in my hand—a six-pointed metal star attached to a shoelace.

"Do you know what it is?"

Groggy from almost-sleep, I look around the unfamiliar outlines in the semidark space that is my room now. I must have been dreaming I was still in Siberia, with Babushka, under a thick blanket of quiet. Reaching up to rub my eye, I almost poke myself with one of the six edges.

Mama arranges her long curtain of hair over her left shoulder and smiles at me. "Did Babushka ever show you?"

I shake my head.

"It's not her fault," Mama says. "She'd want to keep you away from trouble."

"What is it, then?" I ask, definitely intrigued now, at the thought of Mama sharing a gift of *trouble* with me.

"It's Jewish," Mama says. "It's me and your babushka. It's you."

"Jewish?" I turn the thing over. "How can a thing be Jewish, except a last name or a nose, maybe?"

I hang the star around my neck. It seems a bit crude—no elegance in it—just a metal shape plus a shoelace. Yet there is something about it. Something magical, bold. I grin. A star has got to bring luck to someone who wants to shine. Using my nightgown for a parachute, I soar out of bed and land on the hardwood floor.

Mama shakes her head, making the long curtain of her hair ripple about her.

"Are you ever going to grow up, *devochka*?" she says. "Is it possible? You're still exactly the same as I always remember."

At this, I stand up, straighten out my star, and face her. I'm not—the same. Or at least I won't be. She'll see.

I spin around. The star flies with me, tracing a circle in the air around me.

"I'll wear it to school," I say.

"Ah, Sonya, what are you saying?" Mama says. "Did you fall off the moon? You can't do that."

My bewildered look subdues her hard, worried words.

"This is a *Magen Dovid*, Sonechka. A powerful symbol. A Jewish star. You don't need that kind of attention."

Perhaps not. Still, I don't surrender easy.

"*You*'ve gotten all kinds of attention," I remind her. "Attention from the KGB, for example."

"That was different."

Of course. Things have always been *different* for Mama. Fighting, flying, making trouble in the world—those were her rules, that was her life.

I had to stay warm and ignorant and safe. A hatchling in an egg, yet to poke her nose out.

Sitting back down on my bed, for the first time in my life I truly wonder what would it have been like to grow up flying by her side.

Never mind. I banish the thought with a shake of my crazy tousled hair.

I am here now, Mama. Here to be what I should have been always—a dissident's daughter. Fierce, bright, unstoppable. Running my finger over the outlines of Mama's present, I smile at her. It must be quite a strange sort of a smile, because Mama grips my hand and gives it a shake, as if to awaken me.

"Don't even dream of it, you hear me, Sonya?" Her eyes bore into me. "Even I would never think of wearing a Jewish star in public."

"*You* don't have to," I say, and she knows what I mean. Mama's looks are her Jewish star.

"Sonya, Sonya." She gets up. "There's so much for you to learn about who you are. For me too, really. But now isn't the time. This, all this—" she motions around my room, toward the shadows of the wall unit, the plant sleeping on my windowsill, "—is too much for you to take in, already so much for you to feel, to think about. You should get some rest for Monday."

I would sigh if it weren't for her word "Monday" filling my lungs with too much air.

"True enough, Mama," I say, exhaling.

For Monday I have an eggshell to crack open. No, a kingdom to conquer. A New Life to claim.

"That's my good girl," she murmurs, closing the door behind her.

"Where should I wear it, then?" I call after her. "Your present?"

"In your heart," Mama answers from the foyer.

In the darkness, I take the Magen Dovid off and put it under my pillow.

I think of Babushka warning me, in her favorite language of proverbs, "The tallest blade of grass is the first one to be cut down by a scythe." I wrap my fingers tight around the shoelace under my pillow and whisper, "The times have changed, Babushka." All night I dream dazzling dreams.

But come Monday morning, will I easily find her, the girl who slept on a star?

4

Colors

"I'm Andrei." A man with long messy hair thrusts his big hand at me. "Also known at home and abroad as Clown Samoyedov." He chuckles. "What, never seen a real-life clown before? Nice to meet you, *dochka*."

I barely just woke up, and already I am having trouble breathing.

Is it the assortment of suffocating cooking smells oozing out from the neighboring doors that clogs my nose and throat? Or the word "daughter" this blond, sun-tanned stranger just called me?

Mama stands on her toes as she reaches for him. "The deputy director of the Moscow Concert Hall called," she whispers. "Looks like you have a spot in next week's show."

"Hello to you, too," he whispers back.

He looks even younger than Mama, and I didn't think that was possible. I've seen his pictures, but somehow I still wasn't prepared for him—the hair hanging down to his shoulders in blond tangled strands, the huge hands, the sharp smell of cologne and gasoline when he bends down to kiss me.

A memory floats to the surface of my brain, another image from faraway across my life. A yard, like any yard, with chestnut trees to make shade over gossipy babushkas on benches. Two girls, like any girls, small-nosed and frowning, hands on hips, standing before me. Their singsong voices rattling the air.

"Your mother is a criminal."

"—a druggie—"

"—and a whore."

"She's not," I said to them in that characteristically pale voice of mine. I barely understood their words at six years old, yet somehow I knew they were lies.

"*Da?* How come then you have never even had a father?"

I don't remember the girls' names, but right now, standing inside my *two-room* Moscow Region apartment as a man *known at home and abroad as Clown Samoyedov* leans over to rub his unshaven cheek against mine, how I wish those girls could see him, looking more like an American movie star.

Except, when he wraps Mama in his arms and their lips touch, I turn my flushed face to the wall for a second.

"So, what would you like to start with, *princessa?*" my new father asks. "Tea or gifts from the West?"

In the living room, enormous suitcases snap open. Unnecessary light from a small chandelier pours luxuriously over bright-colored plastic bags with foreign letters. I survey a scene so surreal it could have come from a science fiction story.

But Mama's wide smile has tempered.

"You're spoiling us, Andrei," Mama says. "All of this . . . must have cost a . . . fortune . . ."

"Ah, but look how hard you're working!" He slips his feet into soft-looking foreign slippers, then turns around and gives me a wink. "Your mother." He shakes his head. "An amazing woman. "Heaps of freelance assignments. Translating, copywriting, dissertation writing, and God knows what else. And I'm not counting all that studying—all that drama—"

He pronounces the full name of the prestigious theater arts university, and finishes off with a whistle.

"Sh-sh-sh, don't whistle in the house." I look in surprise at the hard edge in Mama's voice now. "That's bad money luck. And the stash of savings won't replenish itself automatically."

Andrei looks at her, as though seeing her for the first time, and his smile fades slightly. Sunlight streams through the golden drapes over the window to the balcony. Competing with the light from the chandelier, it bounces off the polished wood of the wall unit, reflecting newness through mirrors, china, and glass. It shines on an imported bottle of cognac Andrei places on a small corner table.

"Want a glass?" he asks Mama.

Mama frowns. "Let's not start off with a party," she says, her voice quiet. "Your show's only a week away. You'll want to be in top shape, no?"

"And I will be. No worries, Comrade General." Andrei wrenches the top of the bottle open and takes a long—*long*—sip. "Ah," he says, wiping his mouth with the back of his hand. "*Now* we're ready." Then he pushes a big suitcase toward me. "Dive in," he says. "It's for you, *princessa*."

"All of this for me?" I look back at Mama. She tries to smile at me.

I hesitate for maybe one more second. Then, like the undignified proletarian that I am, I do as he said: I *plunge* into the heap of gifts.

Even in my dreams, I have never seen things this *fantastic*. The suitcase is filled with colors of all kinds. The pinks not the color of roses, the greens not the colors of oak leaves. I grab them all—soft colors, plastic colors, denim colors, wonderfully smelling colors. I toss them all in the air and I laugh with them.

"Thank you, *Papa*." The word feels wonderfully normal in this shiny room.

I jump into my new father's arms as if I were a toddler, blocking out the sour smell of alcohol on his breath. I try on my new colors, twirling in front of every reflective surface I can find, running my fingers over neat, barely visible stitches on a miniskirt. I stare at a reflection of this shiny new girl no one from my Old Life would have recognized.

Farewell, old clothes! Goodbye, frilly flowered dress that looks more like a house robe! Goodbye, thick round "boat" shoes that would be considered beige for lack of a better definition. And of course, the school uniform dress—a brown trap of wool, plus a white lace apron—*forget it*!

I strut around the apartment in tall, bootlike sneakers with high heels. *What would Babushka say?*

I shake my head. She'd want me to be happy. She'd say, "*Nu*, isn't this what you have been longing for?"

Andrei calls me "The Queen of Beauty." And I beam back at him.

"*Ey*," he says, "maybe you can wear this outfit to my Moscow Concert Hall debut?" But I have a better idea.

I string plastic rings with radioactive-color stones all over my fingers. Both my parents are finally smiling. *Look at them*, I think. *A pair of parents*.

"Ancestors," I mouth, using the slang word because I am cool like that now. Still, I don't dare say it loudly. Mama cocks her head. They didn't even hear me.

It's all right, though. Because—look at me!

No one will mistake me for a quiet little girl when I wear all this on the first day of school!

5

Shining

U nder a sky the color of unwashed laundry, strangers gathering on the steps in front of the faded school building look up in gloomy surprise, drop their conversations mid-sentence, and whisper, "Who is she?"

Shy little first-graders in uniforms widen their eyes at me.

I turn around to double check: Is there someone unusual walking behind me?

The jaunty September wind crawls under my new, low-cut pink polyester shirt, covering my skin with bumps. Clouds shift in the cool air, promising rain. I quicken my pace, swinging my legs from underneath my new denim miniskirt, almost twisting my ankle in the new high-heeled sneaker.

A boy with dark, curly hair leans against a tree, his long nose buried in a thick book. He is probably the only one who doesn't notice me today. A lanky upperclass hooligan whistles low.

My feet pick up speed. My long pigtails, wrapped up in new fluorescent ribbons, skip with me. My breasts jump, too, practically out of my shirt. My "charms," Mama called them at breakfast, frowning. Now I see her point. A tall teacher with a neat gray bun atop her head, her icy eyes scanning and scanning the crowd, gives me a once-over and scowls.

The pink-gray Regional Lubertsy-City School Number Eight looms before me in all of its bedraggled solemnity. The red Soviet flag waves in the wind. The schoolyard is a blur of new faces and voices, faded jeans and brown uniforms, backpacks, shoulder bags, and old-style briefcases like I used to carry.

"*Privet!*" Greetings are flying all over the schoolyard. Robust shouts, giggles, squeals. "Where were you hiding all summer?"

"Are you performing in the first-day-of-school-assembly?"

"You crazy? What am I, a *botanik?*"

Under my feet a matchbox sags with dew, on the lawn littered with dandelions and brownish pieces of beer-bottle glass. Above my head, giggles and gossip twirl and the sun blinds me. It makes me want to find shade to hide in.

"Interesting, who he'll choose next, now that he has sampled practically every *chiksa* in Moscow Region. . . ."

"Sh-sh-sh! Shut your fountain. He's standing right here—"

"Ey, who is this bird?"

My shoulders want to hunch. My eyes fix to the ground, glued to the rusty Pepsi can under my feet. The can is lying around, neglected like it's some ordinary beer bottle instead of a piece of magic, an imported novelty. I straighten. I did not come here to hide and hunch my shoulders.

With a tip of my high-heeled sneaker, I send the Pepsi can flying across a spiky patch of grass. Making a wide half-circle through the air, the can lands with a *bryak, bryak* at the foot of the staircase leading up to the school doorway. It lands among numerous feet and legs, making them scatter. Conversations halt. I feel it all more than I see it. Shivering a little, under the heat of stares burning holes through the back of my dress, I tell myself it's a good omen, the arc that the Pepsi container made as it flew toward the stairs like a welcoming rainbow from across the seas.

I'm about to follow the Pepsi can toward the building when I turn around to toss one last look at the courtyard—and I freeze.

A boy is walking up to me.

The boy is on the shorter side. And definitely on the cuter side. Light hair cropped close to the scalp. A pale serious face. Eyes at once intense and mocking. He takes a long puff of his cigarette without lifting his stare off me.

I have a chance only to notice a hint of a mustache above his thin upper lip before I am taken in by his strange oval-shaped eyes of an unidentifiable color.

"Careful there, *beautiful*," he says.

"Eh . . . what?"

"I don't think Electrification will approve of you playing soccer with *Pepsi* cans." His voice has a raspy edge.

"What Pepsi cans?" I say. "Ah." I look down under my feet, realizing. "I was just . . ." I try to think of something clever. Nothing comes.

"A piece of advice?" He steps closer, closer. "Keep out of her way today." I stare deep inside those eyes, still confused.

"Stay out of whose way?"

He smirks at me. But his eyes are so serious. How does he do this?

I take a step back.

"Electrification tolerates it when people don't wear the school uniform. Still, I don't think she'll much like your outfit."

"Who's Electrification?" I squeak.

What is Electrification? And what kind of eyes are these, anyway? How can a person's eyes contain so many shades and no color, except a kind of gray-muddy-blue?

"Elektra Ivanovna." He leans close, exhaling cheap Soviet tobacco. "We call her 'Electrification,'" he says. "You *know*. As in 'Communism is . . .'"

He waits. His hypnotic eyes bind me, summoning me to finish the phrase, one of those meaningless quotes every Soviet child learns practically in nursery school. *The Communist Party is—intellect, honor, and consciousness of our epoch. Communism is—*

"—collectivization plus . . . *ah* . . . electrification of the whole country," I recite, my voice breaking.

He pulls back, satisfied. "Good girl. Good little Soviet."

I take a shaky, indignant breath. "Name one person here who doesn't know this."

The boy smiles, his gaze softening. "Sometimes we call her 'Dictatorship of the Proletariat.'" Curving his lip, he nods toward the school building. "You'll see why."

"Who . . . is she?" I whisper. "The . . . principal?"

"No. The principal, Anatoly, he's classy. Electrification's a history teacher. And the head teacher of Class 10B. Which makes her my class teacher, unfortunately."

His words send my heart pounding fiercely. I hope he doesn't notice a wave of red wash all over my ears. Class *10 Б*. 10B. I am in that group.

His face reaches close to me again. "What's the matter?" he asks. "Scared?"

"Me?" Shivering right now like it's 20° Celsius, I meet his teasing gray-muddy-blue eyes—or at least I try to—without getting lost in them. "I am a dissident's daughter," I tell him, trembling. "I'm not scared of some history teacher."

"Really?" He cocks his head.

"I saw some tanks passing my taxi on the way here, a few days ago."

"Did you?"

"And I wasn't scared."

"No?"

And here I go again, blushing hard. Didn't I just sound like a preschooler, bragging: *I wasn't sca-red?*

Then I realize: he is looking at me differently now. His eyes travel slowly down my body like he's fitting me for a dress.

That's when I remember that I actually have a body. With legs, and knees, and feet. And so I flee, past the stares and the whispers, up the cracked concrete steps, through the school doorway unevenly painted peach.

"Don't run into any more tanks on your way to the assembly!" the boy calls after me hoarsely, soliciting more whispers still.

I fly into the dim crowded hallway that smells of chalk and dampness, blushing, thinking, *What assembly?* But mostly, I am thinking, *What was that all about, the way he looked at me?*

6

Blooming Guelder Rose

I run my cold, cold hand along the bright green wall, lined with steam-heat pipes and radiators. Back in my previous life, a life that seems so long ago it could have been a dream, boys' stares never turned the tips of my fingers into icicles.

Under banners that read "First-Day-of-School Assembly" and "Forward to the Victory of Communism," I merge into the crowd of upperclassmen. On the second floor we all pour out into a large hallway lined with classroom doors on one side and windows on the other. Through musty lace curtains strips of sunlight shine on a falling-apart piano at the end of the hallway, and several rows of wooden chairs before it.

The teachers herd the youngest pupils to the front. The tall gray-haired woman with pale blue eyes who disapproved of me in the courtyard gives me another cold stare.

And how does everyone else manage to fit in here? Some sitting, others crowding behind the chairs. Kicking at each other's ankles and stepping on each other's feet. Breathing on each other and sweating in a familiar Soviet-style camaraderie. Even some parent types are crowding in, in the back. A too-young for school *devochka*, shy and dark-eyed, resembles me in old photographs. She leans close to a softly blond, middle-aged woman and I wish *my* mama were here, too.

A smallish man, dried up like a breadcrumb, cups his hands and shouts out a greeting, something about "another school year" and "joy despite troubled times."

Gradually, everyone quiets down enough to hear his quivering words.

"It's a pity that in recent years fewer young people volunteer to be a part of this wonderful tradition. Still, I have here a list of this year's fine, talented performers," he says. Someone behind me snickers.

Performers? I look around, dazed.

"Back in 1982, when we started these first-day-of-school celebrations, in order to perform you had to compete in a contest. Now, I open the stage to anyone!"

I crane my neck to see "the stage" from behind rows of heads and shoulders.

"So, before we begin our planned performances, I summon you," the man calls out, theatrically thrusting his thin arms into the air. "As the principal of this fine institution, I call upon you, my dear pupils, offering anyone who isn't already in this year's program a last chance—a wonderful chance— to participate by opening our First-Day-of-School Assembly. Is there anyone? Who wants to be a star? A first grader? An eleventh grader? Anyone . . ."

All around me, people are hanging back; even thuggish-looking types are trying to make themselves smaller.

The principal's sad-hopeful words about being *a star* make me think of my own star underneath my pillow. The principal is New Life itself calling, reminding me of a promise I've made to myself. I think about the boy with those eyes that made fun of me a little in the courtyard, and at the same time how good it felt when he looked at me and actually *saw* me. I think of what I told him: *I am a dissident's daughter.* My hand rises in the air.

"Back there? Come on up!" the principal calls me.

"Showoff," someone mutters.

"*Botanka,*" somebody else says.

"I am not a nerd," I whisper back fiercely.

I make my way to the piano past all those elbows and shoulders. I almost trip on a wooden chair. My flesh-colored stocking rips at my left knee. But I push through the crowd. My heart pulsates with a steady beat.

Standing by the piano beside the grateful principal, I face the strangers before me, all those eyes focusing on me, and I try not think about the length of the skirt I am wearing, the depth of my neckline, or the hole in my stocking inching toward my thigh.

"Please introduce yourself," the principal says after eyeing my outfit a bit warily for a second. "What's it going to be, then?"

Words, notes call out to me. The classical harmonies, the lyrical Beatles, the harsh lyrics of the once-forbidden bards whom everybody loves now, the catchy but empty *tams, tams, ta-dams* of Soviet pop. I look to the faces before me for the answer—freckled faces, mustached faces, loud faces—and I can almost feel it, feel the answer in my fingers, feel it rising from inside my throat, when I get stuck in a pair of eyes.

Da, those eyes belonging to the smoking boy from the courtyard, penetrating me from the middle of a front row. I freeze. The tips of my fingers feel as though they have been dipped in ice-cold water. My cheeks are on fire.

"My . . . *ah* . . . name is . . . Sonya Solovay," I say, finally. "And I will be performing . . . 'Blooming Guelder Rose in the Field by the Creek,'" I call out the first thing that pops into my suddenly hollow head. Of all things, a Russian folksong from an old music lesson. Someone snickers in the audience. Cursing myself for such a stupid choice, I sit down on the bench in front of the squeaky old thing that passes for a piano and try to pull my skirt down, like it's going to matter now. Dodging chuckles and whispers, I throw my hands all over the keys and my voice into the thick, sweaty air. "*I fell in love with a young fellow*," I squeak. "*I fell in love to my own dooo-ooom . . .*"

The higher my voice climbs, the thinner it stretches, until it's barely there at all. My fingers slide all over the keys. Cringing every time I hit a false note, I wade through the slow, viscous melody. I pick up fragments of giggles, shuffling noises, chairs moving, teachers shushing. It's over. I breathe and bow, but the shuffling and the conversations continue as before. Except for the applause—sharp, even, alone—*khlop, khlop, khlop, khlop, khlop,* flying at me from the audience. I dare lift up my head and then I catch it: his thin shadow of a smile.

Someone in the front row snickers. "Looks like our *Don Juan* found himself a new girl toy for September."

"Nice choice, Ruslan."

"Chip off," Ruslan calls out in a calm husky voice, his unsettling eyes on mine all the while, his hands clapping.

The applause ripples through the crowd and multiplies, drowning out all sound.

7

Beauty

"*Lubov*," says my desk neighbor.

"What?" I ask, reeling. *Lubov?* Love? What is she hinting at?

Everything about this girl is pale. Even her skin is the color of a swan's feather. *Like a swan princess,* I think, jealous.

"I'm not . . ." I say. I'm trying to fight off an incoming wave of blush. But it's useless. "It was just a song. I . . . it . . . didn't mean anything. I'm not in *love*," I say fiercely.

"My name, little fool." The girl seems amused. "Lubov is my name. Luba."

"*Ah.*" I exhale. "My name is—"

"I know your name," she says. "We all heard you earlier, *songbird.*"

The walls of the history classroom are peppered with images—soldiers on posters, prehistoric tools, slogans, the flags of the Soviet republics, all fifteen of them: Russia, Ukraine, Georgia, Lithuania, Latvia, and all those others. It feels as though this room has not four walls, but at least a dozen.

I keep glancing at the swinging poster-clad door for any sign of Ruslan. One of the posters, *Historical Development of World Societies,* is organized chronologically. Slavery, the Middle Ages,

and industrial society are marked "the past." Communism—
the future.

On the teacher's desk, a stack of old gray textbooks with
the year 1984 on their spines remind me of my quiet Old Life,
the times before perestroika.

Above Electrification's desk, the portrait of Lenin is
watching me, the way he has been all of my life, from the wall
of every classroom I've ever been in since the age of seven.
Grandpa Lenin, I used to whisper, *am I being good?* Peering back
at his bearded physiognomy, I might as well be seven, eight,
nine, ten years old. It might as well be 1984, Gorbachev a year
or so away from becoming the new general secretary, Mama in
hiding.

For one panicky moment I wonder if time has reversed
itself, if I will awaken back in my childhood and find that a boy
named Ruslan doesn't exist at all.

Students stream into the dark, cavelike space, and
every single one of them looks me over freely. When not
staring at me, they chat about the *dachas* and the food
shortages, some upcoming party (*"Bring your own alcohol!"*)
and an imminent communist coup. Only one boy neither
chats nor stares.

He sits in the front row, his long nose stuck in a thick
tattered book on his desk. He has curly hair and the longest,
darkest eyelashes I have ever seen. The boy is a first-rate *botanik*.
A real nerd. The boy's legs are so long, they don't fit under his
desk properly. And how dark his small curls are.

"Luba?" I lean toward my neighbor. "This boy . . ." I start
to ask. But I don't seem to have her attention. "Over there. . ."

"Shhh. Enough with the boys."

She doesn't understand. That I feel like maybe I've seen
him, like I know him, somehow, even though I know I don't.

Maybe it's because the way he reads so quietly, oblivious to the world, reminds me so much of me—the old me. Maybe it's for the best that I don't get a chance to ask her. The bell jangles and the door to the classroom rips open.

"Hello, class."

Everyone jumps to their feet as one. It takes the long-legged, book-absorbed *botanik* a moment longer than everyone else to scramble up. A moment too long. The woman on the threshold snaps her gray-haired head in his direction immediately. Silence falls.

Except for a *took, took, took,* the click of the teacher's heels knocking against the parquet as she approaches the boy's desk.

Except for a faint thud—the boy drops his thick book on the floor, by the side of his desk.

I cringe.

The corners of the woman's tight, tight mouth stretch into a dreadful grin.

"What's this?" she asks sweetly. "Been doing some reading?"

"I . . ." the boy whispers. "I'll just . . ." he bends over to pick up the book.

"Let me see." She extends her hand.

Silent and blushing deeply under his tan, the boy places the book in her palm. She turns it over, wrinkles her nose and places it face up, right on the floor where it was lying.

"Leave it there," the woman says. "And next time, please refrain from bringing unapproved *heresy* to my classroom."

The boy stares at her.

"You may sit down."

He shifts his weight from one foot to another. "This isn't heresy, Elektra Ivanovna," he says. "It's . . . history. My history."

I study the woman, this Electrification Ruslan warned me about in the courtyard. The cold blue of her eyes reminds me of a river in Siberia. A thin mouth, scowling—the very one that bent in such disgust at the sight of me earlier today. Deep wrinkles create a pair of parentheses around her mouth. An impressive gray bun towers over it all.

Electrification narrows her cold eyes at the boy. "So . . . you have your own personal history, I see?"

"I do," the boy says, his voice fading fast. "At . . . at least that's where I stand." I barely make out these last words even in this deathly quiet.

"That's where you stand?" Electrification mimics. "In that case, won't you remain *standing* for the rest of the lesson?" She turns away from him. "You may sit down, class."

I plop down onto my seat, this dark classroom feeling more and more like something out of Stalin's times, when one could be sent to the labor camps for reading forbidden literature.

"Now, before we get to our lesson, there is one more piece of business I must take care of," Electrification says, pacing the room. "Hello, new girl." My heart drops down to my high-heel-sneakered feet when she stops before me.

I can feel the entire classroom hold its collective breath. "Is this what they wear to school in Siberia?" she asks, after a pause.

I already know that the softness of her voice promises nothing good, absolutely nothing.

"I . . ." I've never been much of a talker.

She cocks her head, waiting. I wish my explanation was as powerful as that *botanik* boy's.

"My father . . ." I try. "My stepfather . . ." Neither word sounds right. "He went to Germany . . ." Her face changes. Her eyebrows squeeze together. She crosses her arms in front of her chest. (I wish I could do that right now, to cover up the glittery *Princess* script.) "He was touring . . . with his clown troupe. And . . . he . . . he brought me . . . I just wanted to . . . I thought . . ."

"You just wanted to join your stepfather's clown troupe," she says. "You thought this school was a circus."

The class buries me with laughter. Except my curly-haired classmate, still serving his "time" standing up beside his desk.

I lift my eyes to meet those of Electrification. She would have liked the old me. For my uniform, for a braid modestly trailing behind me. She would have liked the fear so ingrained into me it was probably written on my face with sweat beads.

She would have liked me for my silence.

"Don't you know what the great Russian writer Lev Nikolayevich Tolstoy said?" Electrification asks me. "He said, 'Modesty beautifies.'"

I inhale. The standing boy gives his head an almost imperceptible shake—a silent warning signal. A memory of Babushka's worried eyes flashes before me.

"Anton Chekhov was a great Russian writer, too," I say, willing my body not to collapse back onto the chair before this woman. "And he said, 'Everything in a person must be beautiful. His mind and his body, his soul and his clothes.'"

Electrification flinches.

"Very well," she says. "Come up here, our *beauty*."

I stare, disbelieving.

"To the board," she says, cheerfully now. "You will stand there for the rest of the class. You might as well show your *beauties* to your classmates. I'm assuming that's what you intended?"

I drag my wooden legs across the floor, trying to pull my skirt down, even a centimeter lower. I wheel around beside the blackboard, and then almost fall over.

A boy is standing by the threshold. He is leaning on the side of the door, arms crossed at his chest, and infiltrating me with his cold-hot-muddy-blue stare. I know this boy. His name is Ruslan. They say he's a *Don Juan*. Romantic. Dangerous. I don't know this boy. And yet, falling, falling deep into his stare, it seems as though I begin to know him. He uncrosses his arms and smiles at me. The tips of his hands touch each other, again, and again, and again, in a soundless applause.

"*Ah*, look who decided to make an appearance." At the cold sound of Electrification's voice, Ruslan straightens and drops his arms to his sides. "Late?" she asks, as she strolls up to him, her heels clicking. "On the first day of school? To *my* class? That's a bit too much, even for you, Valentinov."

He meets her eyes. I watch, breathless.

"I am sorry," he says. "I was looking for . . . *eh* . . . someone," and then, incredibly, he looks away from her and his eyes flit to *me*.

Cheeks, neck and ears blushing furiously, heart floating, head dizzy, I barely pay attention to the punishment Electrification doles out this time (come to this classroom an hour early tomorrow morning). When he walks past me, his hand brushes mine, just barely, sending a jolt of heat through my body.

Once again, the standing dark-haired boy fixes his dark eyes on me. I drop my gaze down to the floor and watch Ruslan's worn Puma sneakers step softly, across the front of the classroom, away from me.

"Open your textbooks to page 16," Electrification says. "You." She nods at the poor *botanik*, like he didn't get enough suffering. "Start reading, right here under the 'Expansion of the Family Brotherhood of the Soviet People.'"

To the accompaniment of the boy's surprisingly resonant tenor reading the lies from an old textbook no one should be using in a classroom anymore, I watch Ruslan's sneakers slow down beside a thick tattered book sprawled out on the floor, forgotten by all, except its curly-haired owner.

"'The Soviet People extended the hand of help toward its brothers . . .'" The boy's voice melodious voice rises and falls, like a sonata, now *forte*, now *piano*. The words he reads pull me—pull us all—deeper in between the covers of the old textbook, trapping us in Lenin's never really fulfilled dream of a peasant-worker paradise, where all the People love each other and work together for the common good, where the neighboring republics have not yet started spilling each other's blood, and no middle-aged Lithuanian women have yet grown bold enough to wave their placards and scream, "Russians go home!" on Central Television.

As the boy reads, I cannot take my eyes off Ruslan's sneaker, the left one, as softly, gently almost, it lands atop a page. "Expressing the will of the overwhelming majority of the population . . . declared Soviet authority on the liberated territories . . ." The boy's voice hesitates, then drops lower. "Take your boot off my book, Valentinov."

I watch, transfixed, as the sneaker pauses on the book, then twists in place. The sound of a ripping page tears through the hushed classroom.

"Read on!" Electrification barks.

"'The class battle exacerbated, and a revolutionary situation formed in the Baltic states. . . .' You're still standing on my book."

"Oh, pardon," Ruslan says. "I didn't realize it was your *Talmud* lying in my way, *Aizerman*."

"*Valentinov!*" Electrification's voice crackles. "Are you having difficulty finding a seat?"

I don't know what a *Talmud* is, I don't even know who I am right now, but the nerve-tickling voice whispering this last name, *Aizerman,* in what sounds like a taunt, forces a blast of air to rise inside my throat. Of course. The dark, dark eyes. The exotic curls. The last name. The owner of the book is a Jew, an obvious one, like Mama. And Ruslan Valentinov's sneaker is still grinding its page.

Just now I wish I had worn the Jewish Star instead of all this, whatever Mama said. I lift my eyes up to meet Aizerman's dark, velvety ones. *We're of one nationality, you and I,* I imagine calling out to him, in the spirit of one of my favorite books, Rudyard Kipling's *Mowghli.* But when he starts reading the textbook again, his eyes hidden beneath the curtain of those luxurious lashes, my own eyes are pulled to another spot, just a few desks behind Aizerman's. For the rest of the lesson I stand on weakened knees, collapsing under the weight of stares, but mostly disintegrating under Ruslan Valentinov's gaze, which is at once scorching and freezing.

8

Russian Hero

After history class Aizerman is free to leave, but Electrification informs me *my* punishment isn't over. Only she doesn't call it punishment.

"Look how dusty the place is," she says. "With all this disrespect taking my attention away, I forgot to mention at the beginning of class that I think my classroom can benefit from a little washing. A little lesson in humility wouldn't hurt you, Solovay. So I thank you in advance for volunteering. I'll see you here at the end of the school day."

Outside the class, some of my classmates surround me in the hallway. Dimpled cheeks. Thirsty smiles. Jealous eyes. They throw their names at me all at once. *Yurik. Dimon. Diana.*

Someone's fluttery fingers latch on to my hand.

"Poor thing," Luba says. "To be on Electrification's Enemy of the People's list already—oh, I don't envy you." But then she pinches the sleeve of my shirt and sighs with longing.

A thuggish-looking type saunters toward me. Overgrown straw-colored bangs hang over his eyes.

"Welcome to Moscow Region," the hooligan drawls, turning the *o-o-ohs* into the *a-a-ahs* in an exaggerated Moscow accent. *Not that this is exactly Moscow,* I remind myself, bracing. *Just another small town, an hour's ride away.*

The protective layer that my classmates have formed around me breaks before him. Diana hooks her arm around Luba's. "Take it easy, Kuzmin."

Their light-haired heads float down the hallway, bobbing together.

I look at them wistfully. I haven't had a best friend since preschool.

With rough, thick fingers, this Kuzmin thug pulls on a hair strand hanging by my forehead, which must have escaped from one of my loosening pigtails.

"Take your hand . . . no—" that's no hand he's got, "—I mean, take your *paw*—off—my hair."

Kuzmin does, chuckling. His eyes scour down my shirt. "I look forward to getting to know you better, cutesy," he drawls. "Need some help cleaning after *schoo-ool*?"

"No thank you," I mouth, though I am not even sure he hears what's left of my voice.

After the last lesson of the day, Electrification hands me an aluminum bucket filled with water that smells of iron and a toilet, and also extends a gigantic gray tattered rag.

"Looks as though some hooligans have already managed to break the mop," she says. Her old face wears a tired expression. "You're going to have to use your hands. . . . Oh, cheer up, Solovay! Labor builds character. Here, a few more, just in case." And she throws some more disintegrating rags in a pile on the floor.

The door closes behind her.

"What are you doing here?" I hear her scold someone behind the door. "The school day's over. Solovay doesn't need any help. Here, let me walk you out."

My heart speeds up a little. *Who was that behind the door?*, I wonder, as I wipe the laminated *Historical Development of World Societies* poster. Whoever it was is gone now. I smudge something dirty and gray over "Communism—the future."

I dip the rag into the cold water. I see my reflection diluted inside the bucket, the face of this supposed new Sonya peering back at me. Holding the rag carefully in between my thumb and forefinger, I let some water drip back into the bucket. I take off my boots. Then I get down on my knees, the way I've seen Babushka do it back in my quiet Old Life. I think of her now, her emerald eyes, the severe wrinkles lining her forehead. I think of the last time I saw her, wiping her soiled kitchen hand over her breeches, her wrinkled face not crying, her large cozy arms squeezing me. Squatting on the dusty floor, I work the floor by the blackboard, the denim mini sliding up my behind. Some Queen of the Class. Then I hear a familiar grating drawl and I whirl around.

"No, don't stand up, *plea-ease*, keep on working." Kuzmin moves toward me through rows of desks covered with upturned chairs, a broken broom in his hand. "I rather liked the way you looked in that position."

I stand up abruptly, trying to pull my skirt down with freezing wet fingers.

"Hello, cutesy." He takes a step toward me.

I try to face him, tough and immobile, but can't help retreating toward the wall as he advances, his frame towering over me.

"What's the matter?" he asks, when I hold up my dripping rag like a shield. His mouth twitches into a smile. "Don't you like the attention?"

I look around the empty classroom, as if the soldiers in the posters could come to my aid. As if, high above Electrification's desk, Lenin could give me advice from inside the portrait. I once thought he could.

He grabs my free arm, then squeezes it hard with his fingers.

"Roll away from me," I say.

"You know what your problem is, *microbe*?" His breath reeks of roasted sunflower seeds. "You don't know your place, that's what. You think you're *so-oh* classy—" His hand brushes down the front of my shirt. "Just cause you've got an imported shirt and a pair of boobies?"

I step aside and knock over the bucket of water. The cold splashes over my feet, bringing me out of a stupor, giving me back my voice, a voice with which to pierce this quiet. "*Auuaouyeerohaaaah!*"

He lets go of my arm and takes a step back.

"What are you screaming like that for, schizophrenic?" he says.

Numb, I watch the water from the bucket float over his oblivious boots. And then Ruslan's raspy voice floats into my ears. "What are you doing?"

Kuzmin's boots retreat a few more steps. "Talking to this pretty little Frau." He sneers. "Is that allowed?"

"I think she's finished talking with you." Ruslan's voice is even, his eyes fixed on Kuzmin.

"I understand." Kuzmin smirks. "Vah-len-tinov, the protector of the weaker sex, lingering in empty school buildings. How *noh*-ble."

Silence hangs heavy in the dimly lit classroom until Kuzmin's boots finally splatter away with affected indifference.

"When you tire of her," he says from the door, "let me know. Not to worry, cutesy." He winks at me. "It won't take long."

Ruslan comes up to me and takes the rag that I've been clutching all this time. I command my half-naked chest to stop shaking.

"You're too beautiful for this place, new girl," he says. This time his eyes aren't laughing at me.

He takes off the navy blue jacket of his uniform. I steal a glance at the skinny torso and bulky shoulders underneath the thinned-out material of his white shirt. "The protector of the weaker sex," Kuzmin called him. No traditional Russian beard on this rescuer, just a thin line of hair emerging above the lip, the eyebrows thin and golden, barely brown, like his hair. A real-life *hero*, better than in any fairytale. He comes up and places his uniform jacket over my shoulders. Suddenly I *am* weak, wonderfully weak, sheltered under that jacket reeking of cigarettes, and the long school day is over. He rolls up the sleeves of his shirt. Then with a grin and a mischievous sideways glance at my bare feet, he unties his own worn Puma sneakers and slips them off along with his socks.

A pair of firmly planted, self-assured feet, the rows of tidy toes—I find it hard to take my eyes off them. I don't think I've ever seen a boy's bare foot this close before.

"Here is how you do it." He places his hands over mine.

The skin of his palm is thin, like wax paper. His nails are cut so short they aren't there. Or does he chew them when he gets nervous, the way some people do? I can't imagine this perfect boy ever getting nervous about anything. He shows me how to twist the rag dry over the half-empty bucket. Together we twist it this way and that, twist it forever, long after the last drop of water is gone. I survey the shiny floors, wishing there were a dusty spot we have forgotten somewhere.

He doesn't ask if he can walk me home—just takes my backpack in his hand.

9

Silence Is A Habit

Outside the school, the late afternoon sun pushes through the clouds.

"So where do you come from?" he says, lighting a cigarette.

Siberia. The Urals. Everywhere and nowhere.

"Myshkin," I say, surprising myself, surprising him too apparently, because he almost drops his cigarette at my words.

"The town of Myshkin?" he says. "Seriously?"

Seriously. I was born there, in a small Volga River town, where Lenin Street is a dirt road leading down to the river.

I haven't been to Myshkin in eleven years, though.

"I know that town," Ruslan says. "Visited it just this spring with my *babulia*, on a tour of the Golden Ring cities. *Ey*—" He smiles at me. "—Maybe I saw you? Walking by the side of the road? Standing over a candle in one of the churches?"

"*Nyet,* Ruslan."

Last spring I was in another time zone. Sitting in Siberia under some oak tree after school, my butt denting my briefcase, a book open on my lap—something science fiction, about an amphibian-man's trek through the sea, or an old Russian fairytale, something faraway. If you saw me then, you'd see my eyes abandoning the pages often, fluttering through the still-bare oak branches to the top of the sky.

"Such a pretty place, Myshkin," Ruslan says. "There was the . . . Uspenski Cathedral, right? And the other one—what's it called?"

"Don't remember," I mutter, looking at weeds pushing through the cracks in between asphalt squares.

Does he even hear me?

"I know the town legend, too." He drops a cigarette butt on the ground and searches his pocket for another cigarette. "A prince fell asleep on the grass on the bank of the Volga. And a mouse—a *myshka*—ran across his face, waking him up just in time to save him from a, venomous snake, was it?"

"Uh-huh."

"And so the prince founded a town, named it Myshkin, in honor of the mouse. Correct?"

I shrug, stepping over his latest cigarette butt. "I don't remember any such story."

He stops in the middle of the asphalt path and turns toward me.

"Don't—" He fixes his eyes on me, forcing me to look up, submerging me in his stare. "You feel ashamed . . ." he says quietly. "Ashamed of being from a small town named after a mouse. Don't be. Because—it's beautiful."

"It's quiet," I say in a voice see-through, like his smoke.

"*Da*, it's quiet," he says. "Sort of like you. Underneath all this . . . glitter . . ."

He puts down my backpack. His hand flies toward my arm. It touches the sleeve of my shirt, right under his own uniform jacket that hangs over my shoulders like a cloak. Down my arm it glides, his hand, brushing against the thin polyester sleeve down to my wrist, where it lingers.

"I only lived there with my mama until I was four," I say. "I remember watching the white cruise boats glide down the river. I don't remember leaving."

I realize I want him to know it—everything, that I'm more than a Myshkin girl.

So I tell him about Mama. How she wrote poetry. Poetry about freedom to believe in her own paradise, not the communist one. Poetry making fun of our elderly general secretaries, their many chins and many medals. I recite a line she shared with me once: "*I wear my own hair.*"

We walk by an empty clothing store with nothing displayed in the display windows. We pass a dairy store packed with people, women coming out hugging small jars of sour cream. A stale soup scent drifts through the open door of a cafeteria. Ruslan clutches me in his stare, sucking one cigarette after another, throwing the butts on the weeds under our feet. I tell him how the authorities didn't much like what she wrote, or the like minded-friends she hung out with. How the KGB watched her every move, called her daily to question and harass her.

I tell him how she left me with Babushka, far from the dangerous life she led, four years in the Ural Mountains, six years in Siberia, the city of Irkutsk.

Time circles with us—past, present, and future—as we pass along an asphalt path around a wrinkly pond, in and out of iron gates framed by diamond-shaped ornaments, through a yard with a rusty merry-go-round. Oaks, maples, poplars, skinny Russian birches—we weave in between their trunks, swimming in the sea of green. I tell Ruslan how Mama floated from one town to the next, trying to get this job, or get into that university. How she dreamed of drama. How of course no one wanted to even be seen talking to someone with her political baggage. I tell him how meanwhile Babushka taught me to keep to myself, lower than grass, quieter than water. How the neighbors whispered, how they told their children not to play with the daughter of a saboteur.

"Silence is . . . a habit," I say. "After a while, the quiet just grows thicker. Until you can't hear yourself anymore."

I don't think I have ever talked this much in my entire life.

I tell him how, when I was five, I made my bed impeccably each morning, knowing that Mama had a magic mirror through which she could see me whenever she wanted, no matter the time or the distance. I try to imitate a throaty and contemptuous laugh Mama emits sometimes when she tells her stories. Instead I inhale too much of Ruslan's cigarette smoke and cough. His hand traveling softly up and down my arm makes me swallow the cough back, somehow.

"*Nu?*" he urges when I grow quiet.

His hand makes its way to my back as I tell him more. About Mama burning her poetry after the KGB threatened to put her in a psychiatric hospital. Me playing and playing the piano, to fill the quiet, as I waited for Mama's life to get normal again so she could take me away.

We sit on a log in the middle of some yard. Two small apartment buildings shield us from the world.

"What does she do now, your mother?" he asks.

"She is studying," I say. "Drama, literature. The National University of Theater Arts."

He doesn't seem impressed. "What else, though?" he says. "She was a rebel. A *dissident*. Shouldn't she be . . . famous now? You know, publishing her poetry?"

"She burned her poetry."

He looks at me, incredulous.

"She told me once—she told me—she never wanted any of this. She never wanted to be this *dissidentka*. Or maybe a little, when she was really young. . . ." I pause to take a breath, to collect years of scattered words whispered here and there. "She said that what she had always wanted the most was simply to live—not to live the life *they* would grant her—but to believe in her own dreams, to live her own way, the only way she knew how."

I smile at Ruslan. "I guess . . . now she's finally living. She wants to write a play."

"You are a lot like her, *da*?" He touches my hand. "You trimmed Electrification good today. She won't soon forget it."

"You heard it?"

"Most of it." He shakes his head. "No one—*not one of us*—has ever stood up to her before." Sunlight skips across his face.

He stretches his legs out next to mine. His Puma sneaker bumps playfully against my own high-heeled one. A single tiny needle sting of a feeling makes me jerk my foot away from his.

"No," I say. "I wasn't the only one who stood up to her this morning."

He wasn't there, didn't hear it. *It's history, my history*, Aizerman had said to Electrification's face. "This boy, *um*, Aiz—"

"Stop being so modest." His foot finds his way back to mine. "I love what you said to her. How does that go again? '*Everything* in a person must be beautiful,'" he imitates me, taunting softly. "'His mind and his *body*—'"—at the word "body" his eyes do a quick sweep over me—"'his soul and his clothes.'"

"Stop it."

"Did Chekhov really say that?" he asks, his eyes dancing.

"I think—maybe. I don't remember the exact quote. Something of the sort."

He laughs. "That expression on Electrification's face—you could get high just looking at it."

With the high heel of my fancy sneaker I draw a circle in the dirt. The uneven shape looks too much like a heart. I smudge it with my sole, trying not to think of Ruslan staring at my leg the whole time, trying not to sway with the unreality of it—a boy praising me, first for my beauty, then for my courage, all in the space of one day.

"What about you?" I ask him.

"What about me? I'm on your side," he says. "I hate it. What their big dream of communism did to people like your mama, what it did to our land. I hate what it turned us into. Someone like my *babulia*, I mean . . ." He trails off.

"Your *babulia?*" I prompt him.

He doesn't answer.

"What about *your* mama?" I ask. "What does she do?"

He looks at me sideways and grins. "My life is rather trite, I'm afraid," he says. "Not like yours."

"You make it sound like I've had these adventures," I say. "But really, things were so boring, until . . ."

"Until?" he prompts me.

Until you looked at me in the courtyard, I could say. *Until now.*

We settle into silence. I think of all the questions I could ask him. What's a *Talmud,* Ruslan? Why did you call Aizerman's book that, and why did you step on it? Did you not see where you were going? A possibility pierces through the impossible sweetness of the sunny afternoon.

Could Ruslan have known what he was doing? Could he have purposefully ripped—could he have hated . . . ?

No. Not this soft-spoken lyrical boy, who believes in all the right things.

I remember how it was in this school and that, the shifting alliances I watched from afar. Some people are friends. Others just don't like each other. I remember the strain in Aizerman's voice, *"Take your boot off my book, Valentinov."* Obviously, Ruslan and he have some kind of a bad *history*.

A woman in a house-robe, wearing galoshes over her bare feet, comes out of an apartment building, dragging a bucket full of garbage behind her.

"My mama might be home now," I say. "Would you like to meet her?"

I pull him by the arm as if I have known him all my life, as if I truly am this new Sonya.

"What's the hurry?" he asks, while we dash across Lenin Street, not bothering to wait for the traffic light to change.

I keep on running. Why waste time on chatter when Mama awaits us, right now, my dissident Jewish Star? One look at her by him will answer all my questions.

10

I Live Here

I turn the giant key in our apartment's door. An acid smell of burnt potatoes bursts into my nostrils. My parents' muffled voices reach us from the closed door of the living room.

"Mama! Andrei—I mean, Papa!"

Ruslan puts my backpack down in the hall, keeping his own on.

I clutch his arm and lead him swiftly through the hallway, maneuvering around cardboard boxes filled with Mama's papers, hoping he doesn't notice the tangle of wires hanging by the door, green paint peeling off the radiator, of that little corner just near the armoire, where the super-fashionable relief wallpaper is peeling a bit.

The sight of a closed living room door brings us to a halt.

"Mama. Papa? I—"

"Sh-sh-sh." Ruslan pulls on my arm, suddenly.

And that's when I hear it.

"Your fucking orders, Comrade General." Andrei's voice, so distorted, I don't recognize it at fist.

The shuffling of feet. Chairs scraping across the living room floor. I hear Mama's voice. A loud, piercing voice.

"You need to stop drinking and start rehearsing!"

The voice of my new father. The high-pitched, liquid, swimming voice.

"You . . ."

"That's enough, Sonya," Ruslan whispers, as their voices intertwine, thickening.

He tries to pull me away, but my feet do not move. Something breaks. Ruslan unglues me from the hardwood floor and practically carries me out. The door bangs shut behind us.

I am walking—somewhere, anywhere, away from this place that isn't home right now. I will never bring Ruslan there again. If something happens between the two of them, will Mama lose the apartment? What about me, then—back to Siberia? Never. I'd rather live at this construction site that looms before us if I must.

Mama told me that she had named me "Sonya," because as a newborn, that first day, I did nothing but sleep. And all my life, that's what I have been. A sleepyhead. A *sonya*. Feeling more awake than ever, I grip the hand of the boy by my side, a boy I didn't even know existed yesterday.

We make our way to a massive block, surrounded by a mess of iron tubes, beams, and concrete squares. Ruslan is out of cigarettes. I have run out of tears. "*Cheerik, cheerik,*" the sparrows argue above our heads.

Our shoulders brush as we watch the outlines of the moon together. And suddenly this world before me is the only world there is. Scattered blocks look like the stone steps of a castle, a metal construction crane near ruins. There is just me and him, and the cold catacombs of iron tubes and concrete blocks.

"I feel like I live here," I say, and I don't even worry whether or not my words make any sense. "Welcome to my castle."

Ruslan shakes his head at me and slides even closer. The chill of the evening reaches me under the smoky roughness of his uniform jacket. "It's too bad I'll be away," he says.

"*What?* Away—where?" I stare ahead, hoping the incoming dark hides the feelings on my face.

"All I can tell you is . . . it's political. All right?" He takes my face in both his hands and turns it toward his. I quit breathing. "We are organizing a demonstration."

I widen my eyes.

When Mama was my age she went to a demonstration, at a time when no one did. Now, it's the latest squeak of fashion: *protests, meetings.* Except it's not that safe. Names noted and stored, faces remembered. Babushka warned me. Things can turn anytime, everyone says so. It's happened before: after Stalin, just as people started talking, just as the truth started to come out— *BOOM*—one fine morning the general secretary of the USSR suddenly retires for "health reasons," and the nation grows quiet once more.

Staring at Ruslan's pale face framed by the darkness, I can just see it. A file somewhere in some KGB basement, a black folder with sturdy pockets labeled "Ruslan Valentinov" in some bureaucrat's neat handwriting. On top of the first one, another folder marked "Sonya Solovay."

"Are you sure you'll be safe?" I blurt out.

He shrugs. "Who knows?"

I turn away. I don't want him to see my forehead creased with worry, like a babushka's. But his hands are warm on my shoulders, steering me back.

"Look at me," he commands. He is grinning. "I was just kidding. It *is* safe. No one ever dares harass us."

"Us—who?"

He shrugs again.

"Then take me with you!"

He smiles, even as he pulls his face away. "A demonstration isn't a tourist attraction," he says. "Or a place for girls," he adds, touching my cheek with a tip of his finger.

"Not for girls like you."

"Why not?" I say furiously. "What sort of coward do you think I am?"

He laughs, and I am grateful for the darkness that hides the heat of my cheeks. "You're too . . . gentle," he says. "Too innocent. And—" He smirks. "Too crazy for your own good, *myshka.*"

"Who are you calling a mouse?"

"You." He smirks wider.

I squeeze my lips tight together so I don't smile back at him by accident.

"How long will you be gone for?" I ask, trying to sound like I couldn't care less.

He catches hold of my hand, ice cold inside his warm one. "Till the rest of the week. Sunday morning I'll be home." He plays with my fingers. "Maybe I can stop by your apartment—"

"No!" I say. *My apartment smells of burnt potatoes.* "But my . . . um . . . *stepfather* is performing on Sunday night. What do you think about . . . another trip to the center of Moscow?"

He stops playing with my fingers and starts rubbing my hand, then my arm. Higher and higher his fingers climb, under the sleeve of his own jacket.

"That's a little unusual, don't you think?" he says in a throaty wheeze. "A woman, asking a guy out on a date?"

Now I allow my smile to grow. "I may have been born in a quiet town called Myshkin," I say. "But I'm no *myshka*. Not anymore."

11

Nearsighted

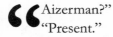"Aizerman?"
"Present."

The roll call always starts with Aizerman.

He is sitting alone, center section, first desk, his spot in every classroom. *Maybe I can talk to him,* I catch myself thinking. *Would he be surprised if I showed him my secret star? Would I have the courage to do it?*

The morning trembles, so unsure, through the naked classroom windows, as though the day is having second thoughts about beginning.

I too have second thoughts. And third, and fourth.

"Borodin?"

"Present."

"Vagonina?"

"Present."

"Valentinov?"

"Absent."

It's been just a few days, and the whispers are turning into murmurs. *"He is cutting school already? Whoa!"* I hear his friend Dimon whisper to Yurik Stepkin behind me.

I look for something to concentrate on. The tall stand on my desk with lots of metal rings to hold the vials. The burner with thick cable, the big aluminum knob to turn it on and off. Mendeleev's Periodic Table of Elements above the blackboard in the front of the room. I examine the elements intently, so no one catches it on my face, how much I miss him.

Without the possibility of his hand brushing mine in the hallway, the magic of New Life seems to be fading from this place, the first day of school now a colorful dream. Without those gray-muddy-blue eyes looking into my soul, I feel unseen. Small. Colorless.

Quiet.

"Solovay?"

"Present."

But am I?

"*Psst!*" A rolled-up paper ball hits me on the shoulder.

I turn around. It's Kuzmin, from a few desks behind me—grinning, whispering, "Where is your prince?" loud enough for everyone in between us to hear.

"Whose prince?" someone whispers.

I turn away. In the classroom so white and beige, my cheeks glow and glow.

Something swishy grazes my ear. A paper airplane. Some lines are scrawled across it in annoying green ink. *I liked your outfit better on Monday.* I whirl back toward Kuzmin's desk. "If you don't leave me alone . . ." I mouth at him.

He beams, grabs his backpack, and gets up from his chair. One noiseless stride, two desks down, and he plops into an empty seat right next to me.

"If I don't leave you alone, then what?" Kuzmin whispers in my ear. For some reason—no good reason at all, really—I glance helplessly at Aizerman.

Half the class is eyeing Kuzmin and me with quite some interest. Only Aizerman in the front row doesn't bother to turn his head. His full attention is—of course—on the chemistry textbook before him.

"What are you gaping at?" Kuzmin whispers. "Looking for a new rescuer?"

The teacher, Klavdia Maximovna, puts away her attendance book, takes one look at the class, without really seeing our faces, and plunges straight into formulas.

"On the desks before you please find acids of various strengths, water, and a few concentrated base solutions," Klavdia Maximovna says.

Kuzmin nods back at her with a solemn expression, grabs a vial with clear liquid, and gives it a vigorous shake.

"Get back to your desk," I say in what I hope passes for a savage whisper, not a desperate one. He scrapes his chair closer to mine.

"Remember, acid molecules donate protons to other molecules, while base molecules accept protons." Klavdia Maximovna paces the front of the classroom, nodding at her own words, oblivious to my misery.

The clock on the wall must have broken down—it can't possibly move this slowly, time just can't run out of breath this way. *Hurry up, clock.* The week is almost over. I move my chair away from Kuzmin, closer to the window. He moves his closer still. I turn away from him. Looking at the already brightening Friday I think of Ruslan at his secret demonstration, making trouble, *mattering,* while I must remain behind, as always. Mama's little girl, a good pupil, back in the scratchy brown school uniform dress I thought I'd left behind forever, listening to the chemistry teacher's excited explanations about the beauty of chemical reactions. I try to imagine Ruslan, in ripped jeans with holes, shouting the way they do on the Independent TV Channel, "Democracy!" "Freedom to the Republics!" "Real freedom of speech!"

In the gray shimmer of the ever-stretching morning, it's easy to wonder, *What did such a drastic boy even see in me?*

And will he still see *me when he returns?*

Kuzmin's hand lands on my leg. I jump up from my chair.

A faint buzz rises in the classroom. Finally, Klavdia Maximovna notices. Aizerman swivels his head and stares at me.

"Why are you standing?" she asks me in a suddenly high, irritated voice. The buzz of murmurs dies. "What's the matter—can't see the formulas?"

Formulas—is that all the woman ever thinks about?

As Kuzmin snickers beside me, I flash a pleasant smile back at the teacher, and, trembling with sudden inspiration, say, "It's true, Klavdia Maximovna . . . The formulas? Can't see them too well from here. I . . . was wondering if maybe I could move closer to the front?"

If it was Electrification, she would have asked, *Does your sudden nearsightedness have anything to do with your new desk neighbor?* But this woman in a strange mid-length cream-color dress that resembles a laboratory coat with its buttons in the front, is impatient to move on to ionizing.

"Go ahead, you may sit beside—him." She points to the front of the classroom.

I grab my backpack and, sending Kuzmin a sparkly farewell smile, leave my old desk for the empty seat beside Aizerman.

Aizerman doesn't sit alone in most classes—just in some, I guess. I was wrong when at first I thought him invisible the way I was in my old life. Guys give him friendly nods as they pass him by. I've heard him chat, throw out a joke. Once or twice, I saw Diana Komissar examine his eyelashes with curiosity. It's just that he doesn't seem to mind being alone.

Did I mind it, in my old life? Even as I hid in my books, and dreamed and *slept?* Maybe I did, just a little.

I slide behind his desk. Aizerman greets me with a quizzical glance, a quick flutter of eyelashes.

"You aren't nearsighted," he whispers.

I stare at him. Is he saying he doesn't want me here? Well, maybe I don't want to be here, either. Maybe I wish I were in the center of Moscow, right now, doing more important things.

"No, I'm not nearsighted," I whisper through my teeth. "But maybe you are?"

Now it's Aizerman's turn to look up, surprised, from the vial of NaOH he was fingering. His black eyebrow arches into an elegant curve.

He throws his hands apart, palms out. "It was just an observation."

"Didn't you *observe* that jerk bothering me?" What started out as an unnerved whisper has grown into a full-fledged voice.

"What is this?" The teacher's voice explodes in my ear. "Had I known you would start such a bazaar..." She shakes her finger at me.

Aizerman gets up from his chair. "I am sorry, Klavdia Maximovna," he says firmly. "It was my fault."

Immediately, I feel bad. It wasn't Aizerman's job to watch over me. "No." I get up, too. "Actually, it was mine."

Klavdia Maximovna just sighs at us both. As soon as she troops away, he turns to me. A subtle layer of a blush, a sort of a glow, makes the tan on Aizerman's face appear richer, deeper around his cheeks. "I . . . I wasn't paying attention . . . this—" he nods at the teacher, pacing between the rows "—it's one of my favorite subjects." He extends his hand, like a grown-up, except he does so under the desk where the teacher of his favorite subject won't notice. "I'm Misha," he whispers.

"Sonya." Our hands clasp under the desk. His handshake is warm and tight. His hand feels like something I have touched many times before. A sunny feeling seeps through me, making a smile appear, just on its own, across my face. Have I just made a friend? Is it that easy?

On the other hand, nothing is easy about chemistry here in Moscow Region.

The Os and Hs on the board now connect, now scatter. We fill the vials with clear liquids. Klavdia Maximovna assures us some of them will change colors when mixed and heated. She paces between the rows and gives out instructions. I crinkle my forehead in concentration, then point at the corner of the board. "What type of acid is this one again?" I whisper.

He shakes his head. "Look, the thing that distinguishes a strong acid from a weak one is how it . . ." He throws a weary look toward the back of the room, where Klavdia Maximovna has just finished helping a confused pair of hooligans. "How about—maybe after school? Or before. Sometimes I am here early in the mornings." He shrugs, as if to let me know that this way or that, it doesn't matter. "I . . . can't do it today—I have to be in Moscow—but maybe—"

"In Moscow? What, don't tell me it's something *political*?" I whisper.

"Why? No," he whispers back. "It's more . . . religious, I'd say."

"You go to church?"

"Not church, no." His dark eyes penetrate mine. Absent-mindedly shifting the vials on our desk with his long fingers, he doesn't seem focused on chemistry any longer.

"How about Monday?" He leans close. No pickles or sausage, no tobacco on his breath. Just the warmth of being human. "I'll come to school early. If you need help, you'll find me in history."

"Thank you . . . I . . . do need help, but . . ." All I can think is, *Monday*. Ruslan will be back by then.

"Or—*hey*—hey—" He lowers his voice, looking around. "How about tomorrow?"

I look at him doubtfully.

"Sunday?"

"I can't. I . . . have a date on Sunday."

He blushes. And right behind him, the now absolutely furious chemistry teacher is flying toward our desk.

"In the end of ends!" she shouts. "I see this is too easy for you. You have it all covered, don't you? In that case, I am giving you all a *controlka* on acids! Everyone, be ready on Tuesday!"

"What?!"

"A quiz? The second week of school?!"

The class collapses with groans.

"So . . ." Misha asks me when everyone quiets down. "Who's the date with? Anyone I know?"

My cheeks blooming, I look away and get back to chemistry.

12

His Girl

Bus number 346 shakes our bones as it drives us along a patchy road. The air inside is nothing but fumes and breath. Space, too, is in short supply, a rare commodity like boots, refrigerators, bread, sausage, or just about anything. But Ruslan's hand sliding down the sweaty railing and landing on mine at each traffic-light jolt more than compensates for these inconveniences of life.

I've never been on a date before.

A true one. The kind they write in books about.

Fellow passengers push their weight onto me. They shove their thick shoulders into my nose. I grin through their wrinkled faces. They look at my smile as though I'm touched, like my head has departed. Maybe I wouldn't be smiling, either, if, like them, I was on my way to a hunt for fresh meat and socks in the capital, net sack at the ready.

In the inside pocket of my new pink leather jacket is a pair of second-row Moscow Concert Hall tickets. And my Jewish Star. I stuck it in there this morning, for, I don't know, luck. For courage. Maybe I'll show it to him today.

Not now, of course. Not in this angry crowd.

"How was, you know?" I wink at him, through all those people. "The *secret* thing?"

His hand stays on mine. His mouth moves to my ear. "It was good," he whispers, his hot breath tickling me.

"Will there be more?"

He nods. His thin smile. How I've missed it.

"Maybe next time, you'll take me?"

Demonstrations. That's the best place to be in Moscow. Better than a concert hall. Better than the McDonald's they have just built in the city center, where Ruslan promised to take me today, before my father's show.

The growing crowd reshuffles yet again at the next stop. *Hmph*, a puff of salty-sour air flies toward me in a foul-smelling snort. It comes from an odd-faced man with pockmarked cheeks, his eyes glazed over. Even when the bus slows, the man can't stand straight.

"What you gaping at?" he asks me, roughly.

Now I stare, transfixed, at the strange man's yellow teeth. Ruslan tries to pulls me closer. But when the bus jumps over a pothole, the man leans into my face again. "Nice jacket," he says.

"Just don't look at him," Ruslan hisses into my ear.

I turn my head away, and face instead a cranky-looking old man in a checkered cap, muttering, "Let me through! I'm an invalid! I'm a veteran!"

The man's voice rises over the noisy shaking of the bus, about how he fought the Germans, got a bullet in his calf, and deserved a seat. The sour-smelling barely-standing drunk beside me tries to latch onto the sleeve of my jacket, but misses.

Arguments rise up slowly, thickening like the dust pouring out of the back of the bus, then settling over us like the soot covering the windows.

"What, you think *she* doesn't deserve a seat?" A younger man with a thoughtful face points at a harried-looking woman with an empty net sack, whose shawl is falling off her shoulder. "She works all day, probably has a child to feed, no?"

"We deserve one, too, as we'll be standing in line for McDonald's for two hours at least, right?" I ask Ruslan cheerfully, earning scowls from all sides for us both.

"The country upside-down . . ." the veteran mutters, shaking his finger at me.

"McDonald's . . . isn't that nice?" the drunk echoes him. "Hard-working . . . people . . . can't find underwear in a store— not a sausage in a refrigerator . . ." His wavering voice grows. " . . . while some teenage *Jid* struts around in a *pink* leather jacket and stuffs herself at a McDonald's restaurant."

I clutch the railing, gritting my teeth hard. I don't hear the rest of his nonsense, not after that word—not again—trailing me like a cursed shadow.

Heat covers my face. When I look at Ruslan's, for a second I don't recognize him. His eyes grow hard, as though something just closed within him.

"What did you just say to *my girl*, dumb asshole?" Ruslan wheezes.

"Ooooh, you love your little *jid-ovochka,* eh?"

Murmurs rise all around us. Ruslan gives the drunk a shove on the chest. The crowd behind the drunk shifts, and he staggers backward.

"What's this country coming to?" the checkered-cap veteran says. He raises his index finger in the air and points it at me, at Ruslan, at the drunk, who is scrambling back up again.

"It's the *Jidy*, I tell you," the drunk slurs.

"I said, shut it, you fucking idiot!" His face completely unrecognizable now, Ruslan rushes headfirst at the drunk, though several pairs of arms restrain him. My heart hammering, I press against him. The young man with the nice face appears before us, standing tall, separating us from the drunk and the veteran, both.

"Calm down, comrades," he says evenly.

Ruslan holds me under the arms like I am some kind of a doll, his hands so close to my chest on either side of me. I don't move them aside. His breathing slows. "I won't let anyone hurt you, *myshka,*" he whispers. Whom he is trying to soothe, himself or me, I do not know. "*Sh-sh-sh,*" he breathes into my ear, rocking me a little. "Don't you mind him. I bet he's on drugs. I bet he was hallucinating."

And yet, somehow, the drunk saw right through me, Ruslan.

The doors of the bus jerk open, letting in fresh diesel-filled air. More people pile in at each stop, pile on top of me. They thaw the early autumn chill off each other's bodies, breathing, coughing, sweating, smelling of smoke, trying to separate me from Ruslan in their fierce search for a better spot. But he keeps his hands on my waist, or at least I hope they're his, holding me tight, saving me from the shifting crowd, shielding me from a drunk who blames everything on Jews. I tremble in his arms, less now from fear and more from the excitement of being his *myshka.* I am his *girl,* he said so. He said so.

13

Not Ours

I am sitting across from Ruslan, our faces so close, with barely any space in between us at the horseshow-shaped table crowded with wonders. A hamburger each. A packet of fried potatoes cut into neat yellow rectangles. To wash it all down, a pair of milkshakes. Mine is strawberry, the color of my leather jacket.

As for dessert, Ruslan said he didn't want any, a bit glumly, I thought, as he smoothed out his crumpled-up rubles and thrust them at a drastic-looking *chiksa* in a magenta uniform. She smiled at us from behind the counter. I gaped back at her. A sales lady, *smiling?*

University student-age guys and girls weave in and out of the crowd, picking up trays, directing a stream of hungry people to this corner and that. One could hardly call them waiters the way they look right back at you and smile. Who wouldn't be proud in such bold-color uniforms, working in this exotic place?

I have lined all of my little boxes and packets along the sides of the table, which is much longer than it is wide. After the hellish bus ride and the four-hour wait outside, I don't hold back. I take bites of this and that and everything together.

Ruslan stops chewing on his fried potato and watches me. I am fascinated with a packet of ketchup. I try to rip open and squeeze the tomato paste onto my plate, like space food.

"For God's sake, Sonya," he finally says, and I look up at him. "What, your mama doesn't feed you?"

I stop, mid-bite. "*Nu* . . . Of course she does . . ."

All around us friends snap each other's photos behind bright posters of giant sandwiches and drinks half the size of a person. Even respectable-looking middle-aged ladies giggle and slurp, the warm meaty smells inside the enormous restaurant having melted the anger of a long wait off their faces. Except for Ruslan's face—an ice statute.

"Try the apple pie, Ruslan."

He scowls.

"I haven't even finished this thing." He gestures at the humongous sandwich lying on his plate, untouched, except for maybe three bite marks.

"A *hamburger*," I say.

"Whatever it's called."

I dare meet his stare, so suddenly flat. It reminds me of the way he looked at the drunk in the bus. The cold lump of sundae burns my throat. I force it down.

When I had first showed him the concert hall tickets out at the bus stop, he squinted at me. "Let's see, the show starts at 8. We'll have a heap of time to hang out. What would you like to visit in the capital?"

"McDonald's," I blurted out.

"Are you sure?" And he shrugged, frowning at me.

As if for the first time, I look at the surface of our table. He is sitting so close to me across the horseshoe table. I think we were supposed to sit beside, not across from, each other. Our knees touch. He shifts them.

"What did I do wrong?"

He puts down his hamburger and reaches for my hand, his eyes softening.

"It's just that it's disgusting, all of it," he says. "All right, maybe not so much the food. But the line to get in here. The sight of us Russians—" He pauses meaningfully, letting his last words *us Russians* settle over the food, settle into a tiny lump inside me "—Salivating at all this when, truthfully, it doesn't even taste that great."

Us Russians. But I am not Russian. At least by mother I'm not. What would he say if he knew my real nationality?

He wouldn't care. I am *his girl*. What does it matter if I am Ukrainian, a Georgian, or a Jew?

He wouldn't care. Of course, he wouldn't.

Ruslan keeps on talking. He is doing something with his voice. I think he's trying to make it sound low. Like he's a man philosophizing at a dinner table. Except he doesn't even have stubble on his cheeks, only a thin mustache, and his voice is but a rasp in my ear. "Are you going to tell me you've never eaten anything better than this before? That this is more chic than the Russian flat pancakes with homemade strawberry jam?"

"Magical." I say it so quietly.

"What?"

"This. This place is magical. Like . . . you know . . . something from . . . another world."

For a moment, he's speechless. Only for a moment. "That's what the problem is."

With one gesture he pushes aside both his tray and mine, and they almost topple off the table. "We like it because it's *foreign*. It's cool because it's not *ours*."

He looks at me expectantly. I'm thinking, *What's ours?* Fresh rye bread with smoked sprats. The barely-there sweetness of birch tree juice. Babushka's nesting wooden *matryoshka* dolls I played with endlessly as a little girl, fascinated with how one fits into another, and another, and another. Cloth dolls with big skirts sitting over samovars. A chorus of drunken voices yelling a folk song at a wedding. Why does the *ours* feel so *foreign* sometimes? Am I *ours?*

I am Jewish, Ruslan. Is that all right? The words almost make it out.

But there is so much more to it than that. How can I explain to him what being a Jew really means when I myself barely know? *Jewish* is a nationality in your mother's passport. It's the color of your mother's hair. It's the dirty word a drunk calls you on the bus. The teachers tell you to be proud of your home, "the best country in the world," but it feels more like a room some sweet money-needing babushka is letting you rent for the rest of your life.

I am Jewish, Ruslan. But he is on a roll, talking and talking. And I don't want him to frown at me again.

"We don't need this." His hand sweeps over the multilevel, multicolor space around us. "When we have our own treasures. Communism took so much of it away from us, for such a long time. And just when we started getting it all back, who knows how long we'll even hold on to it for? The old-guard communists are pushing Gorbachev hard to reverse his course—or else."

The old guard. *Old Life.*

The memory of the stupid tanks passing outside the Volga front window flashes in my mind.

"Maybe by this time next year, they will have closed all the churches, except for the guided tours on architecture." His eyes fix on me, suddenly severe. "The Uspenski Cathedral in Myshkin, you don't even remember if you've been there. And here we are sitting at a *McDonald's*—" I think of Misha beside me in chemistry, blushing so hard that it had felt as though the fire on his cheeks had spread to mine. Misha Aizerman doesn't go to church. *Where does he go?*

"*Myshka,* are you listening? You know our biggest treasure of all?" Ruslan has gotten so animated. His hands run all over, overturning things, playing with ketchup packets. His legs bump mine underneath the table. His sneaker tears briskly past my leg. That Puma sneaker.

"Our biggest treasure is a—what?" He stares. "*What?* Tell me what's on your mind right now."

"Your sneakers," I say, obedient as ever.

"My sneakers." He just looks at me.

The words tumble out before I even know what I'm saying, plop onto his now cold food. "They're imported. Why do you wear them, then?"

He looks down on the floor, startled, down at his own feet he looks, like he has never seen them. "It's only one pair of sneakers," he says. "It's just . . . my father . . . Sometimes he gets me these idiotic presents."

He seems it so small and wretched as he says it, for a moment I cannot look at his pale face without having to control every muscle on my own.

"Where is your father?" I prompt him in the smallest voice. "Your mother?"

"Look, you're changing the subject." His voice rattles. "The biggest treasure is our soul, *myshka.* The Russian soul. And none of these pitiful little packets, none of these sandwiches could ever hope to feed it. Please tell me you understand, *moya myshka.*"

Once again, there is no escape from his eyes.

He sees me as a girl with light hair, a small nose like his, with speech Russian-neat, what they call "pure." A Russian treasure is what he sees across the table. His own little Russian treasure. "*My* myshka," he just called me.

What more could a girl like me ever want?

"Don't you understand?" he asks again.

"*Nu* da," I say. "I understand. But—" *I have to make you too understand, somehow.* "—don't you ever wish you were an American? I mean," I add, trying to think, blushing harder, "They have *all kinds* of people over there, and they all seem to belong." He squeezes his eyebrows together, like my words don't make sense. "I mean," I rush on, before he interrupts me again, "Wouldn't it be cool to be like them? Loud? Brave? Not caring what other people think of you? *Smiling?*"

He frowns more deeply. His lips grow thinner.

I keep trying. "Sometimes . . . it's hard for me to believe I was born in this country. Sometimes, it seems . . . as though it adopted me or—something. Sometimes—" His fingers catch mine, surprising me. He squeezes them—my fingers—so hard it hurts. The words tangle inside my throat.

"You can't say that. No matter how long the lines, how spare the sausage, you're a Russian! Promise, promise me, *myshka,* that you will never forget who you are."

He sounds just like Mama. Sitting on the edge of my bed before the first day of New Life, handing me my present. "It's you," she had said, giving me my Jewish Star.

"Well . . ." I say. His hand moves over mine again, and again, owning my palm, my fingers, everything, "Actually, I'm not . . ." I stumble, because my eyes catch his and get swallowed up by his much too attentive stare. From somewhere deep inside my brain, something reaches and grabs my almost-uttered words and shoves them back inside me.

"Promise you'll never forget who you are," he repeats.

I smile back. "I promise."

He lifts his milkshake glass to toast this. I take mine. Then, smiling, a boldness tearing through me, I put my glass down before Ruslan and take his glass out of his hand. He grins back at me. We raise our switched glasses. With a dull clink, they touch each other. They say if you drink from somebody else's glass, you'll know that person's thoughts. Maybe he can read all about me in the cold strawberry softness. I slurp the thick vanilla swirl from Ruslan's glass. His unsettling gray-blue eyes never leave my face as we drink. I don't know anything about his family or how many girls he dated from our class. I don't know what he sees when he looks at me the way he does right now. All right, maybe I can't read his thoughts. But I can taste his feelings.

14

A Dog's Life

Stuffed, warm, and drunk from each other's milkshakes, we float out of McDonald's. The early evening sky is the color of a gasoline-filled puddle. The wide boulevards are free of mean drunks for now, our hands are hooked, and we are almost late for the show.

He holds my hand in the dark auditorium pierced by multicolored lights, to the parade of songs, the pounding of changing rhythm patterns, to the even sound of hundreds of hands beating together. People in glittering costumes throw their affected voices at us, shake their behinds, and joke and fuss on the shiny stage before us. A clown in a wig with two ponytails flips, dances, and falls with fake clumsiness. The clown is wearing a deliberately foolish bone-covered nurse uniform I've seen hanging in our armoire. A guitarlike instrument but smaller, not pear-shaped, dangles in his hand.

"Look, that's him—that's my father!"

"He plays the *balalaika?*"

I nod, beaming, clapping, forgiving Andrei Samoyedov for an occasional drunken night. Clown Samoyedov sends an unmistakable wink in our direction, then plops onto all fours, loftily catching the balalaika with one hand, and barks into the audience.

Laughter greets his rolling and balalaika-juggling antics. *"A do-o-og bites like a do-o-og when she leads a do-o-og's life,"* the music howls.

"Who are you?" my father half-says and half-barks at another clown crawling on all fours. That other one is wrapped in thick shiny real-looking fur. The second clown doesn't twirl and flip over his head as skillfully as Andrei—my papa! But he squeezes a fluorescent-color ball into his mouth.

"I'm an American bulldog," the clown replies, his words muffled with the ball stuffed in his mouth. "And you?"

"Just a Russian mongrel," my father says, setting the balalaika aside.

"So, is life better under the perestroika, friend?" asks the American bulldog.

"Oh, much better," Papa says. "Well, they did move the bowl of food out of reach just a bit—" He twists his leg, and scratches his wig with his foot "—but the chain's much longer, and they let you bark as much as you please."

I don't clap to Papa's woofs and howls, because my hand is in Ruslan's grip again.

"Your father is incredible," he says, his face in mine, my eyes in his. "You are incredible."

My skin soaks in Ruslan's soft breath. Suddenly, we are alone in this large auditorium, alone in Moscow. His mouth moves toward mine. My breath gets stuck inside me.

A rude heel bores into my foot. I don't even realize that I've let out a shriek until I notice people's eyes, people's faces everywhere.

A large woman with dark hair over her face shoves her pompously dressed body and her enormous feet though the narrow passage in front of our seats. Here goes her shiny square shoe over my other sneaker. I scrunch my face up in pain.

"Watch where you're walking, *Jid*-face," Ruslan tells her.

Slowly the poisonous word sinks its teeth into me. The woman, who probably wasn't even Jewish—or maybe she was—is long gone. Ruslan's thin lips are moving, I think they are asking a question. I think I'm even answering. The clowns bow before me, pressing flowers to their hearts. They make way for singers and dancers. I watch them all, pretending he didn't just say what he said. I sit in the dark, unable to cry or feel or take my freezing hand out of Ruslan's grip.

Part II
Secrets

15

Curses Never Make Sense

Inside my room the piano releases a pitiful wail when I drop the lid. I look around for other things to clatter or rip and find nothing but green heads of a plant that blooms in December. My backpack on the floor. A mess of heart-shaped erasers on my desk.

Papa is not yet home from the show. Mama isn't here, either. The apartment is empty, smelling of nothing.

Ruslan walked me here. I smiled at him and said, "Bye now."

"Hey, maybe—" he started to say.

"I'll see you at school." I closed the door in his face, with his nose practically still in it, because I didn't want to want to let his hand brush past mine again.

"But wait—"

"Forgive me," I said, through the door. "But I need to be alone now."

And here I am. Once again, all alone.

Five minutes after he's gone, I wish I'd followed. Furiously, I search the inside pockets of my jacket. I dig the Jewish Star from its hiding place. I put it around my neck. *That's all right*, I tell myself. I will see Ruslan in school tomorrow. First thing in the morning. And I'll tell him. I'll tell him to go find another girl to lay his charms on. I'll tell him to take his Russian treasures and shove them. He'll know where.

I take my boots off and throw them violently against the hardwood floor of the foyer, my foot still smarting from the impact with the wretched woman's heel. What was she thinking, walking right over my foot? Didn't she see Ruslan and me leaning into each other?

I put the lights on everywhere. In the living room, I turn on the television, just to shatter the silence.

On Central TV, Channel One's nightly news program *Vremya*, the most famous democrat, Boris Yeltsin, stands at a podium, challenging the president of the USSR.

"The Supreme Soviet of the Russian Republic has concluded that the government of the USSR is not capable of leading the country out of this profound economic crisis," the news anchor reads, frowning at the statement.

Gorbachev and Yeltsin used to be political allies. Now they're enemies. How quickly some people change allegiances. How strongly people hate each other.

I shut off the TV and take the red telephone from its headset on the wall. My finger itches to press itself against the black buttons of what used to be my home number back in safe, quiet Siberia. Dial Babushka: ask her advice.

Maybe even tell her I've had enough of this New Life of Mama's. Tell her she's been right to be worried, political troubles are brewing. Tell her I am going home, back to the place where the rules are clear. I think of my old bookshelf stuffed with books, the comfort of the piano standing right across from my bed, Babushka always knowing how to talk to me. No more boys, no more tangled feelings.

Yes, run away, Sonya, tail tucked between your legs. Run back to a hiding place, where neither troubles nor happiness will ever find you again.

I dial the number.

"What happened, Sonechka?" Babushka shouts at me through time and space, shouts with all her might, as if her voice could cover the distance between us. "Is everything all right? Where is your mama?"

"Mama's resting," I lie, so easily, not wanting to make her wonder.

"How is school? Friends? Teachers? Andrei? How is the apartment? You eating well? Studying hard? Being good for your mama?"

I smile at the string of questions, trying to imagine her pacing inside the tiny square of a one-room apartment we shared, glad she can't see my pale, empty face right now. My fingers tangle with the shoelace of my Jewish Star.

"My mama gave me a present," I say.

"Some pretty new clothes?"

"That was Andrei."

The high-heeled boots. The Princess shirt. How little they matter right now. "Mama gave me a *Magen Dovid.*" I whisper it, but the way she sucks in breath, then grows silent, I know she hears me perfectly.

"This isn't for a telephone conversation," she says finally, her own voice dropping.

I shake my head. "We are not bugged, Babushka. Besides, being Jewish isn't against the law."

"No it's not." She sighs. "But it's not easy, either. Remember, you have a . . ." She trails off.

"Choice," I finish for her. "I know, I know. I'm a half-Russian, half-Jew."

"It's not exactly like that." She hesitates, another long, probably costly pause across the kilometers. "I know someone who is traveling to Moscow soon. I'll send along a package. Some of your old books. Lots of pickled tomatoes. And a letter."

It must be past midnight when Mama and Papa come home at last. Not a glimmer of sleep in my eye, I jump out of bed right in my nightgown.

"Sh-sh-sh," Mama whispers, too loudly, "you'll wake Sonya."

"You're the one who needs to shut up for a change, bitch," Papa slurs.

I freeze, listening to their footsteps down the hall.

I don't dare lie back down for a while or even lift my fingers up to shut my ears. I hate my own traitorous body for trembling so.

In the light of the day, they kiss and laugh at each other. Now that the sun has hidden, they throw more words at each other—ugly, awful, unprintable words, making no sense. Then again, curses never make sense, do they?

I thought I was too numb to cry. And too old. Even as a toddler I was never a crier, and all those years without Mama I never shed a tear over missing her. Sometimes I almost wished I could cry. It seemed so romantic and feminine in all these books and movies. Now my cheeks are coated with salty, sticky tears, as I listen to Mama and Papa lose their voices at each other from across the wall, and there is nothing romantic about any of it.

16

Equilibrium

In the early Monday morning hour, I share the school with the janitor dangling her keys on the way to the history classroom.

"Gabbing about," the janitor mutters at me. "Various types. Hooligans. When all honest children are just awakening, eating breakfast."

"Couldn't sleep." I look away from the janitor, so she doesn't notice my puffy, puffy eyes. *Didn't want to be home,* I don't add, obviously.

I expect her to work the lock, but she just pushes the classroom door open. Light pours out from inside the room. I grow immobile. He is here, already?

Good. Running my fingers over the side of my neck and touching the shoelace of my Jewish Star, I walk into the room and wonder if my fingers will have the strength to pull the star out from underneath my uniform dress.

"Good morning," a melodious clear voice greets me. "I guess you really need help, after all?"

I stare at him. Only it isn't *him*. It's Misha Aizerman, putting a book away, smiling at me from the first row.

He gets up from his chair. "I'm sorry," he says. "I . . . didn't mean to be . . . sarcastic. I guess I didn't really expect you to show up."

I lean against the door as it closes softly after the still-muttering janitor.

He squints. "What's that you got here?"

"Nothing." Automatically, my ice-cold fingers drop my Jewish Star back under my dress. "I should just—"

"Don't worry," Misha says. "I still brought the chemistry textbook, just in case."

Right. Chemistry.

Numb, I float up to his desk. I start to take off the upturned chair beside his. He comes up to help me, placing his hands just next to mine.

"How was your date?" he asks quietly.

My hands start to shake like a drunk's and I let the chair go. It topples sideways on the floor.

"I'm sorry," Misha and I say in unison. Then we grow silent, both of us blushing, as if on command.

Sure, I memorized all of the formulas in Siberia. I read the textbook, answered the questions. But only here, in a deserted history classroom, have I discovered that chemistry can have so much more meaning than that. I have discovered too how easy it can be—just talking to a boy, without your entire body quivering.

"Many acids can be quite corrosive," Misha says, "melt flesh, dissolve metal, whatever you please. Others are harmless—*nyet*, not just harmless—healing."

"Isn't that crazy?" I say, so quietly, watching Misha walk around the room. "The same sort of substance, made out of essentially the same stuff, and yet . . ."

He comes up to me and squats before my chair. His knees bump into my legs. When he is this excited, he forgets to be awkward, forgets to blush under his permanent tan.

His fervor is contagious, making me forget to blush, too, making me forget Ruslan. Almost.

"It's life," Misha says. "Everything is like that."

I nod. "Corrosive people," I whisper. "I know what you mean."

"*Nyet*," Misha says. "I mean each one of us is like that. There are some forces in us that are corrosive and some life-giving."

I stare at his eyes. So dark they are, but how they can sparkle, surrounded by all those eyelashes. I shake my head. "Not you. There is nothing 'corrosive' in you." With each word, my whisper grows fainter.

He gives me a wry smile, then sort of freezes, as if he notices for the first time the way he is stooping before me, his knees to my legs. He doesn't get up.

"I'm only a person." He touches my hand. One of his fingers hooks with one of mine. His skin is warm. His face leans into mine. "Anyway," he breathes out, "no one could possibly be good without a little darkness inside him."

What is he doing? I stare at him. My breath won't come out, like someone had just knocked the wind out of me.

"I thought you were . . . *um* . . . like . . . religious," I squeeze out.

"I am," he whispers. His breath is soft on my face. "It's a part of my religion. The winter, or old age, or even—death— we need it. Tell me this, Sonya Solovay: if it weren't for the darkness, how would the moonlight reveal itself within each one of us?"

Transfixed, I just listen, hardly breathing.

"It isn't a question of us having it: we all have it. It's how much further we allow it to expand within us, how much power we grant it. The evil inclination, the *yetzer hara*, whatever you want to call it—"

"What's *yetzer hara?*"

"Evil inclination, like I said. But it's also, more. It's . . . Never mind." He gets up. "It's complicated." Shakes his curls, like he can't believe himself. I get up, too. Why are his cheeks burning so? And why are mine?

We go up to the board together and he teaches me to balance equations.

"So much of chemistry is about equilibrium," he says. "For example, when a strong acid is mixed with a strong base in equal amounts, the acid gives its protons to the base, correct?" His long fingers grasp the chalk with force. "And a base accepts it." Transfixed, I watch the chalk make furious scratches on Electrification's board, amazed at understanding the words that only a week ago would have run into one another the way phrases do in a foreign language.

"An equal amount of protons is exchanged and we end up with a solution that is neither acidic nor basic any longer. We have achieved equilibrium!" He cocks his head in triumph. I nod.

"Prove now that you understand," he says. "If you do, maybe . . . maybe next time we could move on to metals. . . ."

Next time. The words could fill me. Instead, they make everything come back. The bitter taste in my throat. The dark auditorium. My hand in Ruslan's. The corrosive word he threw at me. Was that just a word he picked up from the drunk on the bus, like a piece of gum that sticks to your shoe, without you even knowing it?

My hand twitches to the shoelace around my neck.

No one could possibly be good without a little darkness inside him. Didn't Misha just tell me so?

"*Nu?*" Misha prods me. "Did you understand?"

I look back at him, my heart beating too fast, my head spinning in confusion.

"Sometimes I feel like I am a walking equilibrium," I whisper, staring at the closed poster-clad door of the classroom, dreading what I am going to have to say and do when the door opens, and *he* walks in, flashing a thin smile at me.

"What are you talking about?" Misha is asking.

"Like water I am, neither base nor acid, all of the protons donated and accepted within me at once. Neither this nor that. Add me to an acid, add me to a base. . . . That's just the way I feel sometimes."

"What are you talking about? You—water!" He comes up to me, holds his hands over mine for a moment, and then drops them, like he's just touched a flame. The tan on his face grows rich. "You're nothing like water."

But as though to prove him wrong, water floods out of my eyes in a rush and I get up, grab my backpack, and run out of the classroom, bumping into my classmates, who are just starting to arrive.

17

Something You Must Know

I barely have time to catch my breath and drop my backpack to the floor with a great thud, when the emptiness around me vibrates with the sound of a door buzzer.

It can't be Mama. Glory to God, she is already gone, in class all day, probably. Papa is still sleeping, though he is supposed to be rehearsing out in Moscow. But, then again, I'm supposed to be in school . . . and . . . look at me now.

I couldn't stay there, with all these eyes watching, all these people breathing.

Not with *him* strolling through the door.

Then again, being here isn't helping me feel better, either.

I can't be here.

I can't be anywhere.

Through the peephole on the door I see a short skinny boy figure, and my heart lifts. The sleeves of his plain shirt are rolled all the way up to his shoulders. The buzzer rings again. My freezing fingers unlatch the lock on the door.

"What do you want?" I ask, trying to sound rude, my heart hammering so hard I'm afraid he can hear it.

"Nothing," Ruslan says, stepping inside. "Just a house call. I . . . May I come in?"

I don't move from my spot blocking the doorway. "Did you follow me home?" I ask in a whisper that barely makes it out at all.

He catches hold of my hand. I don't push his hand away.

"What happened?" he asks me softly, so softly, as if he's afraid to startle a sparrow. "Why did you run out like that?"

Now. All I have to do is tell him that he is my *yetzer hara*. Tell him to roll away as far from me as possible. Deep breath in, and already I am woozy with the odd combination of tobacco on his breath and the simple smell of children's soap on his skin. Come on, this is positively ridiculous. I mean, what's so special about this bristly hair on his head, this seashell curve of his ear, this nose so small and precise?

"I . . . don't . . . want you here." My eyes shut tight as I whisper this. "I don't want you . . . in this apartment . . . anymore." I open my eyes. He's nodding, like he understands.

I look down at my hand, still inside his, look at it like it's a foreign object, this body part I'm letting him borrow.

"It's your ancestors," he whispers back. "They're home. They've been fighting again. Correct?"

I produce a weak noise, birdlike.

"Let's not disturb them, then."

He takes a step back through the still open door, out into the hallway. He's about to release my hand. He's leaving. I blink at him. Is it relief I'm feeling? No, just emptiness. He pulls me out the door with him. The hallway is drenched in a boiled cabbage smell from a neighbor's kitchen. I lean against the wall next to the door to my apartment. My ears pound with a thousand drums.

"You think I care about that—your ancestors, fighting?" He stands so close to me, there is no escape from his eyes. His raspy voice scratches the nerve endings under my skin. "You think . . ." He trails off.

Misha's words in the empty history classroom echo in my brain: his words about the balance of the elements, the moonlight and the darkness.

I cannot think.

"I missed you yesterday." His nose brushes against mine.

"I missed you, too." The words escape in a rush of air.

"Come with me."

It's early—the construction workers aren't even here yet. My hand is still in his, and he is leading me up, higher and higher, among the slowly widening catacombs of concrete walls and staircases of a castle. Climbing up the half-finished staircase, I am afraid. Like my breath is about to leave me, like I'm drowning. I'm afraid to let his hand go. He stops behind three partitions that someday will become walls of somebody's apartment.

"There is something you must know," he says.

No. No! I'm thinking. *These are the words* I'm *supposed to be saying to* you! He releases my hand, and for a moment, crazily, idiotically, I am afraid that he is leaving, that he is done with me.

"I love you," he whispers.

His hands are on my shoulders, pulling me closer. I hear the sounds of truck wheels on the dirt; voices of men; a short, fast metal clanging. But these sounds—they don't matter, nothing does. I breathe in the fragrant breezy air tinged with his smoke. His lips press against mine, and it's like someone tears my heart out of my chest for a moment. It feels like my breath is gone, my heart is gone, I am gone, and I never want to return from there. My eyes see nothing except his muddy eyes taking me away. His mouth is in mine now, and I'm pulled, pulled inside him, all of me weak, submissive as air.

His hand runs up and down the side of my neck, making me aware of a thousand senses I didn't know I'd possessed. His fingers play with the shoelace still wrapped around me.

"I love you," I hear myself say. "I love you, too."

18

Your Aiz-er-man

On Tuesday morning, everyone whispers, *"weak acids,"* *"strong acids,"* *"a quiz the second week of school, how could she?!"*

I glide into the antiseptic-scented classroom. Ruslan's arm hangs over me.

"You missed a big announcement yesterday," he whispers in my ear. "We're going on a class trip to Lithuania for the winter holiday. Imagine? The train. The hotel. The *sightseeing*." His lips graze my ear, and I wonder what sort of sightseeing exactly he has in mind.

His friends Yurik and Dimon are following us, talking and laughing. Misha is sitting at his desk, the one he and I shared last Friday.

"Why are we stopping?" Ruslan asks me, his hand squeezing my shoulder.

Oh, have I halted? Right before Misha's desk? Yes I have, right by that empty seat beside him.

"You're sitting with me," Ruslan says. "Right there, in the back. Come on."

"But . . . last week . . . Klavdia Maximovna . . ."

"Klavdia won't care."

Still, I won't stop staring at Misha. Inside my head I whisper things at him.

I am sorry. You know, sometimes it's much easier to know what to do when you are quiet, when you are invisible. You would have liked me much better as the old Sonya, probably. Except, would you have even seen me then?

Kuzmin is smirking at me from the back row. From my shoulder, Ruslan's hand climbs higher. His fingers slide up and down my neck, wrap themselves in a strand of my hair.

Through a kind of a dreamy fog that has wrapped around me, all I know, all I'm really aware of is Misha's eyes never leaving my face.

"What, you lost something here?" Ruslan asks me. Yurik and Dimon have stopped laughing.

"And what are *you* goggling at, Aiz-er-man?"

"Don't Ruslan," I whisper. "He isn't goggling. I am the one who . . ."

Ruslan doesn't hear me.

"Want something to look at, Aiz-er-man?"

The silence around his quiet words is so deep you would think the quiz has already started.

"Ruslan, enough." I raise my voice, surprised at how hardy it sounds. "Let's go. I'll sit with you, all right? Look, I'm already go—"

Ruslan's palm lands hard against the side of my neck, making a slapping sound. With his other hand, he grips my shoulder. "Watch this! Watch it well, Ai-zer-man!"

He draws his face close to me.

I angle away. "I said I'm *going.*"

Ruslan nods at me, slowly, like he understands, the smile back on his lips. Only it's not a smile at all and he doesn't understand anything.

"You like kisses on construction sites. But you don't like *witnesses*. What, don't think your *Aiz-er-man* enjoys watching?"

I stare at him: his face slammed shut, eyes turned solid as a concrete fence, and suddenly I hate those eyes just as passionately as I love them, I hate the way he says *your Aiz-er-man*.

Da, he's mine, this Aiz-er-man, but not in the way you think. I lean close. Close to those eyes that I want opened and I reach for his lips and I open them with my own. I suck in bitter cigarette taste inside his mouth, blocking out the gasps and whispers "*What a savage slut*," until I pull away and find the eyes that are soft and mince once more and the lips that are curving.

He takes my face in his hands gently, like I am made of porcelain.

How can a boy love me this much, I wonder. I reach for his face and for the second time my lips surprise his. When we he looks around, almost embarrassed, any thought of *Aiz-er-man* (hopefully) vanished from his jealous mind.

But then, as though on a second thought, he swivels back to Misha and stares down at him, with hard, triumphant eyes.

"Don't strain yourself, Valentinov." Misha's clear melody of a voice streams over the totally silent classroom. "You can have your girl. I'm not interested."

My whole face burns. So does the skin of my neck where Ruslan has squeezed me too hard, earlier. But Misha's words, "*You can have your girl* " sting worse for some strange reason— for no good reason at all.

Next Sunday morning Ruslan is away again, on another one of his demonstrations, coming back any time though, he'd said. I wait for him at the construction site, a letter in hand. Among the slowly widening catacombs of concrete walls and staircases of a castle, I have climbed a few sets of shaky stairs until finding a spot I deem both high and safe enough for me. A concrete block makes for a perfect seat in between three partitions that will become the walls of someone's room one day. There, I tear open the envelope.

In her careful writing, Babushka reminds me to keep an eye on the news, to keep warm this fall, to keep up with schoolwork. *"Birds have their feathers, people have their learning,"* she advises.

I skim through her questions, her usual advice, her news of the neighbors. My heart starts racing when I get to the last page.

> *When we last spoke, you told me you're half-Russian, half-Jew. You still don't understand. This isn't accurate.*
> *There are no halves, legally speaking. You are either Jewish, or you aren't.*

I frown. It sounds ominous. Sounds like a big choice to make.

> *Under Russian law, if your mother is Jewish, you're a Jew. But if your father is Russian, you're a Russian. So when you turn sixteen, and the passport clerk asks for your nationality, you can point to your father's name on the birth certificate and say, "I am Russian." That is one gift you could thank your father for.*

I look away from the letter and think about my father, not Andrei, but the stranger who was partly responsible for bringing me into this world. Even if I piece together the reluctant things Mama told me, it doesn't amount to much of a picture.

A pigeon sits perched atop a block of concrete just beside me, so still and gray, it might as well have been a statue. Such perfect camouflage.

There is nothing wrong with being a Jew. That's who I am, and if anyone tried to make me feel any less for that, I'd put them back in their place, I wouldn't stand for it. But look at yourself in the mirror. You have your father's hair. A delicate nose, like any proper Russian girl.

Put the right nationality into your passport, and most people don't need to know more.

It'll all just be easier: jobs, education—it will all be more open to you.

Your mama doesn't have that choice. I don't, either. But you do. The Jewish path, it can be a difficult one.

I lift my eyes from the letter and stare down at a stagnant puddle of water by the dusty road, my reflection rippling in it. Among the cigarette butts and candy wrappers floating there, I spot a heart-shaped leaf that is just starting to turn pink for the autumn. I fold the letter back and stuff it deep into the pocket of my jeans.

19

Another Jew

"Have you heard what happened?" Dry and raspy, Mama's question crackles in my room. The waltz I've been playing is shattered into a hundred notes.

"Have you heard?"

She's been talking to me like this—in a jagged sort of tone—this whole week now. Ever since that night when Papa came back drunk from the postdebut celebration, and they've been losing their voices at each other across the wall.

Ever since Electrification called her in to see her, because of me cutting school with Ruslan that Monday.

My pointing finger presses on a *do*—a calming, sensible note. "What, a communist takeover?" I offer a melancholic guess. I'm sitting on the piano stool padded with black leather, my back to my mother, still.

Mama's voice is a tense violin. "Is that what it would take to get your attention?"

My fingers pick at the keys, salvaging scattered feelings. Feelings were so much easier in Siberia. Here, feelings tease and rage, refusing to dance to my music in neat well-practiced moves. Here, Mama is standing right behind me, and I am missing her even more.

"You're just mad because you haven't been working on your play. And because of Electrification. What, you never broke any rules?" I marvel at how nonchalant my voice sounds, when inside I am vibrating with the wanting to know of how that meeting went, what Electrification told her. Did she tell Mama that Ruslan was skipping school with me?

She sits on my bed, the newspaper crinkling in her hands.

"I hate your Electrification. And I let her know it. You should have been there. You'd have been proud of me."

When I turn around and look at her face, I am surprised to see her eyes glisten.

"Of course, I'd like to know why she says you came to school early in the morning only to leave before classes started. But . . ." She sighs. "We can talk about that later."

She throws the newspaper at me. I straighten out a page and glimpse the picture of a dark-eyed man in a black robe that suits him well. Even the newspaper photo can't hide the stories and sadness in his eyes, the grace of his black and white beard. And suddenly I can tell this is important to me, somehow.

I sit next to Mama on the wide-striped woolen blanket that covers my bed. Each one of us fits so neatly in a gap between two dark stripes.

"His name was Aleksandr Men," she begins. "He was Jewish by birth." And then she tells me.

He was murdered with an axe on Sunday morning. On the day of my date with Ruslan. I feel my face grow hot as if I were the one who killed him.

"It could have been the KGB. Or anti-Semites," Mama says. "Or that savage nationalist group, *Pamyat*. Their symbol is the axe. The Russian axe." At her own words she throws her head aside, like someone just slapped her. Her hair, weaved together in a great loosening braid, plops over her shoulder. Her hair smells of gasoline and crowds. It's beautiful, so beautiful, her hair. "Have you ever heard of them?"

"*Pamyat?* No. They sound . . . terrifying."

"Of course, we'll never know for sure," Mama says. "Don't count on the *militsia* to solve this crime. Sonechka, what, what?"

Feelings, all of them at once, flooding my eyes, gushing out.

She squeezes me in a bewildered hug, pressing my wet eyes against the scratchy glitter on her sweater in the twilight that has filled my room. "What's wrong? What's wrong with you, lately?" she keeps asking. And how can I tell her when I barely know it myself? But I try.

"So much hate in the world," I whisper, in the midst of more pitiful sniffling.

"*Nu, nu,*" she tries to quiet me. "So sensitive." She strokes my hair. "Half a word I tell you, one picture I show you, and like a thin little vessel you overfill, with all the suffering of the Jewish people."

The sounds of *Star Wars* are blasting from across the room. When did Papa turn on the video player? I bet he's sitting there, on the sofa bed, with a bottle of beer in his hand.

"Sometimes I wish I could build a wall around the beautiful dream world of yours, Sonechka," Mama says. "A wall of glass and mirrors that would never soil. But I can't. These are the times we live in. I'm sorry, but . . . the world you were born into—this is it. And you can't hide from it."

Mama uses my hair as a towel for her own wet cheeks, and talks about Aleksandr Men.

"He was born to Jewish parents, but became a Christian priest back in the time when it was forbidden, dangerous. He was beloved by thousands of Jews and Russians alike, worshippers, dissidents, free thinkers, admired for his wisdom, his serenity, and his rebellion at once. But look at him." I stare at the newspaper again. "You can see how he'd irk quite a few people, too. Say the KGB. Or the anti-Semites. If you can call them *people*."

Even on the thin dirty news page his eyes burn, reminding me of Misha's a little. The man's mustache is Jewish dark, yet somehow it matches with his long, old-style Russian Orthodox beard.

"He was young in the face of old bulldogs," Mama tells me. "He was quiet poetry and kindness of steel."

She continues, pausing between each line:

"He was too divine to live too long. Another Jew to die for our sins."

The first star glows outside my window to the sounds of Mama's poem being born. I wonder what Misha would think of this poem. I wonder what Ruslan would think of it.

"I wonder if people ever called Aleksandr Men a name," I whisper. "You know . . . like . . . um, '*Jid,*' for example." The word is lard in my mouth.

"Some may have," Mama says. "But so? There are worse things, Sonya, than being called a name. When they call you a name, there are so many things you can do."

"Like what?"

She fills the dark with examples. "Smash a plate of hot soup onto some guy's lap at a big-deal restaurant. Tell a hairy-legged woman and her ogling husband in line to go home and make love more often, so as to be in a better mood and have less problems to take out on the Jews."

I wonder if the unshaven woman had taken Mama's advice. I wonder if it had helped. I wonder . . . "What's it like, Mama?" I blurt out. "Making love?"

Now she's quiet. My mama, the commander of words.

"Mama?"

"Sex can be most spiritual. Soul-shaking." I stare back at her, careful not to show my amazement. "Or it can be banal. A little awkward." Her eyes stay on my face, looking at once at me and through me. "But this sort of love in the wrong moment of your life, with the wrong person, it can be less than banal. It can be worse than awkward. It can be devastating. Scarring."

Then her eyes focus on mine. I can feel her reaching through the moonlit dark, delving into the things she can see beyond my widened eyes. What can she see in there?

Now it is I who yearns for a change in subject.

"There is a boy in my class named Aizerman," I whisper.

"An Aizerman, *ah*?" She smiles, her eyes smoothing. "You like him?"

"Yes, but . . ." It used to be so easy to tell her things, easy as sleeping.

She studies me. "So now I know his name," she says, a smile in her whisper.

"Whose name?"

"Your boyfriend's. The boy who's been calling."

He isn't my boyfriend, I want to say. Instead, I ask, "Calling?"

"*Nu, da.* That voice. Older. Real raspy." She cocks her head at me. "I have to tell you, he sort of scared me at first."

I sit up on the bed straighter. "*Nyet,* Mama, that's not him! Not *Aizerman*! It's . . ."

She waits. I don't know where all of my words have gone to.

"Another boy?" she asks wryly. I nod. Then, rolling my eyes and sighing, I shake my head. She looks me over carefully, like she is no longer sure who it is sitting on this bed before her. Once more, I change the subject.

"Our class teacher is taking us to Lithuania this winter. A class trip," I say. "Can I go?"

"I don't know, *devochka. Litva?* I'm not used to letting you go far."

"What?" I sit up from the bed. "What do you mean, *you're not used to* letting me go? What, I've never been far enough from you before?"

Her face is a pale stain framed by shadows.

20

Day of Atonement

I never knew this place existed, that such places exist.

"A synagogue," Mama called it.

Inside the aged, gigantic palace on Arkhipova Street whispers and breaths of hungry women form a solid wall behind me. The solemn chanting of hundreds of men reaches me from below. The air rising up in columns separates me from their skull-capped heads. But even from this safe distance, at the sight of the familiar black curls escaping from out of a dark blue skullcap they call *yarmulke*, I almost fall off the balcony. Am I hallucinating from hunger? But no, it's him, Misha Aizerman, with the men down there in the main hall, chanting and singing.

Babushka never told me about a day of atonement, how it comes around early October, on the heels of the New Year, our own one, just for us, Jews. Mama said she didn't know about it, either, not until this year. There are thousands of years' worth of Jewish things we still don't know, she told me.

On Yom Kippur you must not eat. You must be serious and especially well-behaved if you want God to write your name into the Book of Life for the coming Jewish year. Yet all around me the women shove each other as if we were on a bus. Two, three layers of arms, thighs, purses, bosoms, practically squeezing

Mama and me through the heavy wooden boundaries of the balcony in their fight for a better view of the marble floors underneath. There is so much to take in. Tall chandeliers alight with many candles. The holy book they call the Torah. (Not the Book of Life—that one's for God. The Torah is for the people. Mama said it's like the Bible, only without the second part.) A small bearded rabbi with huge glasses looks even shorter, standing beside a tall cantor from America.

"He looks like a Spanish Don," one woman says reverently.

"How I like your pretty hat!" another woman gushes to Mama, and even in this squash, Mama smiles a satisfied smile and shakes her small round black hat decorated with bright flowers and a short symbolic veil. In the main hall below us, the men pay better attention behind heavy dark wood benches. Heads fill the hall, bodies pack the adjacent passages and corridors. Voices chant unknown musical words that sound something like *naj-shemeyeh-ro-kha-nu-einu*, some sort of a secret code only we, all of these people here, are privy to, without understanding a single word.

Once in a while one of the men will point a finger at us women on the balcony, shake his head, and hiss an angry *sha!* to quiet us. Misha doesn't frown and call out *sha*, though. At the distance of maybe three floors down all I can really make out is his dark-haired head bent over the words in a book. I wonder what would happen if he raised his head, turned around, and saw me?

But then the men on the marble steps start singing, and the women stop pushing, the men stop lifting their heads at us and saying *sha!*, and I stop wondering.

The American cantor's operalike vibrato fills the giant hall. The voices of the other men join him in a slow winding melody. The voices fill me. They fill me with so much joy, so much sadness and calling that I cannot contain it, no one human could, and it overflows into the stuffy air that smells of bodies and a little dust and wood. Underneath the solemnity and sadness, the music teases me with happiness and life and defiance. I wish I knew the mysterious words, wish I could let them travel through my own throat.

I look around at the people, ordinary people one could encounter in any bakery. And yet something about them feels close, warm, my own, *ours*. Their bodies are just like mine, filled with voices and magic on this most important day of the Jewish year, and it doesn't matter that Misha cannot see me. He can feel me, I know, just as I can feel him and the dark-haired bearded man beside him who must be his father, and my own mama in her hat, and that old woman, an immovable face caught in memories, lips cracking through fading red lipstick.

At the end of the concert, the rabbi speaks of hard times. "It is difficult now," he says, "And yet look at us all together like this, a new beginning. . . ."

"He is from Siberia," a woman beside Mama whispers.

"The times are hard," he says. "A difficult winter is coming. . . . And when the times are hard for everyone, for us they will be that much harder." He sounds like Babushka. *The Jewish path is a difficult one.*

"But things will get better," he says. He speaks as though he really does know. "We must persevere, we must keep our *'Jewishness.'* Come to the synagogue, not just for Shabbat, not just for the holidays, come all the time."

After the service we're downstairs, the women mixing with the men. Mama's mouth barely moves, though her fingers won't stop dancing, as she plays with the flowers on her hat, telling some blue-eyed singer friend of hers how it was all soul-shaking, incredible. Perhaps finally realizing she might rip the flower off her hat if she keeps fingering it so furiously, Mama takes the hat off. Without lifting her eyes off the blue-eyed singer's, she thrusts her hat at me to hold. My fingers snatch it by the flower. I jam the hat over my head.

Through a black netted perfume-scented veil the world is just a little darker. Softer. Safer. Suddenly, I feel as though I have entered a dream, where nothing I could do is wrong. I look around through the openings in the small black net hanging before my eyes, at the faces of the people all miraculously related to *me* and to each other, at the six-sided Jewish stars everywhere, carved on the sides of the wooden benches, stitched on the velvet curtain covering the place where the Torah lives. My star, out here in the world, not hiding, beckons through the softness of the black veil.

I scan the place for Misha. I find him entering a side door.

"I'll be right back." In the hallway filled with voices, my own jingles with mischief.

21

In the Moonlight

U p, up, up the winding, steepening steps, higher, higher, past infinite doors, past empty rooms, hallway upon hallway, I find him on one of the balconies. With soft, timid footsteps I join Misha, and he doesn't even know it. Past some sort of an old, pianolike instrument, underneath the faded frescoes, deeper into a thickening smell of dust and sweet wood, I follow Misha through a series of doors until my foot sinks into what feels and smells like a carpet of woodchips.

I let the rest of my body follow through an opening inside the synagogue's vaulted ceiling and find myself in a giant dark attic space, suddenly shivering with cold. I don't see Misha's silhouette anywhere. But in the light of the moon shining through the broken window directly above my head, I can make out the gray features of a dirty city bird. One soft step, and the pigeon rises in the air, flapping its wings indignantly. It's only when the angry flapping dies out that I hear the footsteps and Misha's voice that echoes like the clanging of a church bell. "Is someone there?" He speaks in a pleasantly distant tone reserved for strangers. "Do you need help?"

I stare at him in surprise. He doesn't recognize me. Not in this dark. Not in this black hat with a short veil covering my eyes. Not on the day of Atonement, when his serious thoughts could not be further away from some ungrateful girl classmate who once sat with him in chemistry class.

Besides, only married women wear hats to the synagogue services, Mama told me. I smile. That's right. *A married Jewish woman in a hat. That's me, in this dark attic.* I take a moment to think what sort of voice I would use, before answering.

"Incredible holiday, *ah?*" The voice I have chosen pours out slightly nasal, *dame*like.

"Not many people know about this place," Misha says, sounding uncertain. "My papa, he was taking some courses here—not right here." He smiles shyly. "I mean here at the synagogue, and that's how he found out this is a book cemetery."

"A book cemetery?"

Misha peers back at me, looking startled, and I realize I have dropped my *dame* voice. "*A book cemetery?*" I repeat, this time through my nose, adding a small, high-pitched, coughlike laugh for better effect. I push my hat lower over my eyes.

He peers at me harder. "All those years, all those Hebrew books that have been forbidden, or simply not wanted," he says. " . . . The Jews don't burn books . . . They bury them . . . Here."

As my eyes get used to the lack of light, the darkness becomes soft all around, and I notice them. Big tomes, others bigger still, quite a few taller than me by a head or so. Some stand, some lean against the walls. Others lie on the bed of woodchips and pigeon droppings. Books, books, books, everywhere.

"Is that why . . . *is that why,*" I adjust my voice quickly, to make it sound slightly charmed and condescending, as if I am speaking to a child, "Is that why you like coming here? To read the books?"

He shrugs, even as an uncharacteristic little-boy smile flickers at me. "I try to come here whenever I have a chance. . . . This is the quietest place I know. The perfect place to talk to God, I think."

I look up at the circle window. Wind and moonlight pour through the missing sections, beaming over tiny specks of dust in a flood of brilliance. "God is more of an 'it' than a 'he,'" Mama told me. "To us, God is the blowing of the wind, the glow of the stars in the night sky. Yet God hears us and knows us, and God *is*."

I look back at Misha, absolutely amazed, holding back my breath and a thousand questions. Is the Book of Life here somewhere? If I knew how to read it, would I see my name written in its pages?

But he is the one who asks his question first.

"Excuse me, lady," he says shyly, even as his hand reaches toward me and then stops, hovering within a millimeter of the side of my face. "Have we met before?"

My hand flies up to the flower on my hat. Not my hat, Mama's. Who is probably seriously worrying three, four, five stories down below.

I want to sink beside him on the carpet of woodchips and gaze forever at the shimmering moonlit dust. Instead, I shake my head and turn away from him. "I enjoyed talking with you, young man," I whisper on the way out.

When I see him in school tomorrow, I must remember to look away, to keep my smile tucked inside me, along with the memory of his moonlit face.

22

Family Dinner

"The place is enormous—like a museum! For an hour I've *rummaged* it looking for you!"

So this is what it's like. Having a fight with a mother.

"It couldn't be an hour."

"Don't you dare talk back to me!" Her voice snaps.

The walls in our kitchen are deep red. When I first got here I couldn't get over the hipness of it. Timid, ordinary people wrap their kitchens in soft-color wallpaper, or paint it some kind of beige. *Not here*, I thought, *not in the home of free spirits*.

But tonight—*or is it already morning?*—I think of this red as the color of blood, the color of communism, the most hateful color. Sitting here in the surreal hour of night, I resent the clown masks staring at me from the kitchen wall. With a fork, I push around the now-cold *pelmeni* on a plate before me. I would savor their soft dough, their neat roundness, their meaty middle, especially after twenty-five hours of Yom Kippur fasting. If I didn't have to sit there and watch a brave woman I have idolized my whole life turn mundane and weary.

"She shows up at home after dark every night, like it's normal," she says. "She cuts class and won't give me an explanation. She barely looks at me anymore! She—she won't even play the piano anymore!" Mama's voice floats, in search of the right words a mother must say to her daughter, even while she stands there, hands on hips, like she's some kind of a big-busted matron with a mustache and unshaven legs, instead of this petite thirty-three-year-old brunette.

"Calm down, Rita," Papa says. "Please . . . sit down." He is the one who prepared the *pelmeni* for us. When Mama and I came home, too exhausted after the service and the fast to even really argue, he prickled my cheek with his unshaven one, and I stared at him, surprised, because his usual burnt after-alcohol smell was missing. But the eyes looking down at me from his towering frame were small and broken. "How did you girls like that Jewish concert of yours?" he says.

"A service, not a concert," I say to my plate.

"How is your play, Rita?" Papa tries again.

"Don't ask," she mutters, poking at her *pelmeni*.

Didn't he see? The living room littered with crumpled up pages?

"Oh, the herring." Papa jumps up from his stool. "How could I forget the herring?"

I stare at him. I have never seen him like this. Serving us both dinner. We never really had a family dinner like this, I suddenly realize. While he pulls a jar of herring salad out of the refrigerator, Mama turns on me again. "You still didn't tell me what you were doing in the synagogue's attic."

"And you didn't tell me what you were chatting so pleasantly about with the blue-eyed man," I say, nastily.

Mama's eyes widen. Papa's fork hovers in the air.

I look past their startled faces, at a signed Moscow Concert Hall poster on the red wall. Papa turns his head to follow my gaze. He gets up from the chair. The ripping sound tears into our silence.

"Andrei!" Mama gets up.

"Didn't want to ruin your holiday," he says. "But I have some news of my own."

I gape at him, afraid to ask what he's talking about. Mama though, recovers immediately.

"It's nothing." She comes up to him. Running a tentative hand over his unwashed hair, she speaks a stream of words into his ear—"you still have your clown troupe" words, "other gigs" words, "my connections" words. But he shakes her hand off his greasy curls and looks at me.

"I hope you liked my debut at the Moscow Concert Hall," he says to me. "Because you won't see one of those anymore."

I look back at the plate of *pelmeni*, sticky and dry-looking, coated in occasional lumps of sour cream mixed in from the neighboring tomato and onion salad, and suddenly I get it: I get everything.

I've heard enough of their across-the-wall arguments to know why the Moscow Concert Hall has let Papa go. One late appearance. Too little practice. Too much beer. And then, the other night, almost twisting his ankle on stage.

I grimace at the memory of Mama's metallic voice enunciating, *"You've been giving me more troubles than my adolescent daughter. Are you trying to get fired just to spite me?"*

Now he looks back at Mama and me. "I . . . I need some time away. I need to find myself again. You know?" He looks at me, his eyes pleading, before looking away.

The cuckoo flies out of the clock. My father waits for the cuckoo to finish all of its cries, and then says, "Just taking a little trip, that's all."

His eyes don't meet mine any longer.

He leaves us on a windy Saturday at the end of the week, wearing soft khaki pants and a clean shirt underneath a dark wooly sweater, looking so incredibly handsome. I can see again, for the first time in weeks, why Mama might have fallen for him. When I kiss the side of his clean-shaven face that smells of nothing but an imported men's cologne, I feel a pang of sadness. That Andrei with greasy hair, weak smile, and an unsteady gait, that ghost of a person who could never quite meet my eye—I couldn't say I'd miss him. But this handsome, put-together father who actually looks me in the eye, why does *he* have to go?

23
Parallel Universe

In physics, Russian literature, geometry, I suddenly get this understanding—*ah*, so this is what it must be like, to be illuminated by a searchlight bright on your face, to be blinded for a moment. My braid thumps against my shoulder as I snap my head around. Sure enough, I catch Aizerman looking at me. His eyes fix on the back of a classmate's neck, go for the blackboard.

Another week passes, and we're still at it. I steal the quickest of glances at Aizerman. He pretends he doesn't see it. I pretend I don't see him pretending not to see me.

We are *not* flirting.

He'd made it obvious that he wasn't interested, and let's be honest, so did I.

It's just that autumn is unwinding in this part of the world, but he and I share our own private winter. It's like Aizerman and I live in 1990, but the walls of our time can collapse, or bend. I like this. This knowing that in our parallel universe it's 5751 and the New Year has already started.

Even if he doesn't know it.

Just that—and wanting to catch a glimpse in between the covers of those books he snaps closed at the end of history class.

That's what all this is about.

The mild-weathered, cool October passes in a flurry of kisses. Kisses in dark apartment foyers, Ruslan's hands kneading the back of my neck. Kisses in damp movie theaters smelling of smoke and mold, to the sound of love-hate–fighting on the big screen. Inside the school shed, behind an empty store, at the construction site, inside a Palace of Pioneers lobby after-hours, but before dark, always before dark, so Mama wouldn't ask questions like, *Where have you been, my little Sonechka?*

Ruslan doesn't talk about his mama—so I don't have to talk about mine. We don't have to talk much, in general, Ruslan's eyes half-closed, his breathing labored—as is mine—his fingers now tracing the outlines of my jaw, now wrestling with the buttons of my jacket so they could find my skin under the scarves and sweaters Babushka sent me. My senses multiplied, my knees buckling with tension, my body aching with yearning, my mind melting when his cold hand makes its way under my clothes and his finger runs across my breast. Why talk at all?

It's never enough time, it's always, "I must go."

And he always lets me, no questions asked. I tell him Mama would send me away if I came home after dark again. His hot-cold eyes darken. "Your mama isn't what I expected," he says.

"*Nu*, maybe she isn't exactly what I expected, either," I say. Somehow, even though he doesn't seem to have much of a mother at all, it seems he is the only one who'd understand, the only one I could admit this to. Mama and I have barely even seen each other, let alone talked together, ever since Yom Kippur.

"Don't call me anymore," I say. "She's asking questions." He looks at me intensely and doesn't reply. "Do you hear me?"

His answers are kisses: the rough, hungry, eager ones that freeze time and tip the world; the soft, ticklish ones, tasting of smoke, stealing my soul.

The first snow falls in early November, brightening the world. It's almost as beautiful as the first snow back in Siberia. For a second or two early in the morning, when I look out the window, the untouched magnificence outside fools me into believing that New Life is only starting, full of possibility.

24

What Girls Talk About

The frost must be painting ornaments on my cheeks, the way they tingle. He had said he would meet me here, but I am alone in my white castle abandoned by both the construction workers and the sparrows, my heart an icicle inside my chest.

December is rushing by at the speed of an Arctic hare. It feels as if it has always been winter, as if the world has always consisted of nothing but the crisp windless whiteness and sky.

"Solovay?"

I whirl around. It's my classmate Luba. I didn't recognize her at first. Usually small like me, and slender, today she's a puffy figure in a short fur jacket, what they call "half-a-fur." She is walking with a bag—actually filled with something.

She looks around carefully. I meet her eyes, bluer than ever in the bright winter sunlight.

"What have you got in there?" I ask when she comes closer.

"Sausage," she says.

"Really?" I raise one eyebrow. It's been a while since we had sausage in our refrigerator.

"I doubt there is any left, though," she says.

"Of course not." I sigh politely, mashing the snow with my boots. My mind is suddenly as empty as store shelves. I wonder, what do fifteen-year-old girls say to each other when they aren't talking about meat shortages?

"Any special plans for the winter holiday?" she asks me. "Are you going to Lithuania?"

"I don't know . . . My mama is deciding, still . . . "

She cocks her head. "So then . . ." she says. "How are things . . . on the *love* front?"

Is that what fifteen-year-old girls talk about?

Is that all?

I take a gulp of frosty air. "*Nu*," I say, "I'm waiting for Ruslan."

"I knew it."

I immediately wish I had kept quiet—or at least come up with something that sounded a bit less like a toddler in a sandbox showing off her new shovel. Sure enough, even squeezed inside a furry hat, Luba's small, frost-covered face takes on this sardonic expression.

"What?"

"It's just a little chilly out here for love, don't you think?"

I didn't know she could make her own name, *love,* sound like sugared poison.

"A date at a construction site—how romantic." She sneers. "What are you two, homeless?"

I look around in embarrassment. There's not much to look at except the occasional passerby's bundled-up body trudging past the abandoned splendor of my castle of concrete. Construction workers stopped coming here around mid-November. Now not even drunks dare stick their noses around these parts. The place belongs to Ruslan and me like never before. How could I explain it?

Anyway, where else could we go? Besides the apartment foyers, the cinema, this place, my place, or . . .

"His place?" Luba's words startle me. My thoughts must have been written on my forehead.

His place.

I suddenly realize how raw my fingers are with cold.

"Don't worry," she says. "In all the time I've known him, I don't think he has *ever* invited a girl home. That's just the way this musketeer operates. He likes doing the visiting."

Suddenly, I am done talking to girls. I stare into the blank sky, wondering why he chose this horrid prickly day to be late, when Luba moves her face closer to me again.

"Poor thing. You don't know much about the guy, do you?"

A part of me wants to whisper, *Do you?*

A wind materializes from behind me, pushing me. I squeeze my hands into fists—two ice balls. "I know plenty," I whisper.

She touches my shoulder lightly. Her smile echoes her words *"poor thing."*

"All right, tell me then, what does his grandmother do?"

His grandmother. He doesn't take me home because he doesn't want me to meet her, I realize. It has to be that. I try to keep my voice steady, and I hope the frosty redness on my face hides my flickering realizations. "I can't discuss it with you," I say.

She laughs. "You're making it sound like she's a KGB spy. When it's so much more mundane than that. Though almost just as scary," she adds, quieter, an after-thought. Seeing something on my face, she laughs again, then makes her eyes large—two bright mirrors.

I make a face of stone, even though inside I am dizzy. Her words and my thoughts are a flurry of snowflakes dancing in my head. *What if his grandmother is a spy? What if Ruslan is with me to get information on my mama for the KGB? Just in case things turn again, and the government decides to send all the former dissidents to prison?*

Luba colors the air white with another sigh. "How about a simpler question. How old is your *boy-friend?*"

"I . . . What a question . . . He . . ."

". . . will turn seventeen a month from now," she finishes for me.

"Sev-venteen?" My teeth chatter. "But . . . he looks young. And he's close to my height—and *I* am, like, the shortest."

She laughs. "He repeated a year once. A long time ago. But I understand—" Her voice is pure sugar. "I understand why he didn't have a chance to tell you any of that yet. Cause his mouth has been *occupied.*"

I cannot believe *her* delicate little mouth can utter such vulgarities. I take a step back toward my castle, reeling from the new idea of a *seventeen-year-old* Ruslan. Even as the images of his serious face and the muscles of his arms dancing when he rolls the sleeves of his shirt up to his shoulders confirm what a part of me has maybe already known.

"That's why I've been trying to warn you."

How I wish she'd leave now and let me find shelter from that wind, among the three half-finished floors, on the bottom of the stairs, underneath a roof. But she is advancing on me, swinging the meat-filled bag, her cheeks red, excited.

"He's way too old for someone like you," she says. "Too . . . *advanced.* Understand what I'm talking about?" She widens her eyes. "Too . . . preoccupied?"

"Preoccupied with what?"

She rolls her eyes. "You *know* what. You aren't in kindergarten. What all boys are preoccupied with." My face flushes hot in all that wind and air. Luba sighs. "You see?"

I lick my chapping lips. My eyes scan the snow-covered ruins in search of something real, something I know I can believe.

"He said he loves me!" I say. *So what if she mocks me more with those pity-filled eyes, for being this naïve little thing from the Siberian provinces.*

She doesn't mock me. It happens so quickly, but I see it. The hurt that flits across her face.

"Now you're lying!" she says. "Because I know *him.* He wouldn't say that to a girl, *ever!*"

"No?"

If I had better manners, I'd probably turn around and walk away, taking care to keep my back as stiff as a concrete panel. Instead, I shrug, and don't bother hiding a smirk that spreads across my lips. But after she leaves, the smirk is gone, and once again I am all alone. Even when, from the height of the future third floor, I spot him at last—a small figure in a too-thin jacket fighting the wind, coming toward me from the distance—the aloneness doesn't go away. Wistfully, I glance to the other side of my concrete castle, where Luba is trudging away in the opposite direction, this girl who could have been a friend.

25

Physical Culture

Ruslan is different here, in "physical culture" class. In the middle of the large gymnasium they call Bolshoi for its size, throwing a volleyball around. In other classes he can be such a boy, but in physical culture class it is alien and scary and exhilarating the way he can be a man, this physical being in a shirt that clings to his back, his sleeves rolled up all the way to his shoulders.

"Come *on—nu!*" he shouts at someone on his team who is being too slow. His screams echo off the walls as more boys join him. This is supposed to be a co-ed class, but most girls seem very comfortable on the shaky bench by the wall, gossiping and giggling at the players beside me.

Vitaly Semenovich doesn't mind the not-so-quiet chatter, the occasional explosion of giggles. He is easygoing, even for a phys. culture teacher. Especially now, as we approach the end of the term, the New Year break almost upon us.

"What's this?" Olya asks Luba, who has a book open.

"It's a journal by this American," Luba says. I glance at a picture of a girl our own age on the shadowy cover.

"So, what's she writing about?" I ask.

"You know." Luba shrugs. "The usual. Drugs. Sex." On that last word, she smirks and looks up, her pale gaze slamming into mine, as though she knows things, things I couldn't bring myself to talk to her about in our too-brief exchanges on snowy construction sites.

"*Da*." Olya sighs, like a grownup, while nodding with a superior air. "Over there, in America, they all do it by the time they reach fifteen, you know."

I curse myself for my traitorous cheeks catching fire as I look away. It is only when Luba starts reading again that I allow myself to let this feeling, a question, creep over me. *What would it be like to do it with him? You know.*

The thing all the boys are preoccupied with, as Luba put it. I couldn't even imagine. Or maybe I could.

"He plays well, your *kovboy*."

The clean tenor voice in a slightly strained tone bursts into my thoughts, uninvited. I hold on to the warm dimpled wall. How long has Misha been standing next to me, watching me . . . um . . . daydream?

"You startled me," I say.

He shrugs. I watch him drop his blue-black bag casually onto a long bench next to the wall. He never bothers closing its half-open zipper. He doesn't tell me what he needs, just stands there like there is something between us needing a *discussion*.

"*What?*"

"Nothing." His voice is clear, echoing. "I just . . . I never seem to catch you alone anymore. Not since . . ." He trails off. "I was just wondering . . . see . . . I had this question—*um*—do you ice skate?"

I used to love ice-skating. I have a perfect view of the pond from my room. I don't ask why he is asking, though. Instead, I tear my eyes away, back to the players, back to Ruslan—too late. In the middle of the hall, I find them, my boy's eyes set straight on me, his face the color of early-morning snow.

The rest happens fast, like these things do. The ball flies toward us. It hits the bench on another end, the opposite from where we're standing. The uneven bench shifts, knocking some bags off onto the floor. Misha's book bag flies off, too. A small paperback book slides out. He doesn't see it. I pick it up, extend it to him. He no longer sees me, just picks up the ball, and, cradling it, runs toward the center of the gymnasium. He positions himself across the net from Ruslan's sweaty figure. Ruslan shifts his stare to him. Misha lifts his chin, straightens. Their eyes lock.

Everything about the game feels different now, sharper, louder.

I watch for a little bit, Misha's book still in my hand. I mean to put it back in his bag after a quick glance, I do. *Babi Yar*, by Anatoly Kuznetsov. The fragile old pages in my hands remind me how long it's been since a book mattered to me. It hits me, now, how easy it was, in my Old Life, to let dreams and stories carry me, to observe things from a safe distance of yearning.

My eyes flit to the volleyball game, then turn back to the book in my hands. No one even glances in my direction anymore. The game seems to be going fine, a game like any game, really. The girls are gossiping quietly, watching. Phys. culture is a class to let loose in. Especially today, on one of the last days of the term, the New Year break almost upon us.

I open the book. Just one quick peek, is all.

The narrator is a Ukrainian boy in occupied Kiev. It is 1941, the beginning of the Great Patriotic War. I turn a few pages.

Bombs shattering in the sky, German propaganda. I run my thumb over the accordion of more pages, catching isolated words, snatches of dialogue.

The sounds of the volleyball game fade.

"*All Jews of the city of Kiev and its environs must appear on the corner of Melnikov and Dokhtorov Streets (by the cemetery) at 8 a.m. on September 29, 1941. They must bring their documents, money, valuables warm clothing, etc. All Jews who fail to obey this order will be shot.*"

Obedient and nervous, the Jews gather. I lose myself in their crowd.

I look up from the book at one point. If only those people could get away as easily as this—just lift their eyes off a page.

At one point, the teacher whistles sharply. The hall explodes with groans, arguments. "You could have broken his headlights, Ruslan!" But none of it quite reaches me.

I try to keep my eyes on the game, but all I see is the space bending, the flat field a ravine, a line of Jews getting stripped, beaten, then tossed into the ravine, some of them jumping. The *dat-at-at-at* sound of shooting explodes, bodies fall, and I fall somewhere with them. A voice rises over the machine guns and the screaming. The voice belongs to Misha Aizerman.

"I'd be interested to know," Misha says, "who gave you the right to *dig* in my bag?"

I blink. He looks fierce with cheeks flushed, skin shining with sweat, a grumpy expression on his face. He brings the flat gymnasium space back to its original dimensions. The reality of it hits me like a splash of ice water. The bright spot above Misha's eyebrow. "What happened to you?" my question explodes.

"Nothing," Misha says angrily. "Just your *kovboy* deciding to use my face as target practice for the volleyball."

"I am sorry," I say, even though I didn't do this. Did I?

Misha's eyes are on the book. "Couldn't you just ask?"

"It fell out of your backpack. I just. Picked it up."

"Anyway," he says, not believing me. "Class is over, as you might have noticed."

No, I didn't notice, actually.

He reaches for the book.

He's tall, so much taller than Ruslan, yet he's got such fragile fingers. I let my eyes rise to his face, the angry brightness over his eyebrow where Ruslan's ball has marked him.

"You aren't really that angry about a *book*?" I ask.

He seems to hesitate, his dark eyes set on mine. Behind him, I notice Ruslan come up in the crowd of bobbing heads. He makes his way toward me in his sweaty shirt. His eyes are set; his mouth looks like a scar across his face. I snap the book closed, stick it under my butt, and close my eyes. A really stupid thing to do, I know immediately.

"*Myshka?*"

I open my eyes. I wonder what I must look like—sitting on a bench (on a book, actually), tears sitting in my eyes, a stare.

"What the devil is the matter?" He turns to Misha. "Get away from her right now."

"I just want my book back." Misha's voice is like a stone.

"What book?" Ruslan asks.

I don't know what I hate more, or whom, the book or the ravine it describes, secrets or fear, myself, Ruslan, or Misha Aizerman.

"*That* book," Misha says. "The one she's sitting on."

Ruslan looks at me. People gather around us, ears popping out of their heads.

"Now if this was *your* book, why would *she* be *sitting* on it?"

"Hey, Ruslan," I whisper. "Let's get out of here."

"Maybe she's a kleptomaniac," Misha says. His words are a slap on the mouth.

"My ancestors are out," I say. "Let's go home. Just you and me. Eh?"

Ruslan takes a step toward Misha, ignoring me. "What did you call her?"

Is Ruslan aware of his fingers curling onto themselves? Does he know his arm is making a slight swinging motion? "Watch it, you—"

Hammers knock in my ears as I stand up and whip the book from under me and shove it at Misha, before Ruslan has the chance to inflict any more harm on Misha's face, so furious and fragile. Misha drops the book to the thunderous *ba-bakh* of the bench hitting the floor, the sound covering any words that may have come out of Ruslan's mouth. People are yelling, calling; someone is laughing. Two boys help pull the bench off Misha's foot. The teacher runs up. I see Misha's unnaturally pale face, his lips clenched with pain. I hear him speaking to Vasily Semenovich, squeezing the words, "It was an accident."

"I'm sorry, Misha," I say. "It *was* an accident."

Misha's features are twisted, beautiful, his eyes a pair of coals right now.

"Roll away from me, Sonya Solovay," he says, "so I never have to set my eyes on you again."

Out in the hallway I try to breathe, try to tell myself that I am now free from it all, my classmates, Misha Aizerman—who needs Aizerman? That's when I feel Ruslan's hand on my shoulder. "Here," he says. "You forgot your book."

26

This Shit

In silence, we enter my apartment, as if he is here by accident, as if we don't even know each other. In silence, he drops his backpack next to Mama's papers box, as if he does so every day. When I take my boots off, I let go of Misha's *Babi Yar* book on the floor by Ruslan's backpack.

He looks at it and breaks the precious silence.

"When I looked at the cover, I couldn't believe you read this shit," he says.

My cheeks flush. I pick up the book and squeeze it to my side, even though I want nothing to do with it right now.

Humanity is shit, I could tell him. I could pull the *Magen Dovid* from under my pillow and ask him if he thinks it's shit, too.

Calm, comrades. I am standing in the foyer of my own apartment as if it's an unfamiliar place, something official. If I let my thoughts go, they will get lost in this spacious foyer, and I will never find them. I keep my face composed. I will not think.

"I've heard all about it, you know." He keeps on talking. My God, he barely ever talks, usually. "We have so many problems right now, real things to worry about." I never knew he could talk so fast, either. "Gorbachev—practically yesterday he was going to rush this country to a free market. Now he has thrown all that to the devil and aligned himself with the hard-core toughie communists. Maybe . . . maybe he himself will organize a right-wing coup!"

"What's that got to do with . . ." I trail off. Maybe I don't want to know.

I drop the book on my desk atop a messy pile—unread newspapers, untouched music scores, undone homework. He glares at it. "Nothing! That's the point—this book—has got nothing to do with real life!"

Ruslan's gotten so winded, he forgets to take off his snow-covered coat and sneakers as he follows me down the hall, walks into my room, sits down on my unmade bed.

"But it happened, didn't it? The author's note says—"

He shakes his head furiously. "You have to know, Sonya, that it's lies, this book. Lies and whining. 'Oh, look at what those bad mean Germans did to us in 1941—'" His mocking voice sounds all wrong—like a symphonic orchestra trying to play on out-of-tune instruments. Thinking of Misha's melodious voice that sent me to the demons less than half an hour earlier, I cannot stand Ruslan's speech in such raspy dissonance.

"Sh-sh-sh." I put my finger to his lips. "I didn't bring you here to talk politics."

Finally, something breaks, something softens on his face. His left eyebrow collapses into an amused triangle.

"*Hooliganka*," he says, pulling me down next to him.

The frost is thawing on my cheeks in the warmth of this room; I can practically hear my skin crinkle. Ruslan takes off his coat, his uniform jacket, the T-shirt sweaty from volleyball. It lands over Misha's *Babi Yar* book, hiding it.

"So," Ruslan whispers, "what *did* you bring me here to do?"

I shiver, staring at the image of a double-headed eagle outlined in blue ink on Ruslan's chest.

He bends over to slip off his shoes, the Puma sneakers. When he straightens up, his chest muscles ripple, and it's as though the eagle is about to take flight. A small silver cross on a thin chain around his neck glints against his skin, in between the two heads. He leans toward me. I move away.

He smirks.

"What?" I ask, offended.

"Stop squirming and shaking so, that's what. You look like you want to run out of the room right now."

"I don't!" I can't take my eyes off his chest. "It's just that . . ." I close my mouth, then open it again and blurt, "I thought only sailors got tattoos." I take a deep breath. "And criminals."

His laughter tastes of smoke. "That's such a Soviet way of thinking. Not my way. Neither should it be yours, *myshka*."

He takes my hand and presses it close to his chest, right against the eagle. The unexpected softness of his skin sears into my palm. He is right. Who is to say what's vulgar and what's beautiful?

Maybe he, too, dreams of wings.

"Don't you think I know how delicate you are?" This time, when he slides close to me, closer than before, I stay still, fighting, floating over a new wave of warmth spreading through my body, hoping he won't hear my heart tremble noisily. But of course he does. He does.

"I'm trying to be gentle with you. Though I am not made of iron, you know." I press my hand harder onto the eagle on his chest, his skin at once taut and soft like the cheek of a baby. "You . . . you aren't planning on hurting *me*, are you?"

"Never," I whisper, shivering.

And suddenly he's kissing me, clutching my face, pressing his soft-hard chest against my body. I hold onto both his arms, circling my fingers around his biceps, pulling on them like they are handles.

His kiss spreads over me. His face looming over mine shuts out the world.

And I let the silence crumble under his weight on my bed. Until I hear the keys dangling somewhere in some hallway across the universe. Until I hear the click of heels tapping energetically along the hardwood floors, heels that can only belong to Mama's imported boots.

My bag in the hall. My coat. My boots. And—oh, the horror—Ruslan's backpack. *Quick.* I try to button my uniform dress with slippery fingers. Ruslan grabs his T-shirt from my desk. Calmly, he puts it on, tucks it into his pants.

"Well, at least I'll finally get to meet your—" he says, and I squeeze my palm against his mouth.

No. No time to explain anything, except to mouth: "Get under my bed," and give him a shove. No time to take in the startled-hurt-close-to-infuriated expression.

He looks at me from the tiny dark space. My body must be doing it again: functioning in spite of me. Because at first I don't quite understand why my hands grab the edges of my uniform dress and pull it off me, and why they rip off the brassiere hanging loosely, uselessly over my breasts right under Ruslan's wide-eyed stare, and search for something in the mess of sheets underneath my cover. My nightgown. I throw it over my body just as Mama opens the door to my room. In one smooth move I shove Ruslan's coat, his uniform jacket and sneakers dripping with melted snow, under the bed next to their owner, and pull the woolen cover down all the way to the floor.

"Sonya?! *Devochka*, what happened to you?"

I stop at the sight of the *Magen Dovid* revealing itself almost fully from under my pillow, perilously close to the cover draping the bottom of my bed. I snatch it by the shoelace and shove it into my desk drawer.

"Are you ill?"

"Yes," I say, meeting Mama's eye, my voice naturally wobbly. "A little . . . tired. I was just . . . sleeping. Do you mind if I . . . finish my dreams?"

I attempt a shaky smile.

"But what's wrong?" she asks, her eyes large, like a little girl's. "Oh God. You look pale. What hurts?"

"I just need a little rest, Mama," utters my innocent voice. "Please . . . let's talk later, all right?"

Mama's eyes just grow larger. "Sonya . . . you aren't . . . pregnant? Oh God!!! Is that why you look so upset?"

"No, *no*, Mama!"

Instead of leaving, she sits on the bed, smiling ruefully at me. The bed sags a little, and I think of Ruslan lying on the dusty floor, listening.

"I was just worried because . . . you remember how you've wanted to talk to me about sex?" *Oh God not now not now not now.* "It was so rare, you asking me questions. Well, once again, I am home. Truly home this time. No articles to write, documents to translate. No university papers." She inhales, and suddenly words rush out of her in an excited flood, a flood of things daughters and mothers talk about, "There is this one really important thing you must know . . . if . . . when . . . before . . . you make love—" She exhales the words at me. "Do you know what *preservativy* are?"

I look at her, horrified.

"*Nu*, it's a real shortage product, unfortunately. And . . . well, a young, unmarried girl absolutely cannot have full intimate relations without—"

"Please, Mama," I say weakly. "Not now."

"The way it works is—"

"Mama, *please*," I mouth.

"But this is really important, Sonya. And—" she cocks her head and flashes a mysterious smile at me. "Of course, I am going to be taking lots of trips to the States now." She smiles mysteriously. "And over there, you can buy those things in any pharmacy!"

I sit motionless on my bed and try to wish my lovely mama into disappearing, while she talks and talks.

"Don't you want to know why I'll be going to America?" she asks me.

I wish I could just tell her everything right now. That there is a guy under my bed she could crush if she keeps practically bouncing, and that I love him, that once he said a horrible word, but I am sure he didn't mean anything by it, Mama. But then she pulls things out of her black patent leather purse, some little papers—strange banknotes with men in wigs who look like English noblemen—and strews them all over my bed and throws them in a heap before me.

"They're dollars." Mama smiles proudly, as if she had painted them and cut them out herself. "The *real* currency." She looks at me, expectantly. "*Nu*," she prods, after a moment. "Don't you want to know how I got them?"

Silently, I help her get all those banknotes back into her purse. She looks at me, her cheeks flushed, and tells me anyway. About her new job—writing and translating advertising copy for American products.

"Mars bars," she says. *"Mentos ze Frehsmaker.* To sell them to us Soviets, like we need convincing. Ha, ha,ha."

"What about poetry?" I ask her, even though I can't believe we're having this conversation now. "And what about Moscow University? What about everything you fought for?"

Mama sighs. "This is called growing up, *dochka.* I'll be going on a *beeznes* trip to America," she says. "Can you imagine? America! Think about it, Sonechka, it's not a voyage I could have taken even a few years ago. . . ."

"When are you leaving?" I ask, despite myself. *Here you go, leaving me again,* I think, even though I hate myself for still being that little girl who will miss her.

"Next week." I don't know what she catches on my face, because she squeezes my hand, her expression apologetic. "I am sorry I couldn't get you a visa. It's quite impossible. Good thing they're letting me go, at least. Ah, stop fretting so. Andrei is coming back soon, so you won't be alone." She squeezes my hand. "It'll only be a few weeks."

"That's fine," I say softly. "That's nothing."

She gets up from my bed, her face twisted with hurt.

"I am trying, Sonya."

Only the tiniest shuffle from under the bed dares disturb the quiet between us. On my forehead, my temples, under the tops of my arms I can feel a wave of sweat coming when she throws a quick glance toward the bottom of the bed. She looks back at me.

"It used to be so easy when you were little," she says softly. "You sang, always. And you always smiled at me. All I see today is . . ." She shakes her head, and I remember how she frowned at me in the kitchen a few months ago for merely staring at my reflection in the window. I blink away tears. "When I visited you, no matter how ill you were—just looking at me would cheer you up and we would whisper for hours. Now I . . ." She sucks in her breath. Her lip trembles. "I feel like . . . like you're a stranger."

"Maybe I am!" I take a deep breath, dizzy with hurt and anger. "Or maybe it's you, *you*'re the stranger! You hardly ever knew me before, and you're right—you know absolutely nothing about me now!"

She flinches.

I stand up, shaking, watching her slam the door. Ruslan emerges from under my bed and I shake in his arms and I shout: "Too bad I turned out to be more than the patient, obedient little girl you imagined!"

But even though I say that, I don't feel like more. I feel less.

"Oh, *da*." I freeze in Ruslan's arms, at the sound of her cold voice, so close, right on the other side of the door. "I meant to ask you. Who left this green backpack in the hallway?"

Ruslan looks at me.

"My boyfriend," I say, staring at the closed door, wondering what I'll do if it opens. But it feels good. To tell the truth.

"He was here? Is it the boy who called you on the phone the other day?"

"Yes," I say. "It belongs to a boy I love. And one who actually loves me back." *He is right here, with me,* I almost tell her. Even as he squeezes me tighter, I stand there frozen, as I wait for her to open the door.

"You don't have to turn everything into this big secret," Mama says. "I already *know* your boyfriend's name."

"You do?" I say, uncomprehending, immobile in Ruslan's arms.

"Of course, I do," she spits out at me. "It's Aizerman. You told me yourself, remember? Back when you still talked to me?"

Her heels clatter in the hall. How sure she is of things, my mama. My head floods with emptiness and rage. The door of the living room snaps shut so hard, I hear china jingling from across the wall.

Ruslan releases me from his hug. His eyes are cold. He isn't asking about Aizerman. "I've got to say, I'm a little disappointed in your mother. 'Are you pregnant?'" he mocks, shaking his head ruefully, a cruel laugh curling his lips. "'Cannot have full intimate relations.'"

"Shut up," I whisper through clenched teeth. "Or your guts will catch cold."

"I don't know . . . "he carries on, putting on his shoes. "I guess I imagined her . . . cooler . . . more progressive." He laces his second shoe. "What now?" he asks, responding to something on my face.

"What about your grandmother?" I breathe back at him. "How *progressive* is she?" He stares at me, frozen. "Who is she, exactly? For all I know, she's some KGB spy!" I try to keep my voice low, keep it from bursting out at him. "Maybe you are one, too, for all I know!"

We face each other like enemies. The silence hangs between us.

From across the wall, a man's voice declares on television, "The dictatorship is coming. I tell you that with full responsibility."

Ruslan slips out to the shouts of People's Deputies arguing. I just let him go. On TV across the wall, a well-known politician, Boris Yeltsin, is accusing Gorbachev of faltering, of not going far enough. Poor Gorbachev. He is the one who started all this. He has been so brave. But not brave enough to defeat the gigantic Soviet fear machine that raised him, that raised all of us, the one that raised me.

I come up to my window and peer into the grayness of the late snowy afternoon.

Just a few months ago, I was so proud to live on the eleventh floor, as if being up here would have given me the wings I needed. I open the top drawer of my desk and pull out the *Magen Dovid*. The night Mama gave it to me I looked around this flower wallpapered space and saw New Life everywhere.

And what do I have left of this New Life now? A boy I thought was my friend swore he'll never set his dark eyes on me again. My new father is gone, and my mother has become a stranger.

There is only one thing left, a boy who loves me, a boy whom I love, and whom I just called a KGB spy.

I press my forehead against the cold glass and the numbing snowy grayness beyond it. If I lose him, I might as well hurl myself down from the eleventh floor, because there is no other New Life I could ever want without a gray-blue eyed- raspy-voiced boy whom Mama calls Aizerman.

Aizerman. I wish I had never heard that name.

His book, I wish I'd never opened it.

Babushka is right. The Jewish path is a hard one.

I open the window wide, wider. The cold air assaults my nose. The wind enters my room. I look down on the snow-covered arms of trees, stretching toward me. From underneath them come the happy shouts of ice skaters forgetting time on the frozen pond. I make out Misha's stripy knitted hat with flaps zigzagging among the others. For a single moment, I allow myself to feel it: the yearning to join him down there, right now, to dance and dance with him on ice well into the night. I let the moment pass. I am calm, mesmerized with my own calmness. It hits me how easy it could be, to not even be here at all.

I could make it happen, right now. One final flight.

I allow myself a turn of the head—just one—back toward my room, a final glance at my flowered pillowcase soaked with tears, the tears of Mama's little girl, the one she never had or would have.

I look down at the Jewish Star in my hand. A homecoming present, was it?

"It's you," Mama had said that night.

That me *is no longer here, Mama. That* me *is but a snowflake melting in the palm of a boy's warm hand.*

I climb up the windowsill, knees bumping the side of the potted December-blooming plant showing off its longs buds, pink and fragile. I turn the *Magen Dovid* before thrusting it into the snowy grayness, throwing it out to the wind like an offering. The black shoelace winds and unwinds itself as the star makes its way to the ground from the eleventh floor.

27

Lies and Whining

"Tomorrow is the last day of the term," Electrification says. "And my list for the trip to Lithuania is rather short. Azimova, Borodin, Vagonina, Valentinov, Gladko, Kuzmin, Stepkin. If anyone else still wants to go, you better come see me."

A class trip. Together. The train, the hotel, the *sightseeing*.

I steal a look at Ruslan. He looks away.

Bozhena Lomonosova raises her hand. "But Elektra Ivanovna?" she asks, standing up, her voice cracking, tentative. "My . . . um . . . parents are worried about the political situation over there . . . um . . . unraveling. . . ."

"Sit back down, Lomonosova!" Electrification thunders, and Bozhena plops her large behind back on her chair as though someone has pulled a string from under her. "*Nothing* is unraveling *anywhere*—you got that?" Electrification says, to the class this time. "Some of your parents are reading too many lies in the sorts of newspapers that should not be allowed to exist in the first place! Now, about homework." Her voice turns bored, and she turns to me. "Solovay. Your essay on the material-technical base of socialism after the Great Patriotic War. It's not here."

"I didn't write it," I mutter.

"First Valentinov, now you. Come up to my desk, Solovay," Electrification calls me. Misha glares at me as I walk between the desks. *I thought you were never going to set your eyes on me again, Aizerman.*

"What's your excuse?" Electrification asks. I look at her old, and still almost pretty face, the glasses sitting atop her imposing bun as if they could help her see farther from there.

"I am waiting." She taps her fingers on the desk.

"I . . . am sorry . . ." I say wearily. "I just completely forgot . . . I . . ." *almost threw myself out the window yesterday, Elektra Ivanovna.* I look down at the dark hardwood floors I once washed for her. She takes my chin in her surprisingly soft, wrinkled hand and lifts up my face.

"So tell the class," she says. "What's going on? What took your mind off your responsibilities?"

Why does she want me to stand there and make up excuses? I could make up a lie. Isn't that what I did yesterday, to my mama?

Whose green backpack is it in the hall?

A boy hiding under my bed.

Electrification keeps my face in her hand. "What were you so busy doing?"

"Busy kissing Ruslan Valentinov," I say.

The silence of her classroom ripples with whispers. Luba gasps, then clasps her hand over her mouth. Someone dares a giggle, even. Even in this dark room, I can see the sudden paleness of Electrification's face. Her hand explodes across my cheek. My skin stings from the slap. Ruslan jumps up from behind his chair.

"Sit down, Valentinov," Electrification says. "Solovay is going to answer for her obscene behavior."

"I only told you the truth," I whisper, facing her. "But that's not what you wanted. You wanted me to lie to you, didn't you?"

"What did you say?" she mouths, but every word is heard in the stunned classroom.

"Well, I am tired of lies," I say, louder this time. "My own lies, and yours."

She grabs my hand. "How dare you!"

"You lie to us all the time," I say. "About equality, even as you play favorites. About the family-brotherhood of the Soviet people. When everybody knows there is none. The Lithuanians are protesting *daily*, Elektra Ivanovna! Because they want to be *free*. Free of *us!* But you refuse to see it. You lie about this wonderful society where everything is wrong, but you keep on pretending that it isn't. A wonderful society where people hate each other and call each other names in lines over crumbles of bread. Where children are raised to be afraid, afraid of you, afraid of themselves, afraid of everything. Where everyone is supposed to be wearing the same stupid uniform as everyone else. Where no one is allowed to stand out against the backdrop of stupid gray unfeeling concrete. . . ."

I don't even know what I'm saying anymore, or what I am weeping about.

"I will not have this, this, this . . ." Electrification is trying to find the fury behind her voice, but it only comes out stiff, small, old. "I will not have you mock this classroom, this subject, this country," she tries again. Then her voice climbs, starting to ring shakily, higher and higher. ". . . Your grade book, right now! . . . Report you to the local authorities. . . ." Then, like a deflated balloon that just realized it's out of air, she looks around and slumps back down on her chair. The rest of the lesson she spends just sitting there staring eerily into space. Some people are doodling. Others exchanging whispers. Mostly, though, the room is quiet; even the faces of the war posters on the walls are looking shocked and lost, more than fiery-angry. High above Electrification's desk, the portrait of Lenin is staring back at me with eyes dead and empty.

After class, she stops me with a hand on my shoulder. "Just a moment, Solovay," she says.

I sit down at the desk in front of hers. I can't believe it: in the always dark history classroom, she has raised the shades. Streaks of tears on her face make her skin look worn. I stare at the gray hairs jutting out of her bun and realize she may be much older than I had thought.

"Elektra Ivanovna?" I mouth. "Are you feeling well?"

She waves her hand at me, like I am a fly buzzing. "I am starting to think your mother was right," she says. "When she came here last time to see me about your cutting class, she said I should have retired from teaching a long time ago. 'You belong in another era,'" your mother told me." Electrification sniffs. "You showed me that today, didn't you? That things . . . things can't be the same anymore, can they?"

I shake my head, not positively sure if she is talking to me—or to the upturned chairs on the desks around me.

"Gorbachev, he means well," she says. "But he's made too many mistakes. Did too many things that should never have been done. . . ." She turns her gaze to the window. "Did you see the way that man . . . Yeltsin . . . talks about him on television? Calling the general secretary of the Soviet Union a coward. How *dare* he?! They did a, what do you call it, a statistical poll? In some newspapers." She pauses. "And only twenty percent of those asked said they still believed in socialism. And now some politicians, these Yeltsin-types—" She sniffs. "They are talking about breaking up the Union? What kind of mind-boggling senseless talk is that?"

I stand up from behind my desk, as if she asked me a question I'm about to be graded on.

"You are too young to understand," she says, "and so is your mother. But you have a babushka, don't you? Surely she remembers. How happy we were, how proud. Our parents woke up with the sun and toiled in the fields and in the factories for our country, for our future. We didn't care about clothes, or erasers, or pink frilly things. We had each other. We had the promise of Lenin, we had comrade Stalin. . . ."

Sitting back down, I stare at her in surprise. With every word, she looks older.

"All those things they write nowadays in *your* newspapers, how he sent all those millions of people to camps . . . They are *lies,* nothing but *lies and whining.*"

At this, I almost jump up from my seat. *Lies and whining.* Those were the exact words Ruslan used yesterday. But he talked about something entirely different—he talked about Misha's *Babi Yar* book. He talked about the bodies falling into a ravine just outside Kiev. She is talking about Stalin killing and arresting millions of people.

The bell for the next class rings. Electrification is talking and talking. Just like Ruslan yesterday, in my hall.

No. I order myself to calm down. *He and I are on the same side,* I remind myself. *She is the one who doesn't get it.*

"Anyway," Electrification says, "who are we to judge Stalin sixty years later? Even if those things they now say were true, maybe they were necessary! Those were harsh times— *harsh times*—we lived in," she says. "Spies were everywhere, trying to undermine us. We had to be vigilant. Any trace of weakness wiped out." She looks at me. And yet I have a disconcerting feeling that she is looking through me, someplace into the depth of history. "Once, seventeen years ago, I knew a woman," she says, her voice growing quiet, "who had to inform the authorities about her daughter's suspicious activities."

I stare, startled at the site of fresh tears streaming down her cheeks.

"But it *had to be* done!" she looks at me, her eyes almost pleading. "The important thing is, back then, our parents *believed!* They fought the war in his name. . . . They taught us songs . . . good songs . . . the kinds I tried to teach my daughter, too. . . . And now it's all gone. There is nothing."

"Elektra Ivanovna," I ask her. "That woman, seventeen years ago, did she ever see her daughter again?"

She shakes her head at me, not meeting my stare.

"You remind me of her," she says softly.

"Who?"

"Lena."

"Who is that?" I ask.

"Nobody."

This woman with her drooping bun and wrinkled forehead, maybe she had blond hair once. Maybe her mother stood next to other young blond communists, grinning on a black-and-white photograph. Her father may have sung "I know of no other land where a man can breathe so freely," meaning every word. What kinds of songs did the people in Stalin's camps sing? The ones who hadn't been shot? What did they believe in?

They believed in the sound of boots in the corridor. In a sharp, insistent knock on the door in the middle of the night in 1937. In a jealous neighbor with hard, vertical wrinkles in between her eyebrows. In daughters being denied their mothers. And what did I believe in? I think of the wind on my face last night, as I threw my star out the window, and something tightens inside my chest.

"Don't you have the next class to catch?" Electrification looks at me, as if she didn't even know I was here.

"Yes, geometry." I get up, backpack on my shoulder.

"Oh, one more thing," Electrification says just as I am ready to leave her wretched classroom. "Just a word of advice to you, really. Keep away from Valentinov." I whirl around, my cheeks on fire immediately.

"Just trust me on this."

Then, looking more collected, she grabs a pen, and starts reading someone's essay, *tsk*-ing and frowning, as if I am already gone.

28

Just One Question, Sonya Solovay

Outside the classroom Misha Aizerman sways slightly in the empty hallway.

"Discussing history?" he asks.

"Felt more like a confession," I whisper back. Then I remember myself, remember that we shouldn't be here, we shouldn't be talking, and I furrow my eyebrows at him. Because damn it, I shouldn't feel this, it shouldn't matter, shouldn't be happening, gladness shouldn't swell and swirl at the sight of him, at the sound of his voice addressing *me,* despite what he said yesterday. His dark eyes, they shouldn't stare at me so. I have long ago given up trying to read the complex ancient expressions that flicker on his golden face like shadows.

I scan the gray hallway space behind him, and his eyebrows bend. "Don't worry so. The *kovboy* isn't here."

I narrow my eyes. I've had enough of his sarcasm. "If I worry, then it's not for myself, *fool.*" I try to sound as cold as possible. It must work, because he actually takes a step back and almost trips. Automatically, I extend my hand to him, then lower it, just as quickly.

"I think he did enough damage on your pretty face yesterday," I say. "Whether or not you get hurt doesn't concern me. I just don't want it to be on my account, that's all."

"Now who is being a *fool*, Sonya? You still think it's just about *you*, the way he washed my face with the volleyball?"

"Oh forget it." *Forget me.* I'm already walking toward the staircase, shaking my head.

"Do you think we were *comrades* before you appeared?"

"He likes *me!*" I call out absurdly, without turning my head, still walking.

He follows me down the hall. He doesn't understand. I've seen it, how frighteningly easy it can be, to lose things—a job, a love, a passion for something. I've seen Mama putting her typewriter away. I don't know what she does, but I don't think she goes to her Theater Institute classes any longer. I've seen the furtive look on the face of a man who was supposed to be my new father when he wrapped his large sweaty hand around mine that late September morning and told me to feel at home in the apartment that I had thought was mine.

"If you are so scared on my behalf, we can talk some place *safer*."

Right outside a closed door of a boys' bathroom, I turn around and present him with the fiercest glare yet. "No need."

"You can always find me at the pond," Misha says. "Skating."

I know. "I have nothing to talk to you about."

"You know," he says, "it was quite impressive, your speech in history class, about lies. There are different kinds of lies, there are the lies people tell each other, and then there are the lies people tell themselves."

I redden. "Stop it—oh, stop it, enough lecturing me, you aren't a *rabbi*!"

He raises his eyebrows.

Reddening some more, I point my finger at Electrification's closed door. "You think you *know* all the answers, don't you? Just like *her*, back there." I lower my voice. "She knows all the answers, too, doesn't she?"

We face off, inhaling the rusty bathroom smell in the deserted hallway. We are standing so close, both so late to geometry. He is blushing now, too, staring hard into me, as if my face is a foreign script he's trying to decipher.

"Listen," he says. He touches the sleeve of my uniform dress for the tiniest of moments. "There was something I wanted to know . . . *eh* . . . Unless I was hallucinating from hunger . . . *nu* . . . It was a few months ago. . . . "

"What are you talking about?" I ask him, still trying to sound as rude as possible over the thumping of my own worried heart. How eloquently he defends the proof of a latest theorem in geometry classes. Now he is looking for words, stammering. "Were you at the synagogue that night, on Yom Kippur? The Moscow Synagogue on Arkhipova Street," he clarifies, as if there are many others. And I can feel the heat I see on his face under my own skin.

"I . . . I don't . . . know" *what you're talking about.* With a desperate look toward the entrance to the staircase, I try to breathe out the words, but they refuse to come out.

He takes a step back, like he means to go. *Go—just go*, I am thinking, though a tiny, crazy part of me is absurdly wishing he would stay. "Just tell me this, then, Sonya Solovay—one simple question, a crazy question, perhaps, and then I'll leave you alone."

"Promise?" I whisper.

He takes a soft breath that I can hear. "Are you Jewish?"

Closing my eyes, just for one moment, to regain control, blocking out the swirling, rushing water noises from behind the bathroom door, I can feel things disappear, thoughts, memories—Mama's twilight words on my bed, *"another Jew to die for our sins";* the electric candles in the chandeliers by the synagogue balcony flickering; the moonlight that streamed through the broken attic window dimming; and, finally, the metal six-edged star glinting on the setting sun as it fell outside my window.

"Sonya?" he prods me.

Sonya Solovay, it sounded like God himself, asking, *are you Jewish?*

When I open my eyes again, I meet his without flinching, knowing the answer, knowing all the answers to my troubles.

"*Nyet,*" I answer, my voice clear, my choice made. "I am not, Aizerman."

The door to the boys' bathroom swings open. "Whatever gave you *that* idea."

And that's when I see him, the face I always look for, even when gazing in the mirror. "Ruslan!"

He doesn't look at me. Doesn't say a word. Just grips my hand. Every muscle on his face is tight. The whole time, he'd been standing behind that door. I rake through my conversation with Misha in mind—what have we said to each other?

But then he says, "Go to class, *myshka,*" and in the way he says it, even as he releases my hand, I know I am still this little Russian treasure of his and a sort of velvety pleasure makes a cushion around my heart at being loved with such fierceness. But within the velvet feeling, a dull dread spreads when I see the two boys' eyes lock.

"Aren't you coming?" I touch Ruslan's hand. His skin feels taut, like cold resin.

"In a minute," he says, his eyes on Misha. I try to pull Ruslan aside, but it's like pulling on a railing.

And why are you standing there? I shout mentally at Misha. *When you should be as far away from here as your long legs can carry you!*

"Don't worry, *myshka*. It won't take long."

"You think so, do you?" Misha says to him, his feet planted firmly on the dirty hardwood floor. I hang on to Ruslan's arm more tightly. "Please . . . don't . . . I . . . we . . . he . . . didn't—"

"I know he didn't. I heard enough from where I was standing. I heard how you put him back in his place. Now, go to geometry. Just give me another minute."

Another minute to do what, Ruslan? I want to shout at him, my legs trembling. Instead, I cock my head and peer at him from behind half-closed eyelids the way I've seen pretty women do in movies. "Why geometry?" I say in a voice I don't even recognize. "It's the last day before break. We won't be doing anything. Why don't you . . . ever . . . take me over to your place, for a change?" I rub his arm until his muscles start to relax under my fingers.

"Why . . . my place?"

Misha clears his throat. "You don't have to keep doing this, Sonya."

"Doing what?"

Of course, I know exactly what he means.

"Go to geometry, like the *botanik* that you are," is what comes out of my mouth. "We are done here, *Aiz-er-man*." I hate the words, the moment they are out. But what Ruslan says next, I hate even more.

"Don't worry, *myshka*. I'll take care of him another time. He won't ever bother you again."

29

Afternoon Off

A wall unit with shelves and shelves. China that shimmers with soft mother-of-pearl shades. A few assorted-size iron weights on the floor in the corner. They remind me of his biceps tightening under my hand.

Wooden chairs and kitchen stools, and the smell of old furniture. A round table covered in cloth stands between two sofa beds facing each other.

"Do you live with your grandmother?" I ask him.

"Don't worry," he says. "She's at work."

"What does she do?"

"Nothing interesting, I promise."

In the middle of the room stands a pretty little New Year's evergreen, decorated with fancy ornaments. I touch them gently: the cones and the painted glass balls, the chubby Father Frost figures and the sweet, smiling Snow Maiden figurines.

"Beautiful tree," I say. "You decorated it with your babushka?"

"Yes." His reply is oddly curt. Is he as nervous as I am? Or still angry about Misha? He sits on one of the sofa beds and pats the space beside him. I throw another look around, awed at how much furniture he and his grandmother were able to fit in this rectangle of a room.

"What happened to your—" *parents*, I want to ask, but he speaks at the same time, his words covering mine.

"What's the matter," he says, smirking, "Never been to a boy's apartment before?"

"Actually—no." His smirk grows wider, then, just as suddenly, he grows serious.

"Come here," he whispers.

The warmth of the radiators melting my cheeks; his hands expectant on my uniformed shoulders.

"Sit down."

I sit on the tacky burgundy flower on his bed cover, wrapped into my own arms, knees close together. I stare at a small wrinkled picture of a Russian Orthodox saint tucked behind his bed.

"Relax," he breathes in my ear. "Would you like some Georgian wine?"

"No, I'm all right." *I'm all right.*

You don't have to keep doing this, Sonya, the memory of Misha's voice rises up from somewhere deep inside my soul. I shake my head at the memory and tell it to go back to geometry.

"How about a joke?" Ruslan plops down beside me on his bed and places his hand over my leg.

"Sure."

The sun is white outside the window. His hand burns on my leg.

His eyes are far away, but his hand slides down my leg, then back up. Only this time when it climbs, his fingers are underneath the skirt of my dress, not above it. *That's all right,* I tell myself. *It's what I want.*

"A *negr*—a black-skinned man—asks a genie, 'pleaze, make me white . . . "

I tune out the rest of it. When he is done, he looks at me expectantly. The laugh he wants from me stays glued to the bottom of my throat. His fingers stroking my leg do not falter.

"A bit vulgar?—All right, how about this one. A *negr* and a Georgian tried to trade with a Jew—"

"No."

He lifts his hand from my thigh for a moment. I dare ⟨ small breath, realizing only now that I haven't been breathin⟨ trying to quiet my leg trembling under the sudden absence touch.

"I don't want to hear any more jokes."

His hand races up my thigh, keeping me pinned. "So ⟨ do you want to do, *myshenka moya*?"

My mouth won't open. The answer won't come. H⟨ into me, reaching for my lips. His breath smells of saus⟨ hands are rubbing my neck. His fingers unfasten the of my dress.

His tongue churns, filling my mouth with his sa⟨

My dress whooshes on its way over my head.

You don't have to keep doing this, Misha's voice w⟨ whispers inside me.

Through the swift breaths, the smears of his lip⟨   s⟨
the too-fast rub of his hands burning on my
skin everywhere, I try to keep my eyes squeezed
cross tickles my skin. I must be strong. I must⟨   "⟨
much I love him, show him that he has nothin⟨
from Misha Aizerman. *Close your eyes. Be brave*   to
But eyes wide open, I take in his uniform ⟨   mo⟨
                                                                         bac⟨

floor. For a moment he stares at me staring at his striped briefs. I slide back on the sofa bed. With my eyes closed, and maybe some Georgian wine right now, everything would be soft, unimportant, the whole world a dream. But I am staring. My bare buttocks rub against his velvet cover. My hands are on Ruslan's chest.

"May I have a glass of wine, after all?" I whisper. My whisper doesn't reach him.

". . . I'll be careful . . ." he mutters in an odd disjointed sleep-talker voice. ". . . This won't hurt. . . . I'll make sure . . ." His chest is a boulder.

This won't hurt. Just like they tell you in a pediatrician's office. *A stupid thought. Concentrate. Relax.*

You don't have to keep doing this, Sonya. But what else can a girl do?

Everything is in sharp focus. His wet lips. The short hairs of his would-be mustache. "Ruslan, wait, wait . . . I just . . . I don't think I . . ."

His eyelids unglue themselves finally. His smooth chest separates from me, looming over my own nakedness. His narrow thighs slide away from me. I keep my gaze fixed on his so hard, my eyes are watering—*anything,* away from his legs, his body.

His eyes meet my gaze, suddenly alert. "Did you hear something?"

Just then I do: a rustling of plastic bags, a thud, a shuffling.

"Damn," he whispers, diving for his clothes on the floor. t can't be Babushka."

I reach for my own dress, exhaling. I am already grateful this woman, whoever she is, for coming in at such a perfect ment. I am grateful, that is, until I see her face, glowering at me, and all I can think at first is, *Thank God and Jesus and a crowd of angels and stars in the sky or whoever is up there who pays attention, thank you that at least I've had time to throw my uniform over my bare body.*

"Aren't you supposed to be at work?" Ruslan asks the old woman on the threshold.

"I took the afternoon off," the woman says. "I guess the two of you did, also." She bends down and picks up my bra from the floor, by her feet. "Welcome to my home, Solovay. Look—just bought some choice pork on the way here." She nods down at the leaking plastic bag in her hand. "Since you're here, you might as well stay for lunch."

"That would be . . . *um* . . . " I stammer—*unnecessary,* I am too polite to say. "Thank you . . . *um* . . . Elektra Ivanovna."

"Oh, don't thank me just yet. Won't you fix yourself up first. Properly." With a smirk, Electrification throws my bra at me. I don't even catch it. "I'll be waiting in the kitchen," she says.

I am standing in the middle of Ruslan's room like it's a forest.

"Sonya . . . um . . ." Ruslan is saying something, his voice a barley-there wheeze. His face is the color of a faded pillowcase on his sofa bed. "Sonya?"

But it's as though I've just entered a cloud. I can't hear him properly. *Electrification*—his *babushka?*

I am speechless. I can't fathom it.

30

Secrets

In the kitchen Electrification spreads some newspapers on the small space between the faucet and the windowsill cluttered with flowers.

"The threat of the collapse of the Soviet Union has emerged," reads a newspaper passage soggy with meaty blood. *"National chauvinism is being whipped up. Mass disturbances and violence are being provoked."*

"We are moving toward dictatorship," another newspaper headline screams. *"What choice will Gorbachev make?"*

"Nu?" Electrification prods me. "Are you going to be standing here reading scaredy-cat headlines, or are you helping me make lunch?"

She drops the bloody mass of pork onto the newspapers. My legs and my stomach are weak from the stale-salty smell of dead pig, and my brain is foggy, like the glass surface of this small kitchen clock, covered in grease stains. I still can't believe it. The loathsome Dictatorship of the Proletariat, Electrification of the Whole County, the Queen of Dark History, is the grandmother of the fearless, democratic boy I am supposed to be in love with. I also can't believe this pork in my hands, in these mad winter days of shortages, when even my mama with her dollars has learned to celebrate chicken soup and herring for dinner.

After my outburst sent her home, I guess Electrification has given up on trying to punish me. Then again—here I am, helping her wash the pork, piece by bloody piece, before packing it into the aluminum grinder she has positioned on the counter. If this isn't a punishment, I don't know what is.

I take each gooey morsel very carefully with two fingers. I lift it in the air and watch in frozen horror as the blood drops onto the edge of my uniform dress. I squeeze my teeth together, mentally pinch my nose, and I wash the meat. Then I drop it inside the meat grinder.

Not that it satisfies my torturer any. Laughing, Electrification takes my hands with her meaty wet ones and rams them into the pork. This, she explains, is to ensure more meat fits into the grinder. I screw up my face and push my hand in there, trying not to think about bits of pork crawling in between my fingers.

"You don't help out your mama at home?" she asks.

"We don't have meat like that, at home. In fact, I don't know anyone who does, these days." That quiets her for a little while.

But just as my thoughts start to settle to the awful rhythm of wash-drop-squeeze-grind, she breaks the silence once again. "Do you know what your lover-boy is involved in?" she asks. I make a small noise, working on the pork with renewed vigor. "He is going to a demonstration soon. Maybe even tomorrow." *Tomorrow.* My hands freeze inside the meat grinder. *A demonstration.* I look down at the blood-smeared pictures of Lithuanians in one of the newspapers. Their faces are exalted, insolent, their mouths open in ecstasy as they call for freedom.

She lets it sink in before continuing. "Hanging around with a bunch of rowdy hooligans. Planning their stupid protests."

She cocks her head, staring at me. I try to slam the next morsel of meat into the grinder. But all it does is make an odd squelching noise that sounds indecent. So I drop the pork and face her. "I know he goes to these things," I say.

Jaw open, now it is her turn to stare. "You *know*?"

"Thanks for the invitation to lunch," I say, wiping my hands on a dry piece of newspaper. "But I am no longer hungry."

"Don't . . . be like that." He grabs me by the shoulders outside his building, by a rusty pole of a streetlamp leaning slightly. I try to twist out of his reach. But he catches my slimy pork hand and squeezes it with his fingers. "Don't listen to her," he says.

I whirl around, and my face almost slams into his. "Well, who else am I supposed to listen to? You won't tell me where you go, or what happened to your mother. What your father is like. Or who your grandmother is—this whole *time*!" He tries to hold on to my slippery hand, but I pull it away. "That's fine though. That's how it is. Have your secrets." *And I'll have mine.*

Maybe it's better this way.

He grabs my arms with both hands and pins me to the streetlamp. "My father has another life, a wife, a family, a cushy government job," he whispers. "Sometimes he'll help out with . . . money and pork and . . ." He looks down at his feet, his cheeks ashen with shame. "The Puma sneakers." He looks up at me. "My mama . . . I don't know where she is."

I feel a lightness on my face—a snowflake. My next breath reaches him in a soft cloud. "I know what it's like. To miss your mama."

He shakes his head. "All this time, and she never even tried to find me." He looks like he wants to stop talking—more than anything—and yet he squeezes the next words out. "Babushka won't answer any questions about her. I think she hates her."

He looks away. And suddenly it hits me. The tears on Electrification's cheeks earlier today, in the empty classroom. Her strange story about how a woman she knew betrayed her own daughter. Her words, *You remind me of Lena.*

I look at Ruslan. His face so close, and yet so far away right now. The cold hardness of the streetlamp pole under my ribs makes me shiver all the harder.

"Did you—do you know your mother's name?" I whisper.

"Elena," he breathes back. "Lena. That's all *she'll* tell me."

Have you ever tried to breathe when your chest feels like someone's pinching it from the inside? *The woman had to inform authorities about her daughter's suspicious activities,* that's the way Electrification put it back in the classroom. *But it had to be done!* Her eyes pleaded with me, as though it were up to me to forgive her.

If I am standing here before him, choking on this knowledge in the frosty air, how can I expect *him* to carry this truth for the rest of his life? I swallow back the words—yet another secret, while he is standing here, and sharing his with me.

"Electri—I mean . . . your babushka . . . as much as you cannot stand her and her horrible politics . . . she's all you have, isn't she?"

"No she isn't." He keeps looking down on the snow-covered ditch, filled with cigarette butts and broken beer bottles.

"Now *you* don't be like that. It's all right. It's great that you told me. You know . . . I . . . too . . . have been keeping something from you." I take a deep breath, for courage. It is time. I must tell him. "I . . ."

He catches hold of my dirty hand again. "No," he says. "I mean what I said. My babushka isn't the only thing I have. Here." He lets go of my hand and reaches with his hands behind his own neck. I watch him pull out something thin and delicate. I can't quite breathe when he puts it around my neck— the small ornate cross on a thin silver chain he wears on his chest.

"I bought it in Moscow," he says. "I used to like pretending that it was hers. My mama's. That she left it for me."

With a pang, I think of my own mama's gift—a real one— burrowed deep in some snow mound by the pond. "Ruslan . . . I . . ." I start to say. "What if I told you—"

"Sh-sh-sh. Just don't say anything. It's already yours." He presses his warm lips to the side of my neck for a moment, as he clasps the silver chain shut.

31
Water

A foreign-brand sedan crunches the snow under its wheels just outside my apartment building. The silver shade of the car is barely visible under a layer of dirt, salt, and clingy old snow. The car door opens and then slams shut.

"Wait, wait, finally, there she is—that's my daughter!"

Mama's jeans—flared on the bottoms. Who wears such hip jeans in pre–New Year's snow?

"Where were you?" she says softly. "You almost didn't make it!"

I look up from her jeans, to my own small tapestry-covered bag in her hand.

"Didn't make it for what?" I ask, my heart dropping.

"Meet Vitaly," she says. "My *chauffeur.*"

"Your *what?*"

A scraggly bearded man nods back at me sternly.

"Get in the car—I'll tell you everything!"

Shadows of my castle's unfinished skeleton lie in patches on the perfect white snow. The sun will go down soon, marking the end of a day where at once too much and too little has happened. Under the sun the snow shines, a soft rug sewn with diamonds. But in those patches covered with shadows the snow is not quite black in its dullness. I now notice pieces of ice underneath it, dotted with soot from someone's cigarette. *Why do I have to—notice? Why do I have to go?*

Vitaly coughs into his beard as they smoke together in front of the company *Mazda*. The moment I get in, I am drenched in the spicy smell of cold leather, cigarettes, and gasoline—the smell of money. Vitaly starts driving, and Mama tells me. About her new boss with an exotic name *John,* whom I am going to meet today, apparently.

"But Mama, I am in my school uniform!"

She laughs. "That's all right, *devochka.* Remember the *beezness* trip to America I told you about? Well." While she takes another drag of her cigarette, I watch other cars pass faster and slower over blackened snow. Separated from their worries by the cool glass of the chauffeured car, I peer at the stoic faces of the People ready, always ready, even if they might not know what they're ready for.

"It wasn't easy to get a visa appointment for us both at the American Embassy," Mama says, "but John pulled some strings and—Here we go!" She waves her hand around the *Mazda*, and throws flashy smiles at me.

"So, that's where we're going?" My voice cracks. "To the American Embassy?"

"Eventually. First, some shopping in Moscow. Passport photos. We'll have a busy week! John is paying for the hotel for us, and everything! Then . . ." She beams brighter with every traffic light we pass.

The chauffeur's eyes meet mine in the rearview mirror, and I remember another car trip, the one from Moscow's center to its outskirts, when I called on New Life through the window with everything I had. I remember the tanks rolling before us like a black cat crossing the street. "What a nice surprise your mother prepared for you, *eh*?" the chauffer says.

Mama directs her smile at him. "As I told John, I can't very well leave my daughter all alone."

There was a time when those words would have made me soar all the way to the moon.

Now I say, "What about the class trip to Lithuania?"

Mama snorts. "I am taking you to New York City, the capital of the world, and you're talking about *Lithuania*?" She shakes her head. "I would not have let you go there in any case. Not with all the unrest. It's just getting worse, the talk of separation."

"So, you oppose it, then?" I squeeze out, lest the words choke me. "'*All that talk of separation.*' You don't think the *Lithuanians* deserve a little *sovereignty*? I would have thought your views would be a lot more *democratic*."

She smiles. She ignores the strangeness of my voice. "Deserve, don't deserve," she says. "I just don't want *you* there, foolish."

"But what about school, after the holidays?"

"It's all right, *Sonechka*. You'll only miss one day, tomorrow. I'll bring you back in time for the next school term."

"One day can make all the difference."

I reach down under my fur coat and finger Ruslan's silver token on my chest. I think of his eyes not meeting mine outside the building. Electrification—*his grandmother's!*—warnings in the kitchen about a demonstration, maybe even tomorrow. I think of the tenderness in his raspy voice, as he told me his secrets, and how steel-gray his eyes were in that school hallway when he promised, *"Don't worry,* myshka, *I'll take care of him another time."*

Mama keeps looking at me expectantly. "I can't leave my daughter alone," she repeats. "Not again."

My next words to Mama are quiet, soft, like a snowflake dancing outside our window. "What if I told you there are things *I* cannot leave alone, Mama?"

"What things?"

I look back at her anxious eyes through the mirror. "My new life," I whisper. "It's here. It might not be exotic. You know, empty stores and birch trees. But it's mine."

Now it's Mama's turn to gape at me, speechless and breathing, tightening the muscles on her face. "Maybe if things were different—if *you* were different—not this pale stranger with a heart of ice, I would have trusted you enough to leave you here alone. As it is, the choice is yours." Her heavy hair slams over her shoulder as she whirls around again. "It's either America. Or Siberia."

"You sound like the Communist Party itself."

"What did you say to me?"

Tactfully, Vitaly turns the radio on. Mama's eyes burn at me through the rearview mirror. An old pop song comes on, in a pleasantly spicy Latvian accent.

I think of Ruslan looking for me tomorrow morning to sneak in a quick goodbye before his demonstration, the way he likes to do sometimes. I think of Misha's striped hat zigzagging out on the pond, eleven floors below my window. I think of his stolen *Babi Yar* book, all alone in my room, hidden in the pile of notebooks.

I think of Misha walking into some empty boy's bathroom tomorrow morning, followed by Ruslan. There will be no one to say, *Can't we go over to your place,* pouting sweetly.

The car swerves a little. Brown slosh splatters onto my window. I watch it run down the glass in streaks of dirty water.

Over my side of the glass, my finger traces *H2O*.

You are nothing like water, Misha once told me.

"What, *what?*" Mama asks me, frowning.

I stare at her beautiful, though tired-looking face through the mirror. *I am thinking about the qualities of water, Mama. How each year it hardens into ice, then thaws, over and over.* I think of the wind on my cheeks, the rush I used to get in late November, when the water turned hard in Siberia. I think of my Old Life, colorless as water, easy as see-through dreams. The afternoon is slipping by me. Once things are set in motion, can they be stopped?

"Stop," I whisper.

Mama turns to me. A fast hand on my knee, warm, restraining.

"Stop the car! I shouldn't be here."

"It's going to be great, Sonya," she says in a beautiful voice, soothing. "Like nothing you've ever seen."

"I know," I say. "I bet America is amazing, Mama."

Vitaly slows the car, keeping his eyes on me, absolutely fascinated. Like he's watching something out of a Latin *telenovella* called *The Rich Cry Too.* I roll down the window.

"What—Sonya? Whatever are you *thinking?*" Mama asks against the gust of gasoline-scented wind.

I am thinking how blissfully easy it would be, to leave it all behind for two weeks, to skip along the streets of New York holding Mama's hand, chewing gum the color of freedom, and picking out another pair of jeans.

"*Sonya!*"

The car has slowed even more. Vitaly has given up his wheel, practically.

"I have already told you—"

At the traffic light Vitaly slams on the brakes. It's lucky he has been driving slowly, this observer of human drama. On the left side of the boulevard, a mass of people jostles for position at the sight of an oncoming bus.

"Sonya!"

I never realized how easy it is. To open the car door. And come out, right on the road. Mama flies out the other side. A chauffeur of a nearby *Volga* sedan rolls down his window for a better view.

"Get back in here and start acting like an adult!" Mama shouts. "What do you want me to do—cancel everything? If we don't make it to the embassy appointment, what of the voyage, the new job, now that I finally, finally . . ."

The traffic light has changed color. Vitaly comes out of the car, shouting. Mama, too, cries and shouts, running toward me. The other cars beep with savage enthusiasm. The drivers curse though the open windows, their eyes devouring us. I maneuver between them all, flying to the other side of the street, thinking, *Is this what freedom feels like, is this how the communists felt at first, when they smoked on their barricades, when they plotted to defy the tsar, this intoxicating feeling I inhale now with the gasoline-filled air?* Mama follows me.

"For the thirty-fifth time, Sonya." She exhales sharply. "You are." Breath. "*Not.*" Breath. "Going." Breath. "To *Litva.*" She is completely out of breath. Poor Mama.

"Fine, I'm not. *Ladno.* But I *am* taking this bus, right here, Mama." I point to it, a sluggish creature, puffing stink and slowing, ready to swallow up the impatient crowd. "You cannot stop me anymore than you can carry me onto the airplane to America."

"All right!" Mama grabs on to my coat as I tear into the savage crowd of competing passengers-to-be. As the bus pulls up to the curb the crowd around us pours forward—a cursing, elbow-jabbing flood. "I am going to call John tonight and tell him the whole thing is off," she shouts at me, struggling against the ferocious crowd all about her, struggling against her tears. "The appointment. The voyage. The job. Let's go home. Everything to the demons."

The cursing, poking flood of people shoves me aside, out of their way to the bus doors. I grab Mama's arm. Someone pushes my face almost into hers. Her cheeks are wet with freezing tears. "You are doing so well right now," I tell her. "I know why we've had all these imported yogurts in the refrigerator in the past month. If you don't go, who is going to feed this family? Papa?" I smile.

She sniffs and twists her lip. "There is something I didn't tell you. He came home." I stare at her. "Andrei is home. He came this morning."

My eyes widen. "He's home?" Her words—my own words repeating, *he's home*, lift me, make me feel lighter than a spare snowflake landing on Mama's tear-stained face. "So why didn't you tell me? I won't be alone, then!"

"I . . . I didn't want you to know . . . before the visa appointment. . . ." Some of her words she gulps in with the wind. "Anyway, don't get too excited. . . . He isn't necessarily . . . He just—"

"I love you, Mama."

"I will call you every single evening—and you better be there, and you better sound good."

"I will."

"And—Sonya, wait!" I dive back into the crowd. I can hear Mama's voice shouting hoarsely behind me, "Wait! Wait! Let me through!" But I have already become a part of the fierce elbow-jabbing flood that is pulling my limbs apart as it carries me into the bus just far enough from the doors not to snap my nose off when they close. Through the grimy glass of the bus door, I catch a glimpse of a shiny slim brunette waving at me through her tears. I know the water in my own eyes could never match the beauty of that shimmer.

32

Dance Partner

When I get home, it's like I had stepped into the wrong apartment. My bed sticks out from my room, half of it out in the foyer.

"Papa? Are you—" But the thunderous noise of moving furniture across the wall drowns out my would-be words. I almost trip on a carton filled with empty jars and cognac bottles outside the living room. *What is this, a pre–New Year's cleaning? Is Papa moving in—or moving out?* Whatever question or greeting wanted to come out dissipates into stale, smoke-filled apartment air.

The window of my room is open. I don't need to look out to know the celebration of the winter holidays has already started down there. Little kids shout. Blades scratch the ice. I change into warmer clothes quickly. Grab Misha's *Babi Yar* book and stick it in my deep coat pocket. I dig out a pair of skates I'd brought here from Siberia. I leave a note on the kitchen table. *Dear Papa, I am out on the pond. Will be home soon.*

Because I won't be long, I'm sure. Just a spin or two to soften up these old skates. Give Misha the book. Tell him to be careful. Tell him that I love Ruslan. I am his girl. That's just the way it is, now. Ruslan is a jealous boy. We can't really be friends, Misha. But I didn't mean it, the way I called you *Aiz-er-man.*

Just a spin or two or three. A quick word under the setting sun, the only place we could talk, really. Then I'll go home. If you can call it that, this lonely space filled with smoke.

It's almost winter break, for God's sake. Just a spin or two or three.

The bright wintry sunlight shines on the frozen lid of the pond. The skaters' faces gleam, framed by hills of brilliant snow.

The littlest children—the ones that come along with a bright-cheeked young mama or an energetic babushka—congregate in corners. The rest of the pond belongs to their taller, pushier comrades. Some of the faces I recognize—a neighbor, a classmate, Diana Komissar with her faithful Luba, Kuzmin, Bozhena Lomonosova. I look at them all fondly. Even Kuzmin is part of it, even Luba, part of that *life* I have—here, right here. . . .

Lacing my skates on a bench that sits atop the hill, already I can feel the increasing rhythm of my heart contracting to the chorus of loud scratch marks, the fierce slamming of the puck. A first skate of the season. My blades sink into snow, as I make my sideways walk down the hill, Misha Aizerman's *Babi Yar* book in hand.

He must be the tallest one here, a lamppost, lighting the place with his fresh forever sun-tanned face. At the sight of me watching, he dashes sideways, squeezing his hockey stick to himself like a dance partner in a furious tango—a flurry of coarse boy shouts—the puck spinning, spinning across the pond. He briefly turns toward me, with a triumphant three-quarters grin, one-quarter glare, before joining the pack of other puck pursuers.

I straighten up, shove the book back into my pocket. A spin first, right? Then I start off, just wanting to show him. One step to the right. One to the left. Do not let the right skate drag behind as a brake.

I try to look ahead, toward the side of the pond the hockey players have claimed—almost half the space they have reserved for themselves with their fierce knocking and shouting. I try to follow Misha's brown eyes shining back at me as he darts closer and closer to the invisible line that separates the hockey players from the rest of us, peaceful skaters. I tell myself not to smile at him, not to concentrate too hard on the movement of my own feet underneath me. But one time he whizzes by me too fast, and I teeter. My arm swings into his side and something gets in the way of my right toe. I try to balance my body back into place. Too late. I am already giggling with a momentary weightlessness. The next second I am sprawled somewhere beside Misha's black skates. Lying there, a heap of parts on the ice, I grin into the blinding sun above me.

Now I remember that it really is nothing. More than nothing—falling is part of the pleasure.

It's just the snow that has somehow crept inside of my glove that is nasty, and so I take my glove off. Without thinking, I reach out to grab another gloveless hand extending toward me. I grin at Misha as he pulls me up. My palm against his skin feels so warm and dry, so ordinary, as if I have held his hand a thousand times.

"You tripped me," I say.

"I tripped you?" A wide smile lightens his face. "You have been teetering, tripping all over the place."

"Pardon me, but *I* never trip *or* teeter."

"You don't know how to skate."

"Then you haven't been watching."

His smile fades a little, and I look down at my own hand and realize it's still clasped around his. The day floods in, as if by command, with its excited noises, the swishing, the scratching, the clatter of the hockey game momentarily ceased, the giggles of Diana and Luba staring at Misha and me, the figure of Kuzmin standing to the side, staring in our direction, too, leaning on his hockey stick.

When I start moving again, it's just like Siberia. Maybe better. I put my face out to the wind. I let my body take over, let my legs lead me where they shall.

Of course. Of course! It's just like playing the piano, isn't it? If you just get out of your own way, your fingers will know, and all you have to do is follow. Wide steps, small steps, forward, backward. Letting my feet spread and then come close together, over and over and over and over. I draw a braid. I weave in between those ahead who are suddenly too slow. I change direction. I float, I fly, my snowy swan wings strong behind me, the ice changing shades under the setting sun. I grin, swinging calmly to the side past a hockey-stick–wielding hooligan skating fast at me. As my blades graze the ice, the evening wind reaches all the way down to my heart and cools the staleness of my insides. I veer and swish, hands on the waist, laughing in this rediscovered warmth of winter, laughing harder, when I see Misha laugh back at me. Two street lights throw scant yellow light over the skaters' faces, and the hills of snow grow gray, then black around us. At one point I look around, laughter scorching my parched throat, when I realize how warmly I am smiling at Misha, how slippery is the surface we are both standing on.

Diana Komissar skates up to me. "You are *such* a flirt," she says, giving me a playful shove on the stomach that almost sends me toppling backward. An image of Ruslan's sad, loving, furiously hot-cold-muddy eyes floats into my head.

"I'm just skating, for God's sake," I tell her angrily, shutting the image out.

In my ears the wind erases the sound of children's laughter, the last of the parents' calls, "Din-ner is rea-dy!" "Na-ta-sha, come home!" "*Da-da-da*, you and right now," the hockey players joking something to Misha on their way out. The people leave all around me, but I just dance to the music of the blades singing against the ice, and I don't realize that I have been dancing until the pond gleams empty, for the most part, and except for the retreating group of hockey players there is no one left but me—and my dance partner.

33
Careful

For the first time, I notice how much his hair has grown since autumn, when I last really looked at him. Some of his curls escape from underneath the front of the hat, falling in short commas over his forehead. I look down under my feet, at the scratch marks that look like messages written in an unknown cursive. In the night, quiet with stars and snow, I can hear a stranger in the dark cough and spit out productively.

"I am sorry about . . . the way I spoke to you . . . earlier," I say, absently poking the ice with the tip of my blade.

"Careful," Misha says, nodding down at my skates. "Are you trying to drown us?"

And then it all comes crashing down. The whole weight of the day.

When I should be as far away from this boy as possible, for both his sake and mine, here I am smiling at him, barely aware of the blade of my right skate knocking at the ice, knocking and knocking.

"Maybe you're the one who should be careful."

There, I said what I came here to say.

We walk toward the bench together. The muscles of my legs are ringing pleasantly. My cheeks are still ablaze from the wildest skate of my life. Yet, a quiet cold starts reaching under my coat and my sweater. Ruslan's silver cross is itchy on my sweaty skin.

The climb is hard on legs that all of a sudden feel unused to skating. At one point, my blade sinks too deep, and the rest of me follows, my knee dropping into the wet snow. Misha slows down to help me. Ignoring his outstretched hand, I pull my body upward.

"Why?" he asks. His voice is measured. I stare at him, not quite sure what he's asking.

"Why should I be careful?" he says. The earflaps on his knitted hat ruffle in the wind defiantly.

Making certain that we keep an acceptable distance as we sit down to unlace our skates, I slide to the edge of the bench. "Because *he* . . ." Misha knows just who I mean. He snorts, taking the time with his laces. I try to explain God-knows-what.

"He isn't like *that*," I say. "He's really . . . nice. He's . . . thoughtful—" I look hard at Misha, just in case he dares argue or snort again. "Deep down, in his own way, without knowing it. He is . . ." *tender*, I stop myself from saying.

Snow has started falling. One snowflake gets trapped in his eyelashes. Despite myself, I slide a bit closer.

"He is . . . jealous. He . . . just doesn't believe in friendship . . ." the word gets caught in my throat—*druzhba*—"friendship between guys and girls."

"What do *you* believe in?" Misha asks me.

I look away and pull off my skate. We stay like this for a moment, sitting quite close on the bench now, looking everywhere but at each other's faces.

"So you live around here?" he asks.

In response to his question, I look up at my building, dotted with windows, some yellow, busy with people, others cold and blank. The window of my room is dark, and I can't see our living room from here. Papa must be done moving things around by now. Drinking something in the kitchen. Hopefully, tea. The wind whips at us from around the corner with new force. *Tea would warm us right up.* The thought flashes, then vanishes, just as quickly.

"I live on the other side of the boulevard," Misha says. He lets a brief silence linger.

Despite myself, I wonder what it would be like, to stop in, one anonymous night just like this one, when the falling snow covers your tracks the moment you make them. . . . To peek inside Misha's mysterious space. . . . *Enough.* I jump up from the bench. He gets up, too. He hands me the skates I have almost abandoned at the foot of the bench. That's when I notice a shoelace, making a loop out of a rather shallow-looking pocket of his coat.

"You are about to drop something, I think." I reach toward his pocket. Then my hand halts. He looks down at his pocket, holds on to the rope.

"Ah just a curious thing I found out here." He pulls it out at first, then stuffs it deeper into the pocket. But not before I glimpse the metal edges glinting under the spare stars.

"When?" I whisper. I don't want him to hear my voice right now. "When did you find it?"

"Just tonight, not too far, in a snow mound. It's just—why?"

He peers at me. I look down at my boots, shrugging. I don't want him to know that I have seen the shiny thing in his pocket. That I held it. Wore it. Kept it under my pillow. That, once, it was mine.

Now the sight of it reminds me that we shouldn't be here, talking together, this late. He leans close to me.

"I have to go home," I say.

"I understand," he says. His feet, like mine, are absolutely still. "Sonya, I never . . ." He trails off, tries again. "I think I . . ."

"You what?" I whisper. The skin of his cheeks glitters with dewlike drops of snow. For this one crazy moment I allow myself to examine the imprecise carving of his nose, the wavering line of his lip. . . . His face floats closer, closer, closer. "I am . . ." His breath warms me, and the coolness of his skin on my nose sends a jolt of heat through me.

"You're crazy, is what you are." I straighten up, my posture regal with belated indignation.

"Crazy?" he grins. "You're one to speak."

"Why am I crazy?"

He raises his eyebrows. "You're here, aren't you?"

With a shake of my head, I take a step back.

"No wait. I never thanked you. For trying to *save* me, for God's sake." He nods vaguely in the direction of some idling passerby or other, smoking in the darkness.

We're still standing by the bench—two idiots. He places each one of his hands over my sleeve. His fingers get caught in the long strands of fur on my coat. The sound of someone coughing explodes through the silence of the night. I whirl around. I think I see a shadow shift somewhere among the trees. Of course, I always see shadows.

Misha looks around. His dark eyes—pure peacefulness.

"Aren't you scared?" I whisper to Misha.

"Scared? Someone like me?" He smiles. "I cannot afford to be."

My cheeks tingle with warmth and frost, as I stand, delaying the night, watching Misha go. To warm my fingers I put my hand in the deep pocket of my coat. My fingers land on the soft, worn-out side of what I immediately realize is—oh how could I forget it *again*—Misha's *Babi Yar* book.

"Misha!" I shout. "Wait, Mi—" I halt, midyell. It might be better that way.

The whole world seems a little unreal on this furry Russian night. I keep my eyes on the brightness of the silly stripes on his hat, on the skates over his shoulders, and on his slow, yet springy steps, as my own feet step lightly over the freshly gathering snow.

Someone coughs loudly. *A smoker's cough*, I think, with a shiver. I dare not turn my head toward the sound. I don't know what's worse, the enormousness of the space surrounding me, or the possibility that the halting footsteps approaching me from behind, *khroost, khroost*, belong to someone I know.

I walk on, forcing imaginary coughing smoker's shadows out of my mind.

34

SOS

Come on, what's the matter with me today?

Leave the *Babi Yar* book on a foot rug outside his door. Good.

Now, fade. Lingering strictly prohibited.

Instead of leaving the wet nasty chill of the drafty hallway, I lean against the leatherlike padding of Misha's apartment door and listen to the merry sounds of dishes clinking musically against each other. What was meant to be a scream turns into a hollow squeak out of my mouth as I realize I am no longer alone. A shadow covers the distant light of the moon through the window across from the landing—the only source of illumination here.

"Good evening," says a shadow of a voice. The air fills with tingly tobacco mixed in with something else oddly raw and sour.

"I . . ." My throat fills. Thoughts race, too fast for me to catch any. The figure in the darkness takes a step back, and upon realizing who it is, I gasp with relief.

"It's *you*! I thought . . . I . . . I didn't know you smoked."

A soft guffaw. "When I've got ci-gah-rettes, I do."

Kuzmin takes a step toward me, his gangly figure and small eyes emerging from the shadow. I stare at the pair of skates, tied together with laces, hanging across his shoulders. I realize I'm holding my breath. I realize he has followed me here from the pond. The momentary relief is gone now.

"Do you live here or something?" I croak.

"No, I don't li-ive here," Kuzmin says. He props each hand to Misha's door, on either side of me. "Do you?"

My feet take an automatic step back. Which means I stand with my back pressed against Misha's fake leather padded door. "I was just . . . dropping off a book, that's all."

"Which book? *Ah*, you mean this one?"

I shift, too late. He has seen it. The tome, lying on Misha's doormat. One hand still firmly planted against Misha's door, Kuzmin picks up the book with the other.

"*Babi Yar,*" he reads the title, then shoves the book quickly under his jacket.

"Give . . . it . . . back . . . or . . ."

Kuzin's face just moves nearer. I realize I haven't been able to see it in such horrid detail since a chemistry lesson on the first week of school.

"Or what?"

"Or . . . I'll . . . rip your head off."

He sneers. "I'd like to see you try, microbe."

"I'll . . . tell . . ."

"You'll tell who? Aiz-er-man? That you followed him home? That you've been standing here, behind his door, doing what?" He laughs. "Or is it your precious Valenteee-eenov that you're going to tell? And you will tell him what, exactly?"

In a swift movement that must surprise him as much as it surprises me, I extend my hand toward his coat to rip out the book. He jerks back, his hand snatching the book back from me. One of his skates cuts into my shoulder. Released from the prison bars of his arms, I turn sideways toward Misha's door and place the pointing finger of my left hand on the round buzzer button.

"Careful," Kuzmin says, dropping the exaggerated Moscow accent. I can see him squeezing Misha's book to his side, underneath his coat. "I don't advise you to upset me." Finger still on the button, I stare at him, hesitating, watching him squeeze the *Babi Yar* book harder to his ribs underneath his coat.

"Relax, little one," he says. "I won't reveal your little game. Your secrets are safe in this little vault." He points at his once-more smirking mouth. "I only want—a little appre-ciation. Let's see—" He puckers his lips and scratches his hat like he's *thinking*. "How about a . . . kiss?"

I narrow my eyes at him. "Get lost."

"Just on the cheek, fool. After all, I've got *principles*." And he takes yet another step away form me, smirking.

My eyes fly open. A breath of relief makes a small noise escaping from my lungs. A kiss on the cheek? It doesn't seem bad, really. Just a small step? And maybe another? A brush of my lips on his skin. Just a shadow of a touch. And away, away, down those stairs, faster than an antelope. . . . He isn't breathing into my face anymore, isn't squeezing me to the door like a soldering press. I lift my hand off Misha's buzzer button.

"And the book?" I whisper, nodding at his coat, hating myself for discussing this like it's some sort of a business deal.

"The book?" Again, he puckers his lips in *thought*, keeping his eyes fixed on me.

"I don't know . . . I'd like to keep it, probably," he says. "A token that symbolizes our understanding, *eh*? But then again—" he adds, seeing my expression. "Maybe I'll give it back. Maybe—if I like the kiss. *Nu*—" His smirk widens. "Let's get on with it? Don't be scared. I don't *bite*. . . ." He closes his eyes dreamily.

"I'm not *scared*," I whisper, though I feel like I am drowning in a snow mound. Then I remember Misha's words. *I'm not scared. Someone like me, I can't afford to be.* I spread my arms, as though I am still dancing on ice with Misha under the setting sun, not afraid to fall, not afraid of anything. My skates fly about me as I perform one final twirl for my astonished spectator. One of my blades hits Kuzmin on the side of his arm, and he lets out a muffled cry, as he stumbles and falls on the floor, more from the surprise of it than from the pain, or at least I hope so. I look at him landing on his knees, and at my skates falling to the floor with a clatter, surprised and terrified at what they've done, I've done. But he gets up, grunting, his small eyes even smaller with menace and fear.

My finger lands back onto the tiny circular surface of Misha's buzzer. The place on the other side of the door rattles with sound, *SOS*.

From behind the opened door, a sharp-chinned, skinny girl stares at me through Misha's fierce dark eyes.

"Misha! Mi-sha!" she calls. In her flannel pajamas she shivers as she takes a step backward, squeezing her back to the full-length mirror on the wall.

From behind the girl emerges a woman in a long-sleeve robe thrown over an ankle-length lacy nightgown. Softly blonde and middle-aged, she frowns as she says, "Who's there?" But at the sight of me, fine wrinkles on her plain but endearing face crease gently on the sides of her eyes. "Are you Misha's classmate?"

"I . . ." I look behind me helplessly.

"See you in school, microbe," whispers a voice from the shadows below me. The stairwell door creaks open, slams shut.

I take a breath. *Nu*. After everything that I have withstood today, I should be able to handle explaining myself to this soft blonde in a nightgown.

"I . . . Misha and I . . . we were just . . ." I smile faintly, even as I wonder how I could be so reckless to be standing on this particular threshold at such an improper hour. I wonder, too, how a small soft woman like this could have born a son so giant and blazing-dark handsome. "Misha and I were skating . . . and I was going to return his book—" I offer another weak smile, "so—here . . ." I look down at my coat and freeze, realizing the book is no longer *here,* fool—*fool, fool, fool*—wishing I could fall through the cracks of the earth.

When I look up, still numb with shame, I find Misha—this new Aizerman in worn leather slippers, pale blue Soviet sports pants with a white stripe on each side, a plaid flannel shirt, and cheeks still burgundy from skating (or from seeing me here, at his doorstep this way?). His long fingers pull on a loose thread on the side of his pants. I should be the one flustered. And I am. And yet, looking at the shy glow of Misha's complexion, God knows why I cannot stop smiling. (*fool fool fool*)

"Come in already," Misha says. His mother smiles at me.

How cold all the endings of my body have gotten in the draft—toes, fingers. When I sniff to clear my nose of cold and leftover tears, the smells of warmth and fried onions fill my nostrils.

I throw a brisk, panicked look behind me. I shouldn't. God knows I shouldn't. But I think of Mama, staying at some friend's apartment in the center of Moscow. I think of Papa rearranging the furniture—what an odd thing to do, when coming home for the holidays. I think of the menacing drafty night behind my back. I step across the threshold.

35

The *R-r-r*'s and the *Kh-kh-h*'s

Misha lives in a fortress of books.

In every apartment I've ever been to, everyone displays a few shelves, read or unread. But here in the light of the small table lamp and the moon glowing grandly outside a tall oval window, we aren't talking about shelves, we're talking about walls—walls of books—practically whole floors of them! Oh, the dusty basement smell of old books, the fresh-baked smell of new ones.

I pull out one book from the nearest shelves. Ray Bradbury.

"Adore him," I say hoarsely. "Short stories, especially."

"Which one's your favorite?"

"Oh God," I reply. "They're all so different. I really don't think it's fair to—"

"Mine is the one about a triangle baby," he says, and here I am jumping up and down, shouting, "*Da, da,* the one where the baby is born in the wrong dimension! And his parents don't know what to do at first, and then they enter his dimension through this special machine, and—" I am speaking really fast and too loud probably for God-knows-what-hour.

"—and they become a circle and a square," Misha says.

"—and then they are happy," I whisper.

He starts pulling books off the shelves for me, books with gold letters, leather jackets. From one of the shelves, I pick up a small tome, wrapped in soft paper the color of cream, *Stories for Children* by an author whose long name starts with *Isaac*. "I read these to my sister," Misha says, watching me intently.

Can it be? *Jewish* fairytales?

I open it, and before I know it, I am sitting on his divan, reading some crazy story about a corpse praying at a synagogue. Misha is sitting next to me, guitar in hand, plucking at the strings and reading over my shoulder.

At one point I look up from the book, and stare at his long fingers on the strings.

I didn't know he played guitar.

The number of reasons for me to get up and get going multiplies with every second. But every time I look around telling myself it is way too late to be here, I hook my eyes onto something I might not have noticed yet. I should think of Papa, or Mama's half-hearted warning, *Don't get too excited,* earlier. I should think of Ruslan, Kuzmin, I don't know, having to wake up early enough for the last day of school tomorrow. Instead I think, *God knows I will probably never come back to this place again.* A few times, I stand up and sit back down.

"What does your mama do?" I ask.

"A doctor," Misha says. "Both my parents are." He is picking and picking at his guitar. *Tram, tram, ta-dam.* "My papa is at work right now. First aid."

My eye falls on a shelf lined with books about anatomy and biology. "So, you're going to be one, too?"

"I would be one, even if they were *chefs* or geologists," he says, a little defensively. "It's just . . . something I believe in." *Tram, tram, tra-da-dam.*

"Believe in?"

"It's a way of keeping up with the repairs. . . ."

"The *repairs?*"

Finally, he loses his seriousness enough to grin.

"My father taught me this, it's a Jewish concept." He glances carefully at me when he says the word "Jewish." "It's called *tikkun olam*, which means, basically, repair the world." He glances at me again. "I figure being a doctor is an easy way to fulfill that a little."

I smile. "I didn't know there were Jewish concepts."

His gaze is piercing, searching my face. "They are just these rules . . . for us to live by," he says. "Some are more literal, like what we are and what we aren't allowed to eat. Like not eating pork, for example."

I turn away from his stare.

"We don't mix milk and—" He stops himself, shaking away the rest of the phrase.

"What?"

"*Tikkun olam*," I say. I like the musical way it rolls off my tongue. ". . . But . . . don't you believe in God?"

"Of course."

"Well, then, wouldn't that be God's job? World repair?"

He shakes his head adamantly, making the locks over his forehead fly. "Our world, our job . . ." he says. With each one of my questions he grows more restless. His fingers keep fidgeting with guitar strings.

But I cannot stop myself. "So what else? What other rules do you have?"

Tram, tam, ta-dam, his fingers sing. "There are too many to learn about in one day. There is a commandment for practically everything—"

"You mean like the Ten Commandments?"

He smiles. "Try 613."

"Six hundred?"

"And thirteen." He smiles.

I stare at him in disbelief. "How do you know all this, anyway? I mean, my babush—" I stop myself, just in time, under his startled stare. "I mean, when you are Jewish, is it just something written on the inside of your brain—*tikkun olam*, no pork, 613 commandments?"

He shakes his head, not lifting those eyes off mine. "My father—he has been taking these night classes at the Moscow Synagogue after work. He has been teaching Mama and me since the beginning of the year. But there is still so much I don't know. Like, I've been trying to learn this song, but the chords are . . . not cooperating. . . ."

"Which song?" I ask.

Just this one time, I tell myself. Wouldn't it be something? To hear the sounds of wind and sunshine through his voice, like the music in the synagogue.

The color on his face deepens. For the first time I notice his little sister leaning in the door frame with an eager face. I wonder if he sees her when he whispers, "*Hava*," his fingers barely touching the guitar strings at all.

"*Nagila Hava*," he says, "*Nagila Hava, nagila ve-nis-me-kha* . . ."

"*Hava*," I sing softly, before he changes his mind—before I change mine, "*Nagila hava, nagila ne veesmekhat* . . ."

"It's *ve nis me kha*," he corrects me.

I can't help grinning at him, ever the teacher. We do it together. Him, me, him, me. "*Hava ne-ra-ne-na, hava ne-ra-ne-na.*" His voice crackles, not knowing how smooth it really is. I fumble. He grows excited.

"Good, just—see if you can accentuate the *kh-kh-kh*'s and the *r-r-r*'s a little more."

It must be at least eleven, maybe close to midnight, even, and yet here we are standing in the middle of the room, grinning at Misha's little sister, and throwing the *kh-kh-kh*'s and the *r-r-r*'s at each other with *r-r-r*elish. The *r-r-r*'s make wind inside my mouth. As for the *kh-kh-kh*'s, so soft they are in normal everyday life, *h-h-h,* timid, hiding. Yet there is a rasp to it, a wheeze, a hint of a roar, if you pronounce it right, the explosion *khlop khlop khlop* of hands clapping.

"*Kh-kh-khava, ne-r-r-ah-ne nah, kh-kh-khava, ne r-r-rah-ne-nah,*" I sing, and still Misha is interrupting me, laughing, saying, "Now you're doing it too much, Sonya!"

"So what?" I say, "I like it!" and I sing, "*kha-vva-ne-r-r-r-r-r-r-ah ne nah,*" until I am left with practically no breath whatsoever. When I stop to breathe, his sister edges closer, cocks her head at me, and asks in a really thoughtful, sophisticated tone of voice, "Are you Misha's girlfriend?"

There is a silence, followed by a sharp intake of his breath, and way too many explanations on my part about the nature of comradeship and the lateness of the hour. Their mother calls out from another room, "*An-ya!*"

Misha has an odd expression on his face, a shadow of a smile playing on his lips.

"What's so funny?" I smile back nervously.

"Nothing," he says.

"What?" I ask him again, my voice tightening.

"Your *boy-friend,*" he says.

I knew it. *What a stupid mistake.* I take a decisive step toward the door. He blocks my way.

"Just . . . the idea of it . . ." he says. "If he could see you right now . . . standing *here,* singing *Jewish* songs."

Even as I look up at him, I can feel my heart dropping.

"You're right," I say. "I am sorry. I shouldn't have come at all."

"No!" he says. "That's not what I—"

"I know what you're thinking. You think he hates you. You think he's—" I can't push the words out.

A negr *and a Georgian tried to trade with a Jew* . . . The words of Ruslan's joke come back to me in a flash. I shake my head. It was just a dumb joke.

I glare at Misha. "You think you are this wise Jewish *man*, the follower of six hundred rules, a *tikkun olam* man, the world-repairer." I snicker. "Aren't you being just a little—arrogant? To assume that the world is broken? And that we—you're the ones to fix it? Is it possible that there is nothing wrong with the world *per se,* nothing except you—*us*—its loud-mouthed bully know-it-all inhabitants?"

He stares at me, jaw practically on the floor. I am breathing hard.

"What are you saying?" Misha whispers.

"I'm saying you're wrong about him." I lower my voice to match his. "You're wrong." I walk out of his room, walk out of his apartment with a half-whispered good-night to his mother and sister, my eyes not meeting theirs.

You are wrong. You're wrong. You are wrong. And I'll prove it.

36

Changes

"You scared me!"

"No, you scared *me*—scared us," Mama says.

She is still in her cool jeans, her hair a black tangle over the beautiful white angora sweater. The living room is a mess of things and clothes are everywhere—my bed positioned by the wall where their sofa bed used to be. Everything is covered by a cloud of tobacco, like a fog. How many cigarettes were smoked in this room, I dare not imagine. The note I left for Papa, *"I'm at the pond, skating, will come back soon,"* lies on a prominent place on the table, beside an overflowing ashtray. The note is stained: greasy fingerprints—tears—my parents worrying.

"I looked outside and there you were," Papa, said. He shakes his head, *Shame-on-you.* "The next thing I know it's practically the middle of the night and you aren't home."

"I thought you'd gone to Lithuania," Mama says, smiling wryly.

"I am sorry—I am sorry," I whisper, uselessly, even as I notice something odd about Papa's face, something, I don't know, small. Defeated.

"I am sorry, too," Mama whispers back. "I knew I should have taken that bus right back home with you."

They don't ask me any questions, or yell—which makes it worse. Papa sniffs hard when he leans close to me, checking my breath. Mama examines my face in the bright light of the chandelier for signs of God-knows-what.

I spend the night sleeping beside Mama, on their sofa bed, which now takes over my room when it opens. I don't ask any questions.

The next morning, I wake up just in time to throw on my uniform and dash to school—and barely even make it to geography class, probably. But my parents are both in the kitchen, fresh coffee and hot buckwheat waiting for me on a plastic tablecloth wiped clean. *In the kitchen, together, once more.*

Why then does it feel like a farewell?

They stare at me so hard, taking in a single strand of my braided hair, it feels like. Looking for signs of anything out of place. I am glad I have tucked Ruslan's cross deep under my uniform dress. I don't dare tell them I need to run along.

They both stand up when I come in.

"We want you to know that it isn't your fault," Mama says to me, her voice robotlike, as though reading from a textbook.

I stare at her.

"We have tried—I have tried, *dochka*," Papa says. "But . . . I just can't do this. I . . . I've always wanted a family. But maybe I'm just no good at it. You know?"

I nod. But then I shake my head slightly, because the truth is: no, I don't know.

"You two are welcome to stay here for as long as you need," Papa says. I look up at the long-haired man—his hairy muscular arms on display from under short-sleeve silky pajamas. The man I thought of as my father, sounding more like a gracious host. "At a minimum, you can definitely finish out your school year."

"Thank you," I say in a barely-there voice.

Then I grow aware that they are staring hard at me. The silence between us has grown taut with expectation. I guess it's my turn to explain.

"After skating, I went over to my classmate's apartment," I say. "My . . . friend's."

Mama's hair is twisted in a tight, businesslike knot behind her head. Her face wears no signs of yesterday's crying.

"We didn't do anything wrong," I tell Mama. "Just . . . read books together . . . and . . . sang songs. He plays guitar."

"Aizerman," Mama clarifies; her eyes on me, not letting me go.

"*Nu* . . . yes, Mama, but . . ."

"I have the right to know, Sonya," she says. "I have the right to know who my daughter's boyfriend is."

Her daughter's boyfriend.

I think of Misha Aizerman's words, *if he could see you right now . . . singing Jewish songs.*

You are wrong Misha, I told him.

As I look up at Mama, I find myself smiling. "Will you be home when I get back after school?" I say.

"I will be home," Mama says. "I have already called John, about the voyage, and he said it was all right. He said—"

But I'm not listening. "We are in love, Mama." She smiles at me. "Real love." *Not like you, guys,* I stop myself from adding. "His name is Ruslan."

She frowns, confused.

"Aizerman?"

"No, wait!" I say. Even though I risk being seriously late, and even though my room—mine and Mama's now—is barely recognizable anymore, I sprint into it, heart hammering, and change out of my uniform dress.

I put on a simple white turtleneck sweater. A pair of imported jeans with a made-on-purpose hole in one knee. I want to look right today. I refuse to be sad like Papa in his faded jeans with a matching expression. *We can stay in this apartment for as long as we want*, didn't he say so? All right, so maybe I don't have a father anymore, but at least I am still the daughter of Rita Solovay, a Jewish dissident.

You are wrong about him, Misha. And I'll prove it.

Mama walks in so quietly, I barely hear it at first.

"How are you taking it?" she asks.

I shrug. "He was gone—then he came back—only to leave. So."

"*Oh, dochka*," Mama sighs. She looks like she is going to cry, and I can't have that right now.

"I'm *fine*," I say, more forceful this time. "As long as we can stay here—" I stop, midsentence, when she picks up something from my desk—a thick white booklet. I read a long beautiful name in English letters, "*Fiorello H. LaGuardia High School for Music & Art and Performing Arts.*"

"How would you like it?" she says. "To study music one day. Or singing. In New York City."

"New York City? Mama, not that again, not when I'm so late for geography class! Besides," I add, "I don't have much of a voice, anyhow."

She touches my cheek. "*Sonechka.* We're going to be all right, you know."

I shake my head, shaking her hand off. "Make us something great for lunch, will you, Mama?" I say. "For me and my *boyfriend.*"

Mama nods, her eyes shining with approval at my outfit, and Papa smiles in the hall, releasing me from his too-tight hug, to maybe even still make it to geography.

37

Hedgehog in a Fog

I don't even have to enter the wrought-iron gates of the school courtyard to know something is wrong. A dissonant chorus of coarse boy shouts tells me so.

Classes were supposed to have already started, the teachers inside. Yet a large group of upperclassmen has formed a circle by the patch of trees in the corner. *Ruslan's usual smoking spot,* I think, my heart sinking. The screaming, chanting crowd of boys has formed a wall, impossible to penetrate.

Until some of them see me, that is. Then, they separate, nudging me with elbows, eyes filled with questions, cheeks burgundy from frost and excitement, cracked winter lips ready to suck in gossip. Inside the circle they have created, I find my boyfriend, ramming his body at a figure much taller than he. The other boy's hands are swinging wildly, now up in the air, now shielding his face from Ruslan's hard fists.

A wave of nausea rises inside me in a tidal wave. "Ruslan, *STOP!*" My voice breaks into a million pieces on the wind. He looks up at me. Then he looks at the other boy as if he has never seen him.

"What the hell do you think you're doing!" I run up to the boy, who is still trying to protect his face. I lift one of the boy's arms carefully, away from his face. The sleeve of his jacket is stained with blood. I cry out.

"It's just his nose, for God's sake," Ruslan says.

At first my heart soars at the sight of the small eyes, the bleeding nose, because the boy isn't who I thought it was. *It isn't Misha Aizerman.* Then, the sick feeling in my stomach returns. It's Kuzmin. Poor excuse of a boy. A horrible jerk, really. Under his feet, on the snow, lies Misha's *Babi Yar* book. I don't pick it up. Just pull a handkerchief out of my coat pocket and press it to Kuzmin's nose, to stop the blood.

Ruslan comes up to me, breathing hard, hat askew. "Feeling sorry for your admirer?" he wheezes. "One of your many admirers, I should say."

I whirl around. "It's not him I'm worried about. It's . . . it's you. You can't—you just can't—do this to people. You . . . you aren't an animal."

He takes a step back. "I barely touched him. Nothing a guy can't handle. Right?" He clasps Kuzmin hard on the back.

"Just a normal boy scuffle," Kuzmin says, finally straightening, and I let out a breath I didn't realize I have been holding.

With a strange, empty look in my direction, Ruslan turns to go. "I'll see you later," he says.

"But, Ruslan, geography . . ." I pull on his sleeve.

"I didn't come here for geography." I look down at his hands curling into fists, and for the first time I notice that his backpack is nowhere to be seen. "I came here to see you. I am going—" He looks around. His face is a thundercloud. "Someplace."

Right. The demonstration. Electrification knew it. She warned me, didn't she?

"I'll see you—"

I don't let him finish. I grab Ruslan by the hand, trying to bring him back, the tender boy I know. His hand, hot and moist with sweat, hesitates at first, but then grips mine back so hard, I feel the bones of my fingers.

"Is it true, what he tried to tell me?" Ruslan nods at Kuzmin's figure, retreating already toward the school entrance. "That you ice-skated with *Aizerman* all night? Him, of all people. I thought you had better taste than *that, myshka.*"

I close my eyes and, ignoring the wind that whips up with new force around my face, almost making me choke, I tell myself that I know this tender, passionate boy before me. I open my eyes.

I'll prove it to you, Misha.

"That's not all Kuzmin told me," Ruslan is saying. "He said that you stood outside *Aiz-er-man's* door at 11 o'clock in the evening, and then, and then—"

"And then I went in," I whisper. I order my legs to stop trembling. My exposed knee is raw from the cold. "*Misha* Aizerman and I are friends, Ruslan." I fix my eyes on his to make sure he believes in my words even more than I do at this moment. "We skated. We talked. We just . . . I mean, you talk to other girls once in a while, no?"

"Friends?" He squeezes my hand tighter still.

"I love *you,*" I whisper. "I trust you. Can you do the same for me?"

He studies me for what feels like a century.

"What time is your demonstration?" I say.

He stares at me in silence.

"Because by afternoon at the latest we should be back at my apartment," I say, trying to squeeze his hand back, even though I can barely move a muscle inside the iron grip of his. "My mama is waiting to meet you."

"All right." He nods, as if to answer a question in his mind. Now it's my turn to stare. "All right, what?"

"I think you're right." He flashes a shaky smile. "A demonstration will be good for you. We better get going, then. Before one of the teachers looks out the window and sees us."

"Are you serious?" I dare not believe my luck. "That's so . . . classy . . . but what made you decide?"

"Because it's time you learned life a little, that's why, you little hedgehog in a fog," he answers furiously.

I lean toward him—his usually ashen face raw now with cold. "You aren't angry, then . . . are you?"

He answers with a kiss that almost chokes me.

38

Silver Coin

Time: nine hours, thirty minutes. Meeting place: Mayakovsky statue, the very center of Moscow. Weather: robust and fresh, just right for one of the last days of the year.

"Calm down, *myshka*," Ruslan says. "This is serious."

"I know," I say.

And I do. I thought—we all thought—democracy was finally here. Now perestroika is unraveling before our eyes on Central Television, and the new freedoms we had been enjoying since Gorbachev became the general secretary are being called into question yet again.

I know it's serious. *Democracy! Freedom of speech! Sovereignty to the Republics!*

Tomorrow, Ruslan is leaving for Lithuania. His babushka is making him, he told me gruffly. I will miss him.

But at least we are here now. Standing for something. Standing together.

"If only your babushka could see us now," I say.

"God, let's please not talk about her anymore."

So we don't talk. We don't have to. We are here to hold to everything we have gained under perestroika before it all slips away from us again. One thing—a coup—a power takeover by someone new—or even just the fed-up tired-faced Gorbachev changing course will turn us back into the country we used to be, the country of my childhood, the country of *quiet*. The land of liars and cowards.

I hold on to Ruslan's hand. I know what we're here for. For the freedom to believe in what we want and to say what we believe in.

But it's not just the *secret* meeting or the possibility that the tanks, the *militia* men could be here, just like in Mama's old stories they were, to threaten us and send us away. It's not just that. It's the unraveling of secrets. His and mine.

Ruslan is silent. And, really, why talk when every snowflake rests upon another in just the right way, and old buildings with fancy balconies approve of us as we walk up the street? There is no need to talk when walking for courage, for history, for truth is as easy as light steps over freshly fallen snow.

We stand in the company of Mayakovsky. He's six meters tall. When he was alive, he wrote poetry made of Soviet steel. Today he stands in a small irregular-shaped square, across from one of the gigantic luxurious yet somber Stalin-era apartment towers, surrounded by indifferently panting traffic.

Little by little they start to arrive, the men mostly. Some of them sport black shirts showing from underneath their opened military-style coats.

I should be getting more excited, curious, frightened too, perhaps, in a delicious sort of a way; I should be here, now, but my greedy heart that wants everything pulls my thoughts ahead.

"I'm taking you to my apartment after this, remember?" I whisper to Ruslan.

"I remember," he says, squeezing my hand.

"My papa is . . . leaving her. But I don't care. Not anymore. Not when I have *you*." Why am I babbling? He said we could stay for as long as . . . " I trail off, when I notice he is barely paying attention. "You'll . . . like my mama?" I whisper to him. "Promise that you will?"

"Sh-sh-sh." A guy our age approaches us, and Ruslan lets my hand go.

The guy asks Ruslan for a cigarette, and while Ruslan shares one, the guy stares at me with glassy eyes. He takes his time lighting up. No, he's not our age. It is his cleanly shaved scalp that made me think that at first. Definitely older.

"First time here?" he asks Ruslan, staring, though at the hole on the knee of my imported jeans and the rose-colored light-for-the-weather leather jacket I wore to school today.

"More like fourth." Ruslan shifts his weight from one foot to the other. I beam at the guy, proud for Ruslan.

"It's *my* first time," I say.

I try to make eye contact. The guy's eyes, they look straight through mine.

"Pyotr," he introduces himself.

"Ruslan."

And so I find myself suddenly irrelevant like the gray statue of the once famous poet before me. He stands in his classic "Soviet Hero" coat, Mayakovsky, small against the background of the Stalin skyscraper behind him, solidified in his lifelong anger. First he was angry with passion for the socialist revolution. Then, he was angry because he didn't know what to believe in any longer.

A new group of people arrives. They unroll a black banner featuring the mean-looking double-headed eagle of the Romanov Dynasty. After a rather reserved exchange that consists of short words and names of places I've never heard of, the Pyotr guy finally unglues himself from us. A man with a megaphone makes his way toward the monument.

"It's good to see so many young people here with us today," he whispers to Ruslan and me. He smiles warmly. "We need as many of you as we can get—" and I no longer feel awkward being pretty much the only representative of the female gender. All I feel is the fresh-cold late December day warm in my veins, until he adds, "to take back Russia."

Ruslan squeezes my frozen fingers. "Are you feeling it?" he asks, making a circle in the air with his free hand.

I answer with a vague smile. My eyes travel over bolts of lightning on another banner. On this beautifully frosty Moscow morning warming with commotion, there shouldn't be a reason not to feel that something Ruslan is talking about. The something that livened the faces of Lithuanians on the newspapers Elektra Ivanovna had lain under her pork. Instead, something aches dully someplace under my ribs.

"Who organized this demonstration?" I ask Ruslan.

"*Pamyat*," he says.

Pamyat. Memory. The name tells me something. Have I once heard it on television? Read it in a newspaper a long time ago?

"We're demonstrating for democracy, right?" I ask Ruslan. "For . . . *eh* . . . freedom of speech?"

"This *is* freedom of speech. This *is* democracy," he says. "Sh-sh-sh. They're going to speak now. I've seen a picture of this guy. He's a famous author. Listen, and you'll understand everything."

I try to follow the rich, warm voice on the megaphone as best I can. But I can hear nothing at first over my own noises inside my ears. The pulse of my heart. Out of nowhere, Mayakovsky's quote about a native passport, "Read it and envy.

I am a citizen of the Soviet Union." Enough. With a shake of my head, I empty irrelevant randomness from inside it to make room for the words pouring over the crowd from the megaphone.

". . . the soul-soothing silences?" the voice asks, as I try to find a connection to something I'd know or understand. "The beauty of Russian villages."

"Too much has been lost!" someone calls out from the crowd.

"Our treasures stolen!" someone else picks up. "Our churches—desecrated!"

Everyone stirs. I stand there, breath halting in my chest, waiting, waiting not knowing for what.

"We have been carrying the yolk of humanity's suffering on our broad Russian shoulders, but who dares talk about that? No, it's all about the *Holocaust*."

The Holocaust?

I look at Ruslan. He squeezes my hand.

"Because everything—" the megaphone continues, "the media, the law, and the arts—is controlled by the Jews."

"Jews assassinated the tsar and his family!"

"Jews are destroying Russian culture!"

"Jews blamed Stalin for the murders they masterminded!"

All thought has become lead-heavy. The air itself solidifies around me. I stare at Mayakovsky. He is the guy who wrote a popular book for children at one point, I think dully, called, *What is Good and What is Bad.* How sure he was of everything.

"Jews deliberately drowned Russia in alcohol!" The megaphone words knock into my ears. "Contaminated us with AIDS, porn, and greed from the West! Russia brought to its knees, violated! Crippled by Zionists and foreigners, sold by the government and the Jews . . ."

People clap and shout. Ruslan claps and shouts. My hand goes limp in his. My legs grow weak. The noise grows into a chant.

"You Jew, give back the silver coin."

Ruslan's muddy gray-blue eyes flash. His mouth opens and his lips, bluish from the cold, repeat those words, the lips that I've kissed, chanting, "You Jew, give back the silver coin."

"You Jew, give back the silver coin!" he says to me.

My arms weigh fifty kilograms each as I lift them. So solid they are, I do not know how I manage to bend them behind my neck. My fingers are too cold and sweaty to be any good. How then do I succeed at pulling open the clasp of the thin silver chain around my neck?

"What's the matter?" he asks.

Ruslan's imaginary family heirloom, his cross, thin and elegant, is soft and tickly in my hand as I open his hand with my cold one, and drop it into his palm.

"What are you doing?" he whispers, covering my hand with his.

"Only what you told me to," I whisper back, leaning close, painfully close to his ornately shaped ear. My cheek grazes against the softness of his skin. His face swims away from me, across an ocean of tears. "*You Jew, give back the silver coin*. So here."

He stands there, his eyes wide, as though hypnotized. Then he takes a step back, away from me. "You Jew . . ." The voices chant around us.

My feet splash in the slush and kick aside the grimy-from-the-traffic snow as I run and run, through the people in military greatcoats, through their pale, murderous faces, their narrow eyes. They shout something at me and pull me roughly by the sleeve, but I run and run, and run, and I don't stop until I step inside my apartment and fall into my mama's arms.

"Where is Ruslan?" she asks. "Where is your Aizerman?"

My answer is a flood—a great flood of tears, my very soul, or what's left of it, pouring out of me, soaking Mama's soft, scratchy sleeve in slushy snot and water.

Part III
Exodus

39

Nothing to See

I enter the school courtyard, my toes frozen in my boots and my heart icy on this bracing January day. *Concentrate, Sonya,* I tell myself. *Just to make sure he is all right,* I tell myself. *So I can properly forget him.*

The winter holiday passed me by in a parade of TV images. All week I stayed home, watching tired men at the Congress of People's Deputies blame each other on the small screen. Yeltsin's hand chopping the air, accusing; Gorbachev's stone face, explaining; while men in gray military uniforms shove aside protesters in Latvia, Estonia, Lithuania.

Lithuania.

I didn't want to watch it, yet my eyes stayed glued to the independent channel showing young men trying to shout, *"Sovereignty! Freedom!"* while the militia men pummeled them with batons. I tried not to think about my classmates. Especially not *him,* out there, with stupid Electrification and a handful of others. *Thirteen dead, 120 injured,* independent radio announced through illegal crackling static. They weren't anywhere near the violence, I tell myself. But how do I really know?

Now I look and look, and my heart leaps a little every time I see a familiar, classmate's face looking back at me. His friends give me a weak wave from their usual smoking spot by the trees. His favorite spot, where he used to greet me each morning. Except today. He isn't there.

My other classmates are, though. I nod at each of the familiar faces with relief. *Luba, Bozhena, Diana, Zahar.* I notice more of them, just like me, are no longer in uniforms, and the dim air of the old school building seems all the brighter for it.

"What's the shortest joke in the world?" Zahar asks Luba in the courtyard, who shrugs and smiles at him.

"Communism," he says.

She nods, her smile sardonic now. I smile, too.

"You've got to look where you're going," Kuzmin says in a drawl, as I bump into him on the way to the cloakroom.

"Argh," I groan. "Not you."

Fur coats and thick padded jackets swish around us with the movement of feet and arms. I am trying to change my shoes among the shoving bodies—boys hanging their jackets on hooks, girls bending over to slip their feet into thin sandals—when the second bell rings—two irritated jangles—and a particularly rowdy middle-grader bumps me on my side, sending me toppling down onto the floor, slippery with muddy melting snow.

"Here, let me help you." Kuzmin reaches his gangly arms toward me.

"Roll away from me." I get up, trying to shake off the wet and the dirt from my stocking as the middle-grader scurries out of my way, fast.

"What kind of a hello is that?"

"It's not a hello."

I walk on, looking for a free hook for my coat.

"Ooh, someone's in a temper." He trails after me. "Had a fight with your boyfriend over the break?"

"I am actually fine," I say. "And he's not my boyfriend."

Kuzmin snorts. What does he know?

Some of my classmates throw curious stares my way, and I look away, wondering what sort of gossip they have heard about me over the winter holiday. As the crowd thins, the space fills with coats. I find a hook in the back of the cloakroom and leave my coat there. When I turn around, I can't believe Kuzmin is still there, blocking my way out of the busy cloakroom. No one seems to care, particularly. I don't, either. This time, I won't look for rescuers. I take a sharp breath, inhaling the almost bathroom smell of tile and freshly washed dust that hangs among the jackets. Then I press my hand against his chest, hard.

He teeters and blinks at me. I stare back at him, in a kind of wonder. The last time I saw him, I was shaking with fear, my finger on the buzzer of Misha Aizerman's apartment. Now I speak to him in a voice quiet and calm, and even though he is a boy, a hooligan, towering over me, of the two of us, I know I am the one who is stronger. "You will no longer follow me around," I say. "You will no longer try to touch me with those paws of yours."

"So that means . . ." He grimaces, trying to recover his dignity. "You didn't miss me at all, eh?"

I shrug. "As far as I am concerned, you could have stayed forever in Lithuania."

He frowns. "What Lithuania?"

"Wait." I blink. "What?"

"Anatoly made Electrification cancel the voyage. She announced it at the end of the last day of school. If you'd bothered to attend classes like a good citizen, you would know. Instead we're going to the Ukraine in the summer. The beau-oo-tiful Kiev. You and your boyfriend sharing the train compartment, *eh*?"

I glare at him, flooded with a mixture of relief and fury.

They never did go to Lithuania. *He* was never in any danger. He just wasn't in his usual spot, because . . . I took too long getting here this morning, and the second bell already rang. He wasn't there smoking by the trees, simply because he didn't have to wait for me any longer. My heart feels half-empty, like this coat-filled room.

"Speaking of Ukraine." Kuzmin rummages in his backpack and comes up with a small black book I recognize immediately. I reach for it. He better not yank it delightedly aside, in his favorite game of cat-and-mouse. He doesn't. Just shoves it at my chest. "Didn't know girls like you were interested in war books."

"What do you mean by girls like me? Did you mean dissidents' daughters?"

He blinks at me, startled. Finally, for one glorious moment, he has nothing to say.

"It's a good book. You should ask Misha to borrow it."

He raises his eyebrows. "It's Misha now, eh? Careful. Your boyfriend won't like that."

"*Nyet.* I am done being careful. And you need to get your wax out of your ears. I *told* you: he is not my boyfriend, not anymore."

"Oh, come on. You and Valentinov are married, practically. I should have seen it way, *way*, earlier. He's been with just about any skirt around here, I'll tell you that." Kuzmin guffaws in a way that makes me want to strangle him. "But he has never, ever tiptoed around a girl the way he does around you."

My heart soars for a split second, then plummets just as fast. "Did he pay you to say that? Or just threaten you?"

He guffaws again.

"Not that it matters." I order my legs to stay solid. I order my eyes to stay fixed on Kuzmin's stupid face. "Valentinov and I are history."

Kuzmin stops his horrid laughter and raises his eyebrows. His hand flies up to my hair. "Are you saying . . . ?"

I smack at his hand, and he lets it drop to his side. He really is an idiot.

"See?" He smirks at me.

"I am saying I hate him!" I turn to go, hating how he made me lose my calm again. "Now leave me!"

"*Oooooh,*" he drawls. "Sounds serious. Sounds like love."

A clear melodic voice startles me from behind. "What sounds like love?" the voice asks coolly. I whirl around. Misha Aizerman is swinging and swinging his blue-black book bag. His eyes are on me, filled with questions. Cringing, I think back to my angry words to him on the last day before the break. *I will prove it.* I shove his *Babi Yar* book back at him. I won't look at him. Can't look at him right now. "You were right," I whisper to my feet.

He puts his hand on my shoulder.

"You liked it, then? The book?"

I lift my eyes this time. "Is it true? Is there really such a place as *Babi Yar*? Or is it just a story?"

"You can even see it for yourself, if you like," Misha says. "If you're ever in Kiev. . . . *Syrets* isn't too far from there at all."

"And . . ."

"And yes, it's true, what happened there," Misha says. "There are eyewitness accounts. There are photographs." He hesitates. Opens his mouth, closes it.

Kuzmin looks from Misha to me, shaking his head. "Careful with that one," he says to Misha. "She's a heartbreaker and a flirt," he says. "Plus—" He nods vaguely at a group of upperclassmen entering the cloakroom, coughing and laughing and arguing. "If I know anything at all I know this. Valentinov isn't finished with her."

The chattering and laughing noises at the cloakroom entrance stop abruptly.

"Good thing you don't know anything, then." My cheeks burn. "Because he *is* finished with me, and I sure as hell am finished with him!"

And then, I glare at those boys coming in, as though they have no right to be here. This time my gaze flies straight into the hot-cold muddy-gray-blue sea of a stare. My knees grow weak. I tear my eyes away from him, my head spinning with rage, the earlier moment of calm and quiet strength gone. How dare he even look at me—especially—this way—as though he knows there is a part of me that is still his? He should know better now. He hates me—always has. The only difference is, now he knows it. Doesn't he?

"See?" Kuzmin mouths.

I shake my head, and hook my arm through Misha's. I make myself look right through Ruslan, as though he is invisible. Because there is nothing to see.

"*Ey* Misha?" I ask in an odd, wavering voice. "Are you doing anything after school today?"

Misha examines me. Then turns his head around. His eyes darken with new understanding when he sees Ruslan Valentinov standing there with his friends, still frozen by the cloakroom entrance.

"Not really," Misha says, though his voice is tense, guarded.

"Great." I tighten my arm around his. "I am coming over."

Accidentally, I brush against Ruslan's side on the way out. A flood of warmth rises from somewhere inside me.

That's not fair.

Walking out, my arm hooked with Misha's, I can feel Ruslan's stare burning a hole through my back.

40

Find Your Own Compass

Instead of sitting on one of the couches in his long rectangle of a room—or on the hard wooden chairs beside his desk—we sit together on the floor, Misha and I, backs to his couch, shoulders touching. Little Anya has been banished from the room, even though sometimes I think I can see her peeking from behind the closed door.

I hold Misha's guitar on my lap. His slender fingers rearrange mine over the strings, as he whispers instructions in my ear. The strings cut into the skin of my fingers.

"I can't take it anymore," I whine. "Look at these lines on my finger pads. One more chord, and there will be blood, I just know it."

Sighing, Misha leans over me. His hands linger on my lap before taking away the guitar.

"Maybe it'll hurt less next time?" I say, smiling.

"It'll hurt a lot for a while." His eyes fix on mine, not letting me go. "But one day you'll be playing a song, and you'll look up, surprised, realizing the hurt has been long gone and you haven't even noticed."

We stay like that on the floor. He plays a soft melody. I close my eyes. On what started out as an empty, cold flurry of a day, I am feeling pretty good right now. The cozy smell of wood, books, and warmth hangs over me, and the salty-sweet taste of the beef stew with prunes he heated up for us earlier still lingers in my mouth.

Earlier, in his small kitchen, I stuffed pieces of bread into my mouth and gulped down the jasmine tea he served, as though I had been famished. Between bites, I asked him question after question.

"Are there any other things Jews aren't allowed to eat?"

"No shrimp, no lobsters," he told me. "No insects. No vultures," making me snort and giggle and cough all at once.

"Do you Jews have other holidays besides the New Year?" I asked him.

You Jews.

He told me about dancing with the Torah in September; a story of Moses, and how he led his people out of Egypt and taught them to be Jews the best he could. He told me how, mysteriously, Stalin suffered a massive stroke on the Jewish holiday of Purim, just as he was ready to launch his biggest anti-Jewish purge yet.

Now, in Misha's book fortress, his hardwood floor under my butt more comfortable than any cushion, I listen to the silence between us that feels as normal as breathing.

Except—Ruslan took me to a Pamyat *demonstration, Misha.* I close my eyes, and in the dark I can still see Ruslan's pale, pale face, looking right through me, the girl he thought he loved so much. *You Jew, give back the silver coin,* he'd said, and I did. I could tell Misha, couldn't I? The whole truth, the rest of it, right now. The guitar music stops abruptly. I feel this slight, ticklish tugging, and when I open my eyes, I almost shout out at the sight of Misha's face so close to mine, his musician fingers fiddling with a strand of my hair.

"This is going to sound crazy," he whispers.

"What else is new?" I whisper back, but he doesn't smile.

"Sometimes I look at you, and I feel like I've known you all my life," he says. His breath warms my face. "And sometimes . . . I look at you and I'm thinking, 'Who is she?'"

"Sometimes I don't know the answer to that question, either," I breathe back.

He nods. Still he won't move his face back to a more respectable *friendship* distance. I don't move, either.

"Are you going on the class trip to Kiev?" I am stalling, whispering, afraid to breathe, afraid to move away, afraid to move closer.

"I can't," he whispers back. "I am going to camp. In Israel."

"The Jewish country?"

Take me with you, I want to say, though I don't deserve to go.

No one is sleeping. No one has died. Still, our faces so close, we keep our voices so soft that our words barely touch.

"I'll be working in a camp, sort of. Like a collective farm. It's called a *kibbutz,*" Misha whispers.

"I'll miss you," I whisper back. "I wish you were beside me always. Like a compass."

I can't believe I am saying this to him, now.

"A compass?"

"So I'd never be lost again."

"Find your own compass, Sonya Solovay." But his face moves closer. Closer. Everything grows dark, except his shiny eyes, his velvet eyelashes. My entire body is a guitar string stretched too tight. His eyes close half way. I look down at the perfect, thin shape of his lips.

If only *Valentinov* could see us right now. The stupid, cheap thought ruins the moment. I look away, toward the door, where the floor creaks slightly—his little sister spying on us. Anyway, I can't do this to Misha. Contaminate his Jewish angel mouth with my pork-eating, anti-Semite-kissing contagion.

41

Spring

In Siberia each spring was a celebration, a thawing of the soul, an explosion of scents, a screaming of birds and children. Spring in Moscow Region is a less fragrant, more washed-out version. Spring here is rainy and humid and cold, a background, a so-what, like the running of some motor at a construction site.

Spring is . . .

In Electrification's words, "like the whole country on hormones."

Spring is . . .

The too-warm, sticky nights on the sofa bed I share with Mama.

"Sonya," Mama whispers in the dark. "Please, stop writhing like a tormented snake. I have to work tomorrow."

Spring is Papa's brand-new clown troupe routine. A new poster hanging in the kitchen. The tinkling of his balalaika on a Monday afternoon.

Spring is . . .

In the living room, sitting between Mama and Papa on what used to be *my* bed on a Sunday afternoon, watching young people on television demonstrate in Moscow for democracy and freedom for the republics and for all kinds of right reasons, despite the Ministry of Interior troops lining the streets, holding their shields and what looks like thick batons of rubber. Despite the fed-up Gorbachev warning everyone to stop demonstrating—or else.

Spring is . . .

The surprising scent of fresh warmth drifting out of the usually stale-smelling empty-looking bakery.

Mama and I throw ourselves into the crowd of fierce shoppers with glee. The tall metal racks that line the walls are still empty, with not even ginger cookies or small ring-shaped *bubliki* rolls you dip into tea. But the smell didn't lie. By the time Mama and I make it to the register, the sweaty saleslady in a white apron hands us one last loaf of fresh rye bread.

Spring is pieces of warm bread flesh Mama and I take turns tearing as we walk back home, swinging our empty bags in unison, like girlfriends.

Spring is . . .

One afternoon, in front of the television, Mama's and Papa's hands finding each other, their fingers weaving together, when they think I'm not looking.

Spring is Mama encouraging me to go to the class trip to Kiev. "Spend time with friends."

Papa nods vigorously. "Have some adventures."

"Don't be such a homebody," Mama adds.

If I do go, I wonder, will I find my family whole again upon my return?

Spring is . . .

Me skinning my knee on our walk around the pond, like a seven-year-old, for God's sake. Misha sitting me up on a bench and checking out my "wound." Me laughing at him: Misha the doctor.

Spring is Misha visiting my apartment one afternoon.

Just me and him, sharing a moment of shyness over Turkish tea.

Spring is . . .

Misha dropping some change into a small rectangular box of white and brown marble on his windowsill.

"Your savings?" I ask him.

"It's a *Tzeddakah* box," he says. "It's where I collect money for the poor. It's a *mitzvah*." He shrugs, then blushes. "Which just means, a good thing."

"Let me guess—a Jewish thing?" I whisper.

Spring is Misha's dark eyes peering so hard into mine that I have to look away and change the subject.

Spring is . . .

A letter to Babushka:

You told me I had a choice, I write. *But I am not so sure. Sometimes our enemies make our choices for us.* Spring is . . .

Misha, all mysterious, joy shimmering on his face, on the day he got the tickets to Israel. This joy that does not include me.

Not that it should.

I don't deserve to go.

Spring is . . .

A broody Monday at the Lenin Library in the center of Moscow, fingers blackened from the old newspapers with news of the Jewish land, which is not entirely Jewish, I discover.

I imagined Israel as a fairytale country of golden sun over sparkling seas, populated with golden-tanned versions of Misha, world-repairers, living gloriously under the palm trees. As the light of the chandeliers above my head burn the sunny day away, I learn that Israel is a thousand-plus year-old dream of holiness built on the ashes of the Holocaust, a home disputed, stuck between freedom and occupation, fear and hate, rocks, bullets, and prayers.

Spring is . . .

The Madrid Jewish-Arab Peace Conference being planned for later this year. Operation Solomon: 20,000 Ethiopian Jews airlifted from famine and war to New Life in Israel. Would they be accepted? Is this what true *tikkun olam* looks like? Spring is the world, just like my heart, repaired here, broken there.

Spring is . . .

Misha's voice in the darkness of his room in the evening, *Hava Nagilah* broken into chords. Misha was right. The song *is* difficult.

Me humming *Hava Nagilah* over homework, making Mama look up in surprise from some papers she had been poring over.

"This song," she says. "I've heard it before . . . It's . . . Jewish."

"*Da.*"

"It's beautiful."

Can such beauty be wrong?

Spring is . . .

Gorbachev changing course, veering back to the left— hurrah!—away from threats and ultimatums, back to negotiation and compromise, back to where he started. The change sneaks up on us all, like the thawing of the snow, like the shifting of the winds. It's hard to pick up on any single event that started it. Just a series of them, one building upon another, like the gradual rising of the temperatures, like the weakening of the ice over the pond.

Spring is birdsong filling the air on the day when the liberal newspapers that the local kiosks ran out of, mysteriously, are suddenly available again.

Spring is . . .

Stupid love songs on the radio that Mama hums to on the morning she gets back from her business trip to America. Suitcases filled with crisp, shiny new clothes. Her eyes brimming with stories, stories of people with accents and crazy hair, colorful clothes, and all-sorts-of-color skin. "Dark chocolate brown, smoky black, caramel coffee-color." Her gushing makes me hungry.

Spring is . . .

Suddenly everyone telling old election jokes, "What's a Soviet election?—it's like if God put Eve before Adam and said, 'Now, comrade, you're going to elect yourself a wife.'"

Boris Yeltsin elected the first ever president of the Russian Republic.

Spring is everyone talking about it, even inside Electrification's dark classroom. Electrification wags her finger at us all and says, "You think it's all over? You wait! You just wait!" At her words, a hush falls over the classroom like a curtain.

Spring is . . .

The delicious smell of gently burnt air when the candles light up for Shabbat. Rosa Aizerman's hands soft over mine as she teaches me how to say a special Friday night prayer.

"Jewish words are like magic—words written on scrolls, whispered words, words recited," Misha's mama whispers. "Make a wish, any wish, put it in words. Tell God about it. Don't keep it locked away inside you."

Spring is me looking back at Rosa Aizerman, fighting a sudden heaviness in my chest, not even knowing what to wish for.

Spring is . . .

The story of Exodus explained to me again over eggs in salt water in the Aizermans' kitchen. At home I memorize the

Plagues of Egypt and write them down in my diary. At night I imagine Ruslan now covered in boils, now with toads on his head. Maybe I should try talking to God about it next Friday.

Spring is . . .

A "common statement on immediate measures to stabilize the country" signed by former enemies. Spring is Yeltsin and Gorbachev shaking hands for the cameras. The president of Russia, the USSR's biggest and most important republic, and the president of the USSR itself working together, at last!

Spring is Electrification's livid face when even the normally careful Luba Gladko dares talk about it on a Monday morning, before class.

"Our president is no longer threatening anyone, no longer trying to . . . shut the people up, right?" she says. The others are nodding. Voices rise quietly, cautiously, then die just as quickly, as Electrification walks up to Luba and whispers something in her ear. Luba stiffens. Her shoulders slump. I take a deep breath, thinking, *She can't do this. The class hasn't even started yet!* After class I go up to Electrification's desk. Luba is already there, her fingers ripping at each other furiously, her mouth a grim, stubborn line, even as she nods slowly to whatever punishment Electrification has meted out.

Maybe Electrification told her to write an extra essay. Forced her to "volunteer" for cleaning duty. Threatened to talk to her parents, probably. Now Electrification puts away a stack of notebooks and eyes me, her head cocked, her eyebrows furrowed.

"What do you need, Solovay?"

Back in the fall, when we talked acids and bases, when we discussed the good inclination and the evil *yetzer hara,* Misha told me there is something good, peaceful, loving, selfless in everyone. Even as I narrow my eyes at Electrification, I think

– 221 –

back to the tears on her cheeks when she told me about her daughter, her fierce faith in the goodness of her country, her sacrificing her own little girl for the good of her motherland, and then raising her grandson alone, all these years, while teaching and protecting him the best way she knew.

She must see that as her goodness. But now I know: pure, misguided selflessness can turn evil, too.

My classmates are throwing curious glances at us as they stream out of the classroom.

"I'm coming, I'm coming," Ruslan's voice is too raspy right now to pass for casual. "Yurik, Dimon, you guys . . ." I tune him out. I remind myself it's Electrification I need to deal with right now, not him. Never him again.

"Stop it," I say.

She furrows her thin eyebrows at me. "Stop what?" I nod at Luba, who is already edging away from us. I gesture around her always dark classroom, covered with the same old Soviet propaganda. "Keeping us quiet. Keeping away the truth."

She shrugs. "How I deal with Gladko in my classroom is not your concern."

"It is."

That day in the empty classroom, when Electrification was crying, I was wrong to see her as a harmless, defeated old woman. She is not harmless, I see that now. I need only to look back at Ruslan walking by with an exaggerated swagger, to see the harm she can do, has already done. Ruslan laughs too loud at Yuri Stepkin's joke, pretending not to notice Dimon, one of his friends, eyeing me. I look away from them all and focus on Electrification again. "Well, I for one, won't keep quiet any longer."

"Hm?"

"I am going to tell about what you do here. How you put us down. What sorts of people you try to turn us into."

"Who will you tell, exactly?" Electrification asks.

I am thinking to tell the principal, Anatoly, and I will do it, too. But she says, "Your precious *mamochka*?"

And on command, my cheeks redden. "Leave my mama out of it!"

Electrification leans on her elbows. "Why do you persist in being so loyal to her, anyway, Sonya?" I bristle when she says my name. "Your precious *mamochka* who abandoned you. Who chose subversive work over you."

"You—*ty*—" I've switched to an informal "you," the kind used between friends. Or enemies. "—You can't criticize her." Breathing hard, anger rising, I can feel it—my *yetzer ha-ra* sending blood to my temples, infusing me with its dark, furious power. "How do you know so much about her, anyway?"

She shrugs. "Oh, I've looked into it."

I narrow my eyes. "The KGB, your pals? Did they help you out? Were these perks worth it, selling your own daughter for?"

Her eyes dart to the side of the room. I whirl around. I was wrong. Electrification and I were not left alone in the classroom. When the door slammed, Ruslan must have stayed on this side of it, his back to all the posters. Now, both hands gathered into fists, he turns away slowly, like he means to just walk out of here. His arms are shaking. He faces the door but does not open it. He merely presses his forehead to one of the posters, the one where "Our Soviet Motherland" is a lady clad in red, her hair tied in a kerchief.

"What is she blabbering about?" he asks into the door, his voice muffled.

Electrification gets up but doesn't move. As I walk toward the door, it's hard to look away from his face, ashen, the loneliness of his dry-eyed stare. He steps aside to let me pass but knocks into me instead, like he is drunk. Our palms brush. I am about to jerk my hand away when he catches it. I freeze as he squeezes my palm before letting go just as suddenly. How cold it is, his hand. How clammy and cold.

I am a Jew. He knows it now. And yet he held on to my hand, just one human being holding another for a moment.

The door closes softly behind me. Even though their family affairs shouldn't matter to me anymore, I linger behind the closed door for a moment, straining my ears for shouting? Accusations? A conversation? But all I hear is silence. My heart jumps when a great thud against the door makes it rattle. The next moment, the door swings open, and Ruslan comes out, nursing his bleeding fist.

I stare at the now open door. He had not broken it—not even made a dent. His fist only ripped into the poster, leaving a gaping hole in a place where the lady-Motherland's bosom had been.

Spring is . . .

Luba smiling at me after school.

"She made it sound like my ancestors would kill me. Sometime ago, they definitely would have. Now, eh." She makes a face. "No one is scared anymore!"

Spring is . . .

Luba and I, in her apartment, "Lambada" playing on her kitchen radio, the Latin beat everyone is dying for, lately, making me want to rock my behind.

Luba notices and grins. "Hey," she says. "I am having a party next weekend. The night before our trip. What do you say?"

I smile back, about to say yes, of course. But then she ruins it. "Your old boyfriend will be there." She winks. I shake my head, hard. "My mama wants me home before dark," I say.

Luba rolls her eyes. "What are you, Cinderella?"

I keep my smile on. "Anyway, why wait that long to have a good time? We are here now."

Spring is my hands on Luba's waist as we swing our hips and kick our legs to the exotic drumbeat. We belt out the Latino lyrics, the sun dazzling us through the lace curtains on her window.

Spring is . . .

Anonymous breathing—the only sound when I pick up the telephone. My heart speeding, as I slam the receiver against the wall.

I know who it is: I can recognize even the patterns of his breaths.

Spring is . . .

The smell of May lilacs and fresh garbage outside my building. The first dandelions dotting the grass by the construction site. The aching that grips me every time I glance there. Spring is red fading to pink on the knuckles on Ruslan's hand.

Spring is a silky sleeveless top from America I wear on the last day of school.

Spring is . . .

Ruslan staring at my shoulders all day.

"Are you going to Kiev?" he whispers to me one afternoon in an empty hallway. "On the class trip?"

I try to sidestep him.

"Isn't your father Russian?"

I whirl around. How does he know this? "What do you care?"

He shrugs and looks away. "I don't. Just asking."

"Chip off, you wretched log," I say, my voice cracking.

Spring is a dream where it's just the two of us, sitting on a concrete panel at the construction site, the sun shining on our faces as we trade kisses. "I know you're Jewish," he whispers into my lips. "And I don't care. I still love you. For you. You will always be my *myshka*."

I wake up happy and mad at once, cheeks warm.

Spring is . . .

His whisper on the telephone, "I am sorry."

Spring is . . .

A familiar small silver cross I pick up on the last day of May, left on the doormat outside the apartment.

Spring is guitar playing that solidifies into calloused pads on my fingertips. If only souls could heal as easily.

42

Swimming

The heels of my new shoes sink into the Moscow asphalt. The pungent smell of sweat hits me as busy passengers brush past. The middle of the early summer crowd: the wide-bosomed women, the elderly ladies in sleeveless flowered dresses, sweaty men carrying fat suitcases. By the steps of platform Number Three, my classmates gesture and shout at each other over the thundering trains and the announcer's singsong calls.

I stare at a collection of empty beer bottles not too far from my fancy feet and wonder why I didn't just stay home and wait for Misha to come back from his Jewish camp?

Stay home and watch Mama and Papa timidly rediscover each other, maybe. Share in their chitter-chatter at dinners. Hang outside, and watch the castle of concrete turn into a mere apartment building. Stay home, and wait for the summer to pass me by.

But what did I want from this voyage, with a wallet bursting with rubles in my side pocket, along with Ruslan's silver cross?

What did I hope for as I packed my suitcase with flirty bare-shouldered sun frocks? Why did I bring along a pack of condoms Mama brought me from America?

Maybe I'll fall in love with a tour guide, I thought savagely, as I pressed them this morning into the back pocket of my tiny shorts. Now Luba Gladko examines my shorts approvingly, as she walks up the steps toward me.

She grins. I stare. She leans close to my ear, really close, the way she does when she offers up the latest secret to her friend Diana Komissar.

"Glad to see you here, Cinderella," she whispers. "I think you should talk to him."

Why does she keep taunting me so? I don't need to ask who she is talking about. Still she nods down to the bottom of the concrete steps, where Ruslan is sitting with his friends. He is the last person I want to discuss in this heat. Desperately, I try to come up with a change of subject in my suddenly empty head.

"He got way too drunk at my party last night," she says, still looking down the stairs. "And he tried to kiss me."

Her words hit me in the stomach. It takes me a moment to recover enough to speak, to remember that I don't care, that he isn't mine. Still, my voice comes out all hoarse and wrong-sounding. "That's wonderful," I say. "In fact, you really don't have to tell me—any of this. You know very well, that whatever he does isn't any of my—"

She grabs the sleeve of my shirt. "Oh, come *on*. He couldn't even bring himself to do it. Kiss me, I mean. I just got up and walked away, because I was tired of watching the guy torture himself so. I told him anyone could see how madly in love he is."

"He can't be," I say, doing the best I can with whatever is left of my voice.

She rolls her eyes. Shakes her head, too. "You *still* don't know anything, do you?"

I don't speak. I can't, not with the lump blocking my throat.

"Look at him," she says, pointing at some loud woman in an opposite direction, being much more prudent and discreet than I am, gaping now at the back of his head below me. "He can't even carry a conversation. Says a word—looks at you, word, you again, word, you."

I steal another glance down the steps. When did my hands grow cold?

"You told me yourself. You warned me. That . . . he only cares about one thing . . . "

She sighs. "I said that because that's the way he acted when he was with me."

I stare at her, numb, turning her words over in my head: "he" "was" "with" "me.""

"Oh, don't worry so." She smirks at something in my expression. "It was last school year. *Before* you. And it was nothing. Just an empty little *tra-la-la.*"

"I am *not* worried!" I shout, but the clatter of a parting train buries my words.

He turns in the crowd, and now I see his face. Diana Komissar is standing beside him, saying something to him. He is answering, though his eyes seem distant, not focused on her at all. Not focused on anything. Luba is still talking, her words floating in the air with soot and dust.

"I never thought he would be capable of anything *magical*, or anything real—" I'm not trying to make out his raspy words in the din of too many voices. "—until I saw him with you." Tears aren't smothering me from the inside. They're not. "Please don't think that it's him that I wanted," she says. "I wanted what you two had."

I watch the incoming train explode into the station, sending dust and dirt into my eyes.

"Want to share the train cabin with Diana and me?" she asks.

I smile back at her, shakily, relieved at the change of subject. "Do you think they have any *pirozhki* left down there?" I point toward a kiosk down the platform steps, a huge line of people before it growing longer by the minute. "Those spicy meat smells are making me crazy. *Nu*—" I slap at the wallet fat with rubles. "I'm paying."

"I'd put that somewhere else, in your place," Luba says, nodding at my slim pocket as we head down the stairs. "It's not a thing to show off in this mad crowd."

I walk through the crowd with Luba, smiling at Diana and Bozhena and Dimon, who smile back, walking right past Ruslan and not caring, keeping my mind on the Georgian little meat pies they're selling. The touch of his hand on my arm is tickle-light, like the wing of some insect.

His voice saying my name crushes me like the heat. "Can I have a word with you, Sonya, please?"

The crowd of our classmates grows quiet. Luba steps aside, her thin mouth curved in a tiny knowing smile, in her eyes a warm, comradely *I told you so*. My heart leaps. My legs shake. I should have stayed home.

"We still have half an hour at least," he rasps. "Can we take a walk around the platform?"

We pass by sweaty strangers pulling overflowing suitcases through the platform, women with straw hats askew, men with dusty shoes, boys spitting over their shoulders.

He stops in the middle of the platform. "Will you please look at me?" My skin itches with memories. I look down at my fancy feet.

"Look at me now and tell me Sonya, that I matter to you just about as much as this greasy piece of foil on the ground.

Tell me that I am from the category of 'kissed and forgotten.' And I'll leave you in peace."

I am silent.

"I know you still love me, Sonya."

"I don't love you anymore," I say to the buckles on my shoes. "I care for you about as much as I care for that stupid piece of foil. Where did it go? You are from the category of . . . how did that go? . . . Dirty . . . anti-Semitic . . . pricks!"

I shake and sniff from having said these things.

He slides his hand around my waist. "If that were true, why would I still be here, talking to you?"

The trains thunder in and out, leaving the black dust to drift in the sky, as we resume our walk. My willpower is depleting, fast. It gets harder to find the words to argue with him.

Still, I try.

"Imagine if they could see you now, with me," I whisper. "Who?"

But then he slows, as though realizing just who I am talking about, before I say it, even quieter: "Your *Pamyat* pals. Imagine what they'd say if—"

"I don't care."

His words crash into me. I try to block them. "There is something I need to give back to you." I start digging into my side pocket, the one with the wallet that carries my money for the voyage, and the small Russian treasure that doesn't belong to me. His hand slides down from my waist to the side of my hip and lands on my hand, which is shaking, I realize. As we walk, my hand stays under his, as though with his touch he rendered it immobile.

In this heat I am burning, melting from the inside out. I need to think, to speak, to stop myself from melting.

"My mother is Jewish," I whisper. "So is my grandmother. So am I."

He nods.

His hand slides further down and circles around my butt, and I do nothing about it. We walk without speaking for a while. His words are both unbelievable and real as the heat of the sun. His hand stops moving all over my bottom.

I am about to turn around, to gaze into his eyes, and tell him, what? I'm still not sure. But he says, "I think you dropped something," and when he picks up three black condom envelopes from the ground, I find myself wishing I could fall through the platform and land straight in hell.

His left eyebrow is arched into an astonished triangle.

"I think they'll be safer here for a while," he says with a wink, the lout! And stuffs them in the buttoned pocket of his checkered shirt.

I stop and stare at him, emitting shame and indignation. "I didn't take them for you, you know!" I shout, hating the surprised-sarcastic triangle of his eyebrow.

"*Nyet?*" he says. "Well, then, who are they for? *Aiz-er-man?*"

"Don't you dare say his name that way again!"

He grabs my hand. "I am sorry."

I bite my lip. I don't know what to say or what to feel. I need more time to think.

"Attention, attention," a pleasant woman's voice announces through the speaker in a slick Moscow accent. "Prepare for the arrival of Express Train Number Thirty-two, Moscow–Kiev. Express Number Thirty-two, Moscow–Kiev, is arriving at platform three."

The train bursts in with a fresh surge of wind, smelling of soot, oil, and burnt metal.

Clutching my hand, he pulls me ahead. We push through the dust and the crowd, knocking over suitcases. The to-be-expected mutters and curses fly at our heels. A man rubs rudely against my hip as we run, leaving a sudden lightness in my pocket.

My wallet! Stuffed with rubles. And—Ruslan's silver cross!

"Ruslan, oh *no!* I think someone just—*Oh* no! I am so sorry, Ruslan!"

"Sorry about what?"

I look around, but all I see is the crowd writhing behind me.

"Let's go Sonya," Ruslan pulls on my hand. "The train! *Nu?*"

I don't want to talk to him about *silver coins*. I don't see the thief, anyway, and so I let myself get pulled, pulled ahead, pulled into the train. Nooks, hooks, and shelves and pockets with nets bang and snap as we settle into a stuffy humid cabin. Luba and I get the bottom shelves. Diana and Bozhena will sleep on top. The cabin door slides open and shut.

Others file into our cabin, chattering. Ruslan by my side, his faithful Dimon, my Luba, and Diana, and about a million others sit together on our narrow shelves as if it's the only cabin in the train. Dimon pulls out awfully cold chicken wrapped in foil. Diana drops a stack of greasy cutlets onto our table.

"Look what I got," someone says in a conspiring voice. And before I know it, Zahar Turin pulls out a bottle of vodka, people dig into their suitcases, and Yurik Stepkin comes up with a large, slightly chipped tea cup.

"In a circle," Ruslan commands. "We start with you, Dimon."

I forget about the pickpocket. I forget everything.

Ruslan pours him a cupful of clear liquid. So innocent, so clear like water. Dimon downs it in one gulp, like an expert.

Then it's Yurik Stepkin. Oleg Kuzmin takes the cup with a weary glance at Ruslan.

"Don't worry, Kuzma," he says easily. "I haven't poisoned it."

Kuzmin raises the cup at Ruslan and me, and drains it.

Luba curves her mouth and wrinkles her nose, but drinks the whole thing. I wonder what Misha would do if he were here. Would he take the cup? Ruslan passes the cup toward me. I screw up my face. Certain kinds of liquor leave a fine, subtle pinch in my mouth. But vodka, with its sour, overpowering taste? How can anyone like it?

I can rudely pass up my turn and not even care. I look at their flushed faces, their silly grins, their eyes warm, neither afraid nor menacing, welcoming me into their sweaty circle, at last. I pinch my nose, and everyone laughs. Then, like a good sport, I take the cup and throw the burning liquid into my throat.

The sourness catches hold of my tongue, takes over my mouth, sticks together the muscles of my jaws. But inside, under the still-itching throat, I think I already like this crazy heat a bit, and I no longer smell the chicken smell or feel the stuffiness of the cabin, only the coziness of friends. Trying not to cough, I drain the rest of the cup. I wonder if I would feel them now, those fairytale swan princess wings—maybe, if everyone would just stop clapping me on the back so hard my ribs hurt. The cup makes its circle, then comes back to me. And back to me. And back to me.

The wheels of the train provide a merry beat. People leave. People come in.

Someone's whisper, "Electrification will be doing a cabin check before bedtime. Don't worry, we'll throw her off your track, love doves," barely reaches me.

More people leave. I have the cup again. I have the bottle now. I have Ruslan's arm over my shoulder. I have my Ruslan back.

I stare into the clear liquid that no longer smells so strong. I find myself swimming in it, swimming in the drunken sea of hot cold muddy gray blue, the sea of his eyes and lips and hands on me, trying to enjoy the swim, but really kind of trying to hold on to parts of who I am, the parts that I thought I'd gotten back, the ones that float away from me now in the darkened empty cabin.

43

A Woman

My eyelids cover my eyes like the heavy lids of the passenger shelves we sleep on. But I force them open into the blazing orange heat of the coming day. The train is bouncing Luba's sleeping body across the cabin from me. Her face rolls off the pillow, lipstick and mascara spread all over it.

On the sleeping shelf above hers, Diana is curled up in a lump, a blanket pulled up to her chin. Above me dangles Bozhena's large foot. I cannot make out the color of the polish chipping on her toenails. Slowly, I become aware of hammers, *took-took* knock-knocking, *took-took*, knock-knocking inside my head in sync with the chugging of the train. I half-rise on my sleeping shelf. A sour wave stirs in my stomach.

Under the table covered with greasy newspapers I find my shorts and crumpled T-shirt. I search for my underwear on the floor. The clothes feel too stiff and rough over my body. I am about to sit back down on my shelf when I notice blood stains covering my sheet in patches. I take the sheet and run it all over the floor, rolling it in gray dust, then stuff it under my shelf, hoping they'll think it's a rag or something.

That's when I notice a torn black condom envelope on the floor by my shelf. I try to smile as I pick it up, though my lips feel puffy. I should feel something else besides headache and nausea. My body—it's a grown-up body now. But nothing is different. Is this what happens as you grow up, grow older? It's still just you, same as before, same as always?

I stare at the green fields outside, murky through the soot-covered window, a woman at almost sixteen, my birthday two months from now. The door slides open. Luba stirs on the shelf across from me. Ruslan's eyes, cold, repulsive, and beautiful, float into my field of vision and last night comes back to me. How I hugged the half-empty vodka bottle and tried to sing *Unbreakable Union of Free Republics* in between hiccups, giggles, and burps, how Ruslan wrenched the bottle away from me, saying, "That's enough," and how I shouted, "What, you didn't think Jewish girls could drink like that?" and how the door of the cabin kept thumping as it slid again and again and again after that. . . .

He stoops down before my shelf, and all I can think is *I am a woman*. He runs his dry hand over my forehead as though I have fever, and all I can feel is, *I am a Jew*.

"How are you?" he asks, and suddenly I find myself crying, mostly from the headache, but also from the possibility of losing myself forever. "Sh-sh-sh, what's the matter, *nu*?" he says.

"I . . ." *am disintegrating from the tender concern in your voice. I am Jew, and your lover, both.* "I am in good shape," I say, sniffing back the stupid baby tears.

Across the shelf Luba groans and turns her face to the wall. Bozhena's foot above me swings hard with each lurch of the train. I wonder if they are pretending to sleep so they can listen in on our conversation, or if they too are suffering from a bad hangover.

"We have free time this afternoon," Ruslan says, gently. "What are you going to do? Want to explore Kiev together?"

Explore Kiev! Or its surroundings. I lurch back on my sitting shelf. And suddenly, I know.

"What?" Ruslan sits next to me. He holds my face, turns it gently toward his. I stare at his eyes. Those eyes, they belong to a guy who loves a Jew. Not them in black coats of hate on Mayakovsky Square. Then, last night, in this empty cabin he held me like he loved me. Now is his chance to prove it. A way for me to know, for sure. To know everything.

"When we get to Kiev once we settle in and all that, I'm taking a little trip of my own," I say, not sounding as casual as I would have liked. "Want to come?"

A corner of his mouth rises in tandem with his thin eyebrow. "I'd better. To make sure you do nothing crazy."

I'm sure no one will miss us. They'll be sitting on oak chairs in the hotel lobby, playing cards at a cloth-covered table. They'll be eating sardines inside rooms with stains on the walls. They'll be soaking in the gently rotting smell of heat while they gossip. They'll be discussing the new Electrification, the on-holiday version of her, wearing a straw hat, unaware, understanding, almost *grandmotherly*. They'll be discussing how easy it was to trick her last night.

Ruslan waits for me in his faded jeans on a wrought-iron bench.

"So, where are we going?"

To a mass grave.

That doesn't sound very romantic, Sonya.

"Ruslan," I whisper. "Will you pay for the taxi? I—I don't have any money." My neck grows hot from shame for the wallet that got snatched out of my tiny pocket back at the Kievsky train station in Moscow.

"*You* don't have any money? Of course, I'll pay," he adds quickly, running his finger across my flustered cheek. "Need you ask, silly?"

"Where to?" says the taxi man with a dashing Ukrainian mustache.

"*Syrets,*" I whisper.

The man considers. "Where to in *Syrets*?"

"*Babi Yar,*" I say under my breath.

The man cocks his head. "*Dobre,*" he agrees in Ukrainian, then adds in Russian,

"Get in."

I slide across the slippery synthetic leather of the backseat, while Ruslan looks at me—only where is he? The blueness of his gray eyes I can no longer find.

"How noble," he says through his teeth.

"What's . . . noble?"

"I can just see it," Ruslan says, seething. "*He* made you promise, didn't he? He couldn't be here, in Kiev, so he made you promise to visit the place out of his stupid book for him."

"He didn't make me—You're the one who's making me—"

"*Aiz-er-man.*"

"Don't say his name like that. Please, don't, Ruslan."

"Why does everything have to be about *him* all the time?"

"No, I am doing it for you. For me. For us. Please—"

"Forget it. I have no desire to go to that particular place."
He is still standing by the open door of the Ukrainian man's

sedan. The sun throws its brilliance into my eyes, making them water.

"I'm not moving from this seat," I whisper to Ruslan. "And you know I don't have even a *kopeck* of money. I'll walk if I have to. And then—" I smile, "—then I might even get lost. Just standing before a monument next to me, is that so difficult?"

Ruslan shakes his head. "We already talked about it," he says. "I thought we could move past—"

"That's up to you, if we can move past it!" I shout at him.

"What's the matter, you don't like *Babi Yar*?" the driver comes to my rescue. "That's too bad. A scenic spot. A historical monument. Anyway, what does it matter where you go with a pretty girl like that?"

Finally, Ruslan slides into the front of the car, bangs the door shut and through squeezed teeth, asks the man for a cigarette. They smoke and they talk about the new treaty between the Soviet Republics Gorbachev is finally going to sign, and they do a comparative analysis of prices between Kiev and Moscow, while my stomach and my heart shake.

44

Babi Yar

Ruslan and I slow our step before a long set of irregular granite steps leading up to an uneven rock the size of a building. I realize the black rock is a mass of granite giants standing in one jagged lump: men and women, naked, pushed and falling almost and forever into the ravine. Birds' timid cries and the distant traffic gently disturb the quiet over the great hill.

"I'll wait for you back there."

I glance back at his skinny figure, the neat shape of his head, shoulders set apart widely, back perfectly straight, retreating toward the road.

"Ruslan!" I call.

He turns around. This little man. This pale guy with a punk-style haircut, a small pimple on his chin, his mouth a thin upside-down crescent shape, his gray eyes almost soulless.

"Where," I shout, "is your soul? That generous Russian soul of yours?"

Slowly, he walks back toward me.

In silence, we make our way up the steps. I read the inscription that names the victims "Soviet citizens." I look up at the giant falling figures, who were small like me once—or maybe

just a bit taller—figures who were more than "Soviet citizens."
One September day in 1941, they were Jews, thousands of
them.

Later, there were the Gypsies, who weren't exactly Nazis'
favorites, either. Then there were others.

Now, quiet as death, Ruslan and I walk back to the road.
"You know what this is called? Us being here?"

He doesn't answer.

"I'm pretty sure it's a '*mitzvah*.'"

He doesn't ask what that means.

I tell him anyhow. "It means, a good deed."

The grass slashes across my ankles. "Good deeds can be
small," I whisper.

We stop by a young twisted tree, over the bones that have
become earth.

He drops a cigarette on the ground and raises his hand to
signal the oncoming traffic for a taxi.

I peer into his mask of a face. "I just wanted you to see.
To feel something."

He is staring at the quiet road, his hand waving up and
down, urgently.

I look back toward the black monument towering in
the distance. "What's the matter, *ah*?" My voice rises. "Why
don't they deserve your sympathy? What did *these* people do
to you?"

"No, you tell me," he says. "Why you're doing this to me,
to yourself, to us? It was going to be perfect. If not for your
stupid pet *Aiz-er-man* . . ."

"I already told you, it's not about him. It's about you."

He isn't listening. "He doesn't even have to be in the same
republic, he can be out of the country and still ruin everything!
That . . . that . . . fucking . . . poodle of yours!"

"*Poodle*? That's not what you were going to say."

"What does it matter what I was going to say!"

"It matters!"

A car pulls up toward us. The driver gestures for us to get in, but I don't move from where I'm standing.

"Get in Sonya," Ruslan orders.

"Not until you answer me!"

"A lot of people died in the great Patriotic War. What makes *them* so special?"

"They died because people hated them." My voice drops low, all the way to the ground it drops. "For who they were when they were born. Or for the way they wanted to believe in God, for the books they were reading. They died because of people like you."

"Why does everything—*everything*—have to be about this precious Jewish suffering of yours? Aren't there other places we could have gone to?" Now he's the one shouting. "Anyway, they never died here—never did—you got that? It's just a story they made up to make themselves look more special."

"They—we—we have plenty of other stories, and we've had them for centuries! We are already special. We live, we dream, we love, oh—" I stumble, as I think of the small dusty attic room under the roof of the synagogue, the wistful sounds of Misha's guitar. "We sing. That's what makes us special."

He looks at me—this time, he really looks. It's as though something about my words awakened that Ruslan, the boy who loves me. Was it the thing I said about singing? Was he remembering the day he clapped for me at the First-Day-of-School Assembly?

"Are you getting in, or not?" the driver asks him.

Ruslan looks at me, hesitating. "I . . . Can't we just forget all this?"

"Can we?" I whisper back at him. *The way we did, on the train?*

He comes up to me, takes hold of my hand. I can't believe it, even as my heart lifts. I grasp his hand tightly. He forces it open. I look down, and watch him trying to stuff something into my palm. Money. *Silver coins.*

No, thank you.

"This is for the ride back, *myshka*," he whispers, eyes on the ground.

I watch him get into the car and slam the door closed.

He wouldn't leave me alone in Syrets, without any money. But he did leave me. He just did. He did.

The way they left all of these people. Here, under my feet.

I spend the rest of the afternoon by that tree, slumped on the ground.

"Do you realize what time it is, Solovay?"

Electrification's worried face drifts into mine. The sun no longer glistens over the ground that was once bones, and before that, skin and blood and love. Gray clouds glide above my head. I almost think it's a dream, but then I watch her scoop up the money with defeated disgust even I couldn't possibly dream up.

"So you wanted to explore historical monuments, Solovay," she grumbles in a private dusty sedan. "But what did ripping up rubles into little pieces have to do with anything, would you explain that to me? I never thought I'd say this to a pupil, but really, Solovay, your unhealthy interest in Soviet history has caused all of us a lot of trouble. I wish you showed this much enthusiasm inside the classroom."

In the back seat, I smile through my empty tearless eyes. "We've never learned about Babi Yar in your classroom, Elektra Ivanovna."

She nods gravely. "Those poor, poor people. It was horrible what happened, Solovay, nobody can deny it—"

"Nobody? Oh, Elektra Ivanovna, you'd be surprised."

Her face sets. "I tried to warn you. Didn't I say, back in December, in my classroom, 'stay away from him?' And then, you told me you knew what sorts of demonstrations he went to. I thought you really knew." She clucks her tongue. "I tried to tell him, too. But he wouldn't listen. He never listens to me."

I sit silent, staring at the beautiful rural Ukrainian scenery outside the window.

She clears her throat. "You—and he—must both understand what's important here. And the important thing is: millions of Soviet citizens died for their country. Jew, Georgian, Ukrainian, or Russian, it doesn't matter."

"It matters!" I shout, and the driver turns his head, frowning.

Can't we just forget all this? Ruslan's question echoes in my mind.

The rest of the week is as slow as a nightmare. Ruslan doesn't look at me, doesn't offer up a single word. Come to think of it, he doesn't look at anybody, doesn't talk to anybody. He, a boy who held me tight in the train cabin, a boy whose hands at once rubbed my skin raw and soothed me, whose mouth shushed me with gentle whispers on my lips. Through the dry tears and the dust of Kiev's summer streets, the sweet incense of its churches, the steep hills, the panoramic views of the wide, curvy river, the sticky feel of chocolate-covered ice-cream *Eskimo Pie* running down my hands, all I can think is, *it matters*. Through the ticklish smell of soot on the train—*it matters*—through the pounding of wheels underneath me—iron against iron—*it matters*—through Electrification's pompous goodbye—*it matters, it matters, it matters*—*Can't we just forget all this?*—*it matters*—all the way back home I keep thinking it.

In the apartment, the couch is still in my bedroom, and my bed in the living room. There is an empty bottle of cognac in the trash, a side of it chipped. I pick up one bit of glass from the floor. Now I know that some things that are broken cannot ever fit together again.

45

Follow the Tanks

The buzz of a doorbell pulls me out of a dream too early on a cold August morning, and immediately I realize about a million things are wrong. First, there is no Mama on the sofa bed beside me. The sounds of television are coming from the living room when it's still dark outside. Most terrifying of all, a rumbling *grr-broooeech-j-j-j-j-j-eeee* thunder-screech spreads, shaking the fragile souvenirs on my shelves. The traffic noise from Lenin Street doesn't usually reach us here, except for an occasional extra giant construction truck. This sounds more like a tank, for God's sake.

A tank?

I sit up on the sofa bed.

"*A mortal danger looms large over our great Motherland,*" an extremely official man's voice announces on television across the wall.

I throw open the door of my room and stare at another surprise, a good one for a change: Papa in his boxers and slippers talking to Misha Aizerman in the hall.

"Misha!" I shout. "You're back?"

He seems taller than before, darker skinned, harder muscled, louder. Like he has soaked in too much sun. He examines me, too. More like stares, and I blush, wondering if he can see what I have become in his absence.

"I got back late last night," he says. "Just in time for this mayhem." He curves his lip sardonically at me, and I grin, even though the TV across the wall keeps announcing those strange things, like, "*Mikhail Sergeevich Gorbachev is no longer able to continue performing his duties due to the state of his health.*"

"What's going on?" I ask.

We walk into the living room, where a pair of oddly pale anchors, a man and a woman, are taking turns reading from pieces of paper that tremble in their hands.

"*The policy of reforms launched at Gorbachev's initiative has, for a number of reasons, run into a dead end.*"

"Wait. . ." I say, frowning. "So is it his health or his reforms that are the problem?"

Papa buries his face in his large hands.

An *Emergency Committee* has been formed and will now deal with the situation, the anchors say.

"What situation?" I say. "And what committee?"

Misha comes up and places his hand on my shoulder.

"Everything seemed fine." I stare at the anchors' corpselike faces, none of it making sense. "Wasn't Gorbachev going away, to negotiate a new treaty with the republics? He didn't look sick—wasn't he just on TV yesterday? And now they're saying his policies failed? On the very same morning as his health . . ." I stop midword, the understanding dawning on me. "The coup. That's what this is, isn't it?"

"Bye-bye, perestroika," Papa says.

"Hello, Emergency Committee," Misha says.

Hello, Old Life.

Suddenly I feel as though I am stuck inside Electrification's dark history classroom, and that the end-of-class bell might never ring.

"I bet they'll be closing the borders," Misha says. "If I had stayed in Israel just one more day . . ." He trails off, and, communist coup or not, I am selfishly glad he is here.

The anchors keep reading one decree after another.

"Public rallies, marches, and demonstrations, as well as strikes are prohibited. When necessary, a curfew is to be introduced. . . ."

A sharp realization hits me.

Mama!

"Where is Mama?"

Papa looks at me with eyes dazed and solemn. "I would have stopped her. But by the time I woke up properly and pieced it all together, she was already—"

"Gone—to Moscow, of course! What the hell was she thinking? Did she not hear those tanks rumbling toward the city?" But even as I ask this, even as I rush out of the room, with Misha on my heels, I already know she heard those tanks. And that is why she is now on her way to Moscow.

I almost run out in the nightgown. At the last moment, I throw on some long skirt and a wrinkled T-shirt, a pair of sandals, and I'm out the door.

"Sonya! Get back here!" Papa calls after me.

The telephone rings or, rather, it beeps—an exotic foreign sound.

I freeze. *Is it her?*

"Olga Borisovna," Papa says. Olga Borisovna—that's my babushka! I feel a pang in my chest—how I've missed her.

Is it a sign—that I should stay home? *Lower than grass, quieter than water,* just like she always taught me to be. "No, Rita isn't here right now," Papa says into the phone. "But don't worry, she's . . ." *in Moscow building an underground movement by now, for God's sake.*

"Let's go!" I whisper to Misha.

"No, no, everything is normal here." Poor Papa is stammering on the telephone. "Your granddaughter is here—would you like to speak with . . . Sonya, wait! I said—wait!"

Misha flies out the door by my side. "I saw a woman on my way here," he says, panting. "Does she have this long hair, really long, jet-black, right? She was standing on the side of Lenin Street, braiding all that hair, and waving at the passing cars, trying to catch a ride."

Damn!

In that case, we have already missed her.

"I am still going," I say.

"So am I," Misha says simply.

I should tell him to go home, to *his* mama, his sister. I should tell him that if I had a brother like that, I wouldn't want him to go. But it's not like he'd listen, anyway.

"You know it's my birthday tomorrow?" I whisper to him in the elevator, just realizing it, myself. "I will turn sixteen at midnight."

"We'll celebrate on the tanks! After we win, that is." He curves his lips.

I lean against his side and inhale his sunshine smell. It's the only thing that feels real right now. When the elevator doors open, I give a start at the sight of a pale familiar-to-the-point-of-pain boy's face.

I straighten and glare at Ruslan Valentinov—even though one small part, a silly little *myshka* part of me thinks it—*Oh my God, he came to see me*—for a split second, before I shut it up. He just stands there, frozen before the elevator, wearing a strange checkered jacket that reminds me of a pattern on a tablecloth. Under his arm, a small beige box crackles with sound. A portable radio.

No one moves.

Finally, he nods at Misha. "Hi." His voice cracks. "I thought you were . . . away."

"I was," Misha says. He sounds surprised. "I came back last night. From Israel." He drapes his hand over my shoulder.

The doors of the elevator jerk to close. Ruslan blocks them with his foot.

I squeeze my teeth together. I take a step toward him. *If he wants to so much as breathe on Misha, he's going to have to go through me first*, I think fiercely.

Ruslan clears his throat. "I . . . was just . . . passing by. I mean, on a day like this, where are you supposed to go?"

"Follow the tanks," I say. My whole body is still tight as a violin string, though I take care to keep my voice sounding casual. *He was just passing by. In a tablecloth jacket I had never seen on him. Didn't know where to go.* "We're off to the center of the capital," I say. "That's where the action is. It's where my *mama* is," I add, locking my eyes with his.

He steps aside, letting Misha and me walk out of that elevator.

He follows us out of the building. "I came here because . . . I couldn't stay away . . . not on a day like this."

We keep on walking, Misha and I, our steps brisk.

"Radio Russia is saying the Emergency Committee is unconstitutional," Ruslan says, pointing to his little crackling radio. "It's calling on all Moscow residents to resist."

Misha stops walking. "I'd put that thing away," he says.

Ruslan sticks the radio under his coat. I stare at him, amazed at how quickly he obeyed *Aizerman*.

"Great. Now you look like you're hiding a weapon under that tablecloth jacket of yours," I tell him. Ruslan snorts, looking down at his jacket. I look up at Misha, my eyes filled with questions as if he is my own personal sage. He shrugs. His eyes meet mine, those deep Jewish eyes offering questions of his own. *Find your own compass,* didn't he tell me, once? *Oh Misha. I am working on it.*

Lubertsy City is a quiet, forgotten suburb, one of Moscow's many stepchildren full of gray apartment buildings and empty stores. Still, even in this quiet place, even for this early hour, the yards and pathways seem eerily free of passersby. Even the birds seem to have grown silent. For a moment, it feels like there is just Misha and I in the world, with Ruslan trailing us all the way to Lenin Street. On the usually busy boulevard, no cars pass, and for a moment, my heart lifts with hope that Mama is still here, waiting for a ride that would never come.

There is no sign of her.

But at the bus stop, a chorus of familiar voices greet us, and the quiet splinters.

"Look, it's her! It's Sonya!"

Luba and Diana are waving at me, whooping, Kira and Olya behind them. There is Tanya. Dimon, Ruslan's friend. Zahar. Marina. Bozhena. Oleg Kuzmin, too.

"What are you guys doing?" I call at them, beaming at the faces that have become familiar.

"Just hanging," says Zahar. "What else are you supposed to do on the day when everything goes to hell?"

"We're checking for more tanks," Bozhena says, in a quieter, more serious voice.

"My ancestors are losing it at home," says Kira. "I needed some air, honestly."

"It's all so crazy." Luba smiles shakily at me. "We need to think, citizens."

"*Nu*, I have already done my thinking," I tell her. "My mama is going to the barricades. We are going to catch up with her, somehow."

"You're going to protest?" Diana breathes out.

"Are you touched?" says Kuzmin, though it seems he sounds awed, a little. "Haven't you heard about the curfew?"

"And the tanks?" Diana says.

"They'll be rounding people up, shooting people!" Olya says, shaking her frizzy curls at me. "This isn't like history class, Sonya. This is for real."

I shake my head, their arguments only solidifying my decision just as—Glory to God!—the bus approaches, farting at us with its black, pungent fumes.

"Do you even know where you're going?" Luba asks. I shrug. "The center of Moscow, I figure" The doors of the fat little bus snap open. "Please be careful out there," says Diana, wide-eyed, pale, and trembling.

"We'll pray for you," Kira whispers.

Marina just puffs on a cigarette, her dark eyes silent and nervous.

I smile at them and step into the mostly empty bus, Misha and Ruslan right behind me. Luba walks in next, followed by Tanya. Oleg Kuzmin and Zahar hesitate.

I turn back at them. *They don't have to do this.*

"Your ancestors will kill you," I point out. "If the tanks don't." I meant to say it as a joke, sort of, but everyone's face grows somber at my words.

"Look who is talking," Luba says. "You know, you might not make it home before dark this time, Cinderella."

And it hits me then: I have no right to tell them to stay home, no more than Mama or Papa do. Because Mama and I, we're not the only ones with voices.

"Clear the entrance, hooligans, or I'll squash you with the doors," the driver barks at us. We get out of the way, squealing, before the accordionlike doors jerk closed.

We all pile in. It's so odd to have a choice of seating. I slide in beside Misha. Ruslan sits with Luba just across from us. For once, Luba doesn't ask silly *love* questions.

Almost a year ago we rode this bus together, Ruslan and I, and it was the two of us against a savage crowd. Now each one of us, an individual, has a stand to take. Still Ruslan stares at me with pleading, muddy-gray eyes that maybe I loved, once, the boy who lost so much to communism, looking at me like he needs my permission to be here.

Find your own compass, I want to tell him.

But I have no right to deny him this—this chance to take a stand for his beloved Mother Russia in a way that would actually count, for once.

The bus shakes us along a potholed road. The sounds of Ruslan's portable radio crackle behind us.

"President Yeltsin demands to know what the Emergency Committee has done with Gorbachev," sputters a young man's voice on the radio. "Yeltsin is calling on every citizen to resist the unlawful coup."

Every citizen. I replay the phrase in my head, thinking of all of us—Luba, Tanya, Kuzmin, Zahar, Misha, Ruslan, and me, together in this bus, our destination the same for a change.

46

It's Crazy

It's crazy.

Only last month they held a huge celebration for Yeltsin, when he became the president of the Russian Republic, complete with the blessing from the Patriarch of the Russian Orthodox Church, broadcast on television. Now, in the center of Moscow, a college student hands us a pamphlet that says earlier this morning Yeltsin nearly escaped arrest by the KGB.

"What has he even done to deserve arrest?" Luba asks, indignant.

Tanya snorts. "That's like asking, what's wrong with Gorbachev's health. The answer is 'absolutely nothing.'"

Rumors travel up and down the metro escalators, along the tree-lined streets.

He was on the list of the most dangerous politicians. Tanks were on the way to Yeltsin's dacha this morning. The KGB has already detained a few liberal Congress deputies, but somehow missed Yeltsin.

"For all we know, Yeltsin is down in KGB headquarters right now," I whisper.

"For all we know, he's dead, along with Gorbachev," Ruslan whispers back, his face pale, worried.

"*Nu,*" Misha says. "Let's not give in to the gloom, citizens."

The subdued early morning city glistens with freshness, and though it isn't raining yet, I can feel it coming. Walking up the hill along a badly paved empty old road, I feel grateful to be here, in the city of my dreams, where history breathes at me from every corner.

On the main thoroughfares the traffic seemed to flow as though it really is just another Monday. But this smaller street is quiet enough for us to spread out in a single line, all seven of us.

"Seven of us to nine of them," Zahar remarks.

"Nine of whom?" I ask.

"Nine members of the Emergency Committee, microbe," Kuzmin answers, all of a sudden a know-it-all.

"Seven is better," I say. "It's a magic number."

It's Kuzmin's turn to look confused. "What?"

I grin. "Haven't you ever read your Russian fairytales?"

Passing by the famous New Arbat Street, normally animated with artists selling their paintings and wares, I am grateful for a cuckoo bird calling down to us from a tall poplar tree. I am even grateful for the uneven land under our feet that makes our legs work harder.

Ruslan's radio is silent, but once in a while it crackles and tells us that Yeltsin is calling on all elected officials to gather in the parliament building for an emergency session of Congress. Passersby glare at us each time the radio awakens with sound and sputters with dangerous words.

The Emergency Committee's takeover of power is illegal, the radio says, over and over. *Yeltsin is inside the parliament building, calling for a general strike.*

"Unless it's a provocation—a trap," an old woman leaning against a kiosk who overhears our radio says with a frown.

Demonstrators flock toward the structure everyone has christened "the White House" today.

"What White House?" Misha asks, frowning at Ruslan's radio.

"The parliament building." Ruslan's voice is rough, scratchy with tobacco.

"I thought that one was in Washington," Misha says.

A shadow flits across Ruslan's face. My body tightens. My hand seeks out Misha's.

Ruslan stares at my fingers as they lock with Misha's. Then he shrugs. "If it wasn't called 'White House' before, that's what it's called now. The important thing is, Yeltsin is there."

"And now that we're here, he need not worry, for the entire Red Army doesn't stand a chance against us!" Misha pumps his fist in the air, pulling my hand along.

Ruslan punches him in the arm, maybe a little too hard. But then he grins and calls Misha a "crazy idiot," and I widen my eyes at them, thinking, *Friendships can be as easy as that, ah?*

It's crazy. Among the seven of us walking along Kutuzov Prospect, the three of us are trading places, nudging each other with elbows. We walk right past the line of tanks, a herd of poorly-cared-for creatures farting and growling. Soldiers sit mounted on their miserable brown-gray beasts.

The crowd of demonstrators swells around us. Students, veterans, long-haired rock-and-rollers, Mafiosi men in suits, big-chested middle-aged women—all dragging pieces of debris to the growing pile of junk spread out before the entrance to the White House. Anything works: a garbage can, a tire, a section of a mesh fence—anything to block the tanks from muscling their way through to this last island of democracy.

I keep asking everyone around for Mama.

The afternoon air boils with slogans written and shouted. Speakers pack the long balcony of the White House before us, calling, "Today we are people, no longer idiots deceived!"

I lose my voice among the others, my right hand squeezing Misha's hand, my left arm hooked around Ruslan's arm, my arms and my legs sweating, my mouth screaming in unison with theirs: "They tried to drive us into the barn but we won't go!"

The three of us, the seven of us, the thousands of us chant "Russia is alive" with rediscovered voices. We chant like nothing would ever tear us apart. Inside the sea of people I sway along, mouth open, unleashing cooped-up anger, hands pumping the air, hair tangled up in ecstasy, eyes unseeing.

When the rally is over, the wave of people recedes, leaving space where thousands have been standing. The sun shines its last rays of the day on the White House. The walls of junk rise before the building—overturned trolleys, bathtubs and rolls of barbwire, rails and beams sticking out—like a messed-up punk hairdo.

Some of the small sloping windows of the giant building slide open. Sometimes pamphlets are sent flying out of those windows. Circling, the flyers fall over people's heads. I wonder which window Yeltsin could be behind, the tough-talking silver-haired square-jawed tower of a man I've seen on television, the president of the Russian Republic, the man we have come here to shield, to die for under those tanks, if necessary.

47

Barricade Builders' Depot

In the twilight that has descended quickly, illuminated by fires and occasional camera flashes, someone is singing a Beatles tune. I hum along, but the sweet and carefree melody feels all wrong in the sudden chill of the evening. Ruslan starts throwing furtive glances at Misha.

I try to hold on to the lovely craziness, the fun of it all.

But our earlier camaraderie seems to be slipping with the last rays of the sun.

"Aren't you going home?" Ruslan asks him.

"Aren't you?" Misha retorts.

Tanya and Zahar both find a pay phone from which to call their parents. Zahar returns shamefaced and somber. "I have to go home." He clasps hands with all the boys and gives me a tight hug, and throws a look of longing at us before departing, taking Kuzmin and Tanya along, our magic seven broken. I think about my own mama. Would she go home? I doubt it.

More likely, she is here, right here, among the demonstrators.

"What about your parents?" I ask Luba. "Seriously, girl. You came here. You did it! You made your statement!"

Luba shakes her head, her mouth thin and stubborn. "I am not going anywhere, not until my country is a democracy, once and for all."

Ruslan and Misha both smile at her, like they can't help it, and so do I. I wish Electrification could hear her words now.

But as the night draws closer, rain gathers in the sky, umbrellas pop up like mushrooms, and our voices grow tense once more. The smiles I saw this afternoon have straightened into thin lines. People are tired. The words between Ruslan and Misha have turned into grunts and syllables.

Someone pierces the night with a drunken shout, "Victory!"

Another voice calls, "Helicopters are on the way here with bullets and tear gas! Yeltsin will be arrested momentarily!"

Men with stockings on their heads and long Kalashnikov rifles under their arms are calling out orders with hoarse voices. "No women or children!"

One of the men stops to stare at Luba and me.

"No women or children," he says. "Take them home."

"I will," Ruslan says. His hand tightens over my arm, and for a second I think he actually considers obeying. I shake his hand off.

"I'm just . . . I'm looking for my mama," I sputter. "She's an activist, maybe you've seen her? She's got jet black, very long, fairytale hair, and her nose is—"

"He hasn't seen her," Ruslan snaps, looking around apologetically, embarrassed, giving my shoulder a hard pat, more like a push actually.

"Leave her be," Misha says. "That's who she came here for, remember?"

"She came here for Russia," Ruslan snaps.

I wrench my arm away from his grasp and glare. "Are you going to start *that* again?"

His gaze, so cold and solid as a concrete fence a moment ago, turns pleading. "But it's true, isn't it?" he says. "You *are* here for Russia. We all are."

"Not like before, though," I remind him.

"Down with communism!" he calls out, flashing a weak smile. I breathe out, relieved. But the moment the tension dissipates, the White House speakers blare. "We're intensifying the movement of military units. The strengthening of the barricades must continue."

We walk along the nearby streets, looking for more barricade-worthy junk, to shield ourselves from the tanks. We walk too far off, into darkness.

"How will we be able to find our way back, let alone drag whatever it is that we find back to the White House?" I ask Luba, Misha, and Ruslan. I don't mean for it to come out sounding so cranky.

Luba chews on her lip, looking worried. Ruslan rolls his eyes all over the gray-brown ceiling of rain. Misha cranes his neck and calls out, "I see just what we need—this way!"

We follow Misha into an empty, half-heartedly fenced-off site with ghostly outlines.

"Welcome to a barricade builders' depot!" Misha says, and I finally realize we're at a construction site. *A castle.*

Panting, smoking, cough-breathing into each other's faces wet with rain, we rummage through brick, cobblestones, and reinforced concrete for pieces light enough to take back to the White House. Ruslan stuffs his pockets with bricks and chipped concrete. Misha has found a cart. While the two of them load it up with boards and pipes, I try to help them, but Ruslan barks at me to *get out of the way, for once,* and when Misha defends me, Ruslan starts throwing bricks into the cart with such savage force that Luba and I leave the two of them to do their men's work alone.

"Let's climb a little higher—see if we can get a good view of where we are," I tell Luba, but she wrinkles her forehead.

"I don't know, Sonya. It looks kind of slippery. I think I'll keep an eye on the boys.

And so I go alone.

I allow myself to really look around, to breathe in the surreal night air, to lose myself in the ruins of concrete and metal, as I climb swiftly atop the half-finished blocks of stairs. I try to savor it, the feeling of adventure. The magic of this night.

It might already be past midnight, I realize. I may have already turned sixteen.

I spread my hands about me as though they were wings and taste the wind that stinks of tanks, even here. I don't know what will happen to us tonight. But I know now what freedom feels like.

Seventy-four years ago, did Lenin and his early communists feel it, too, when they gathered on their own barricades, when they stormed the tsar's winter palace?

Lenin and his Bolsheviks, they had to have believed in things, good things. They believed in equality. And then they forbade people to believe in God. They believed in "power to the masses!" And then they created a dictatorship, where Stalin arrested and murdered people by the millions and the KGB tracked every joke you made.

How do these things happen?

The boys down there below me—and Luba—came here to say the same thing. We don't want to go back to the dark place where one is afraid to share a political joke, be a friend, or express an opinion. We don't want to be a backward country anymore where there are no rich, because everyone is poor. We came here because each one of us—yes, even Ruslan—does not want to be a Soviet person but simply a person, period. The four of us came here holding hands.

Just like I did so many times in Moscow Region at the construction site outside my building, I jump from one block to the next, my hands scooping up the sides of my too-long skirt. From the top of what must be the fourth story or so, I can see it all: the White House, the Garden Ring Road, and the American Embassy, right here, practically underneath me. I can see people rushing about on the street along which we have come, and just across, a crowd gathering underneath the highway overpass formed by a crossing of one road over another.

In the yellow-brown streetlights, one shape jumps out at me.

It's a skinny girl shape, in a too-big jacket. The girl is surrounded by other shapes.

I keep staring at her, I am not sure why, until I realize that only one person I know walks this way. So swift, yet she always gives the impression of flowing rather than marching because of her fairytale hair trailing behind her in a loosening ponytail.

"*Ma-ma!*" I scream.

"*Son-ya!*" Misha calls out from below.

My shout merges with the sound of my own name repeated in the dark over and over again by two boy voices, and Luba's voice. But the young woman with long hair four stories below me keeps marching away from me, oblivious.

She is so close. And yet there she is again, walking away, leaving me again and again, like she is the only one worthy of being here.

"*Ma-ma!*"

"What are you doing up there, you, lunatic?" Ruslan's raspy cry tears through the air.

"Don't move or you're going to fall!" Misha shouts.

I start to descend—God, I wish I could move faster—but I didn't realize how slippery the "steps" of brick, pipe, and concrete have gotten under the rain. I don't know how I made it up so easily. Now my feet float inside my wet sandals and slide all over the place. Misha and Ruslan are making their way up in my direction from below, Ruslan cursing me for my craziness; Misha, slightly ahead of Ruslan, cursing him for cursing me; their hands extended on either side of me.

I take a step and trip on the edge of my long, wet skirt, and just like that I find myself sliding, concrete surfaces moving too fast underneath my feet, the skin of my arms just above my elbow tearing past something solid. A strong pair of arms wraps around me and pulls, and then comes Misha's voice, gentle in my ear: "It's nothing. Just a tiny tumble. I've got you now." His arms are wrapped tight around me. I find myself thinking, *He has gotten so strong in Israel.*

Ruslan is standing just below, his eyes sending arrows at us, as Misha lifts me up like I'm his sister's dolly and then gently sets me down on the last staircase block.

"Now, breathe," he says. "Slow down." *Doctor Aizerman.*

I shake my head. "She's down there—my mama!" I say, out of breath. "I've got to catch up with her!"

Ruslan's face goes from a flat blank expression to something much darker. "I've had it! You're staying here, got it? Seriously, they should have made a rule, no lunatics allowed on the barricades! What are you, a baby, clinging to your mama's skirt?"

"Ruslan," Luba shouts, "what has gotten in—"

Misha tries to say something, too, but I can't hear it over Ruslan's voice exploding, "Keep your snot in your own nose, Aizerman! Who are you, anyway, to tell me how to talk to her?"

"The question is," Misha says quietly, "who are you to be talking for her?"

As the four of us jump down from the foundation block back onto the ground, a sound splits the night sky. Other sounds just like it follow the first, one after another, fast pops.

"What is it?" Luba shrieks.

"They're shooting!" Misha shouts.

"Where?"

But I already know where, and if I had doubts before, they disappear with the new clatter—*Pow! Pow! Pow!*—erupting in the sky. And so I am running, under the black sky breaking with sounds and rain, in the direction of the Garden Ring Road, in which Mama was walking. Misha and Ruslan on either side of me shout, "Wait!" pulling me to pieces, Luba keeping up behind us. The bricks and concrete pieces Ruslan stuffed in the pockets of his jacket tear against my side as we fly through the street. People scream, "Tanks! The tanks are here!" on either side of us.

"It's her, it's her, I see her!" Misha calls. His head towers over the thickening mass of people, and even in this madness I notice Ruslan's face flash with hurt. He doesn't know Misha has only glimpsed Mama just once, on the way to my apartment earlier this morning, when she stood on the side of the boulevard, trying to catch a ride. That quiet morning seems so far away now. Not that it should matter how many times he'd seen her. We catch up with her by the overpass bridge beside the Garden Ring Road.

48

Monsters

The air stinks of sour smoke and diesel fumes. People run toward the tanks. They shout, "Stop!" They spread their arms, as if to hug the approaching monsters. Into the space under the overpass bridge, just underneath freshly painted graffiti demanding "Down with communism!" the tanks are ramming into a line of overturned trolleybuses. They have already passed through one layer of barricades, the one guarding the entrance. But here at the exit they are trapped, five tanks slamming their foul-smelling bodies against a cage.

Just hours ago the barricades had that campfire feel, like it's all one grand adventure. I had turned sixteen at midnight, and just like Misha said, it felt like the entire Soviet military didn't stand a chance against us—against me. Now, choking on diesel fumes, I duck, as though the shouting and the popping gunfire sounds are raining on me from the sky itself.

"Mama! *Maaaa*maaaa!"

Luba trips and curses behind me. On my left side, Ruslan yanks me close to him so hard, I think my arm will rip off for sure. His hand holds me so tight, like he would rather die—or break my hand—than give me up. I feel like shaking him.

Has *he* forgotten what he was here for?

"Today isn't about me, Ruslan, remember?" I shout, trying to work my hand loose from his. He looks into my face—his is twisted with longing and pain. Doesn't he see the tank that is rolling toward us?

"*Watch out!*" Misha shouts.

"You're the one who keeps getting distracted." Ruslan's whisper is hot in my ear. My side rubs against the bricks and concrete pieces in his pocket. "We're here for Russia's new future."

"We are here for the right to be who we are," I tell him, trembling. "Now let go."

His face glows back at me, unreadable and ghostly.

Mama is not glad to see me.

"What are *you* doing here!" she shouts at me. "Tear out of this place, GO! GO! GO NOW!"

I clutch the hands of the two boys that flank me like bodyguards, Luba lost in the crowd behind us. "You want me to stay home, in front of the television, in the shadows of Old Life?" I yell, my voice shredding. "Not today, Mama! Not when I finally, finally—"

The rest of my words drown in gunfire.

One of the tanks turns away from the trolley and plunges instead into the approaching sea of shrieking people.

"Watch out!!!" Misha yells.

I think that's when she truly notices him here, among the mass of people and metal and the smell of burnt air. "Aizerman?" She screams. "That's your Aizerman, isn't it?"

The crowd shifts all around us. Some people are tearing out, others are plunging at the tanks, screaming. Those sitting atop the walls surrounding the overpass shower the mess of tanks and people with sticks and stones. Luba finds her way back to me. I grab her hand. She is shaking, screaming, "Let's get out of here!" Tears roll down her face.

Misha grabs my hand, as though to protect me from the tanks, from my own mama, from Ruslan's furious eyes.

"You—will—take your friends—and get out—*now*." Mama gives me a push on the chest and I struggle to stay upright.

Ruslan's fingers latch on to my wrist, a pair of handcuffs. I tug on my hand. "I said, let go, Ruslan." He doesn't see, doesn't hear me. He turns to Mama. "Get your dirty hands off her, *Jid*-face."

Now Mama sees him.

Ruslan's face glowing with rage looms before me. Blood rushes to my head, pounds in my temples. Finally I tear my hand out of Ruslan's grasp and let it explode across his mouth. The slap makes no noise in the melee of tanks and new gunshots and a hailstorm of sticks and stones descending on us from all sides.

Even as Mama opens her mouth to say God-knows-what, someone screams into the megaphone, "There's live ammunition here! It is going to explode!" and the crowd becomes a creature. A broad-shouldered man wedges himself between Mama and me, and before I know it, the crowd is carrying Mama away.

"*Ma-ma!*"

In the chaos of the night, when my heart thrashes so hard in my chest that it hurts, and more shots puncture the air, I cannot tell what happens next, and how it happens.

Why do Ruslan's fingers linger by his jacket pocket? What is he pulling out of there?

A small concrete block flashes in his hand. Ruslan's face glows white with rage.

Or is he just standing there, helpless, not knowing where to place his hands?

I'm not sure of anything, what I am noticing and what's but a blur of my imagination.

Things are happening somewhere, a million kilometers away, in some fantastic land of beasts and creatures. Somewhere, someone fell off a tank and became a body, with parts caught under the wheels. Somewhere, a tank is moving in a million directions, a savage monster devouring its accidental prey.

I squeeze myself to Misha and watch a small white concrete block sail through the air. I barely feel my body throwing itself over Misha's, I barely see his dazed expression, because for one moment all I see—really see—is the concrete block tumbling on the ground, stained with blood.

"Misha? Misha!"

This is a dream. A nightmare. This cannot be happening.

"Misha!" Luba is screaming along with me.

Fountains and fountains of blood spew from the side of Misha's head, drenching my clothes and his in warm, dark liquid, as he leans on me.

"I am all right," he says, then slumps onto the ground littered with sticks, stones, and pieces of glass.

"I need a doctor!" I shout into the tearing, shifting crowd of people and tanks.

I sit beside Misha on littered asphalt, holding his head with my hands soaked in his blood, and I keep chanting, "It's all right, it's nothing, it's going to be all right." I order myself to believe it.

"I am . . . tired," he mouths through barely moving lips. His eyes pull closed, but he forces them open again. "I am sorry . . . but I . . . ."

"No," I whisper back, trying to stop my body from trembling. "Please . . . don't . . ."

"In Israel. . . . I met someone. . . . I think maybe . . . I wish . . . I'd promised that I'd write. . . . But now . . ."

"Misha?" I want to shake him. "It's all right! It's going to be all right. Stop it!"

"And my little sister . . . Tell her to . . . ask my mama . . . in a top left drawer of my desk. . . . It's a six-pointed metal star. . . ."

A man in a Russian flag bandana leans over Misha and me. Misha blinks. "Who are you?" he asks me softly.

"Misha, please." I taste tears. "You know me."

The man in the Russian flag bandana is saying, "You need to get him to the hospital . . . head trauma . . . As long as it didn't hit the temple . . ."

"And what if—" I try not to think of it, an image of the concrete block and the way it drove into the side of Misha's head, but this time the tremor takes over my body and my voice quivers. "What if it hit the temple?" I squeeze out.

The man doesn't look at me, just leans closer to Misha, grabs his listless hand, and mutters, "Where the hell should his pulse be?"

Somewhere across time and reason, Mama is making her way back toward me, and Luba is crying and crying. Mama holds her hand over her mouth as a scream rips through the night. A boy in a stupid-looking checkered jacket that resembles a tablecloth throws himself over Misha's body, crying in horrible raspy gasps.

"What happened, Sonya?" he says, his voice distorted with tears. "Did you see what happened?" He runs his hand over the side of Misha's head, then recoils at all the blood. "Who did this to him? How—"

"Get away from him. You know who did this. You know what happened."

He straightens. Steps back. "It wasn't me," he stammers, his eyes wide, pleading. "I didn't . . . You know I didn't! And even if I did . . . you know I didn't mean to. You know—"

"*Murderer!*" Somewhere, a solitary girl's shout—I think it is mine—sounds as if a thousand voices are screaming.

49

Baruch Ata Adonai

*D*ear *God, please. Let it all be an awful nightmare.*
That checkered jacket retreating into the night,
melting into the crowd, disappearing into history.

Luba, Mama, and I sitting together in the back of a
stranger's car, listening to the shouts of victory on the dark
streets outside the windows.

"The entire nation straightened its shoulders!"

"Communism is dead!"

"Long live the New Russia!"

Still, I close my eyes and pray. *Dear God, please make it not real.*
Misha's body spread across our laps, his blood soaking my skirt.

Two men in white coats placing him on the stretcher. The
nurse shoving me aside:

"You want the doctor to tend to your friend, or do you
want to give your explanations?"

"Can I at least use the telephone?"

Luba, Mama, and I are sitting on the shaky wooden chairs
in the waiting room, a basement space in an old building with
the low ceiling curving over us, pressing down. I have called
Misha's home, half-hoping, insanely, that he would pick up the
phone and tell me I had a bad dream.

His mama was at work, on duty. But his father, I could barely speak to him through shame and tears. He is already on his way.

Someone put the radio on. The radio voices crackle with joy.

"We did it—you did it!" the voices say. *"The Emergency Committee has surrendered!"* *"Connection with Gorbachev has been re-established, and he's already on his way back from the forcible detainment at his dacha."*

Luba used the clinic's phone when we first got here. Her parents told her to stay put, and this time, she did. After they take her home, Mama holds my hand. Staring at the mold stain in the corner of the wall, I tell her everything. I live through it all over again, and even as the world grows blurry from behind the curtains of tears, my own story—this story—grows clearer.

I tell her that no matter how hard I try, the only thing I really remember is that concrete block glowing in the brown night as it sails through the air. I close my eyes. The tears burn me from the inside, and all I can remember is sticks, stones, glass raining on us from everywhere.

Mama too is crying.

"I am Misha's father," booms a rich baritone.

The tanned bearded man entering the clinic stops at the threshold and looks at me. I meet his dark eyes—they're Misha's eyes, which looked back at me in the Bolshoi Gymnasium last December. I am shaking. *I never want to set my eyes on you,* Misha said then. Oh but how his eyes were burning.

"Follow me," I barely hear the nurse saying.

I move my foot forward, but her hand pushes against my chest. "Not you," she says severely.

Even when I look down at the moldy clinic floor, even after the man's footsteps retreat down the hallway, I can feel the darkness of Misha's eyes on me—his father's eyes.

The nurse comes out in the morning. Standing up on wobbly legs, I blink at her. I register nothing about her, except that her face is somber and her forehead creased with lines, though she is young.

"Misha?" I squeak.

"He is in a coma." She directs her words to Mama, not me, but new hope spreads warmth through the numbness inside me.

"So he isn't—" I start to say. Mama puts her hand on my shoulder. "Does that mean . . . ?" I want the nurse to finish the sentence for me.

The nurse won't meet my eye. She is shaking her head. She is frowning. Mama's hand kneads my shoulder. I collapse back into my chair.

The rest is a blur of voices—Mama's, the nurse's, Mama's. Hands on my shoulders. A curtain of tears hanging over my eyes, making everything sparkle.

"Brain injury . . . Internal bleeding . . ." I make out only fragments. *"If he doesn't wake up in the next three days, the chances of him waking up at all . . . You really should leave now." "His mother is on her way. . . . Give the Aizermans their peace. . . ." "Come on, let's go, Sonya."*

It takes tremendous effort for me to just lift my chin and focus my eyes on my mama. "Misha is gone?" I whisper.

Mama is on one side of me, the nurse on the other. They are supporting me under the arms, lifting me up gently. "Don't think of it that way, child," the nurse says, like she's a million years old. "He is just sleeping."

The rain has stopped, but even in the sunshine, the puddles are here, deep ones and shallow, filled with God's tears. The hot afternoon air smells of washed-out dust. It hits me in the face, fills my lungs, my mouth.

Mama is quiet and sweaty beside me, our hands laced together tight as two strands of a metal chain, as we walk in the middle of one Moscow road after another, many of them barricaded still. In street after street, we pass prickly monument-like barricades, a bathtub here, a tire there, and people, all these people perched like birds on balconies, atop monuments, crawling onto tanks, some of them.

Carnations fly in the air. Numb, I stare at the passersby, their striped shirts and cotton flower-print dresses, and jeans, jeans, jeans, sandals splashing in puddles, tired sneakers stepping over wet leaflets, exalted smiles on faces that are free.

Except, before a makeshift memorial, the smiles whither by a heap of flowers. A woman kneels right on the asphalt and whispers a prayer.

One young man died in the overpass, the people are saying. No—two. No, there were three.

He is just sleeping, the nurse said.

I try to reach inside myself, for even a shadow of hope.

Wake up, Misha. Wake up!

Instead, another thought spreads, dull and cool, coating my soul in gray nothing.

When will the official death count include Misha Aizerman? I think this with the calm of a bureaucrat. My eyes are still wet and my cheeks are sticky, though the tears have stopped. My mouth is dry and my heart is empty.

I call the clinic the next day. Misha is no longer a patient, they tell me.

"Where is he? Where is the nurse who was on duty?" I want to scream at her—some girl on the telephone. But my voice barely makes it.

Outside my apartment building, I make a million circles around the pond. Little kids have gotten their swimming rings and swimming trunks out today. They are splashing and shouting louder than ever, oblivious to the too salty scent that reeks a little of a sewer.

Half a year ago, the green-gray water was solid and white under our ice skates.

I run my hand across the rough trunks of the oaks growing beside the asphalt path I walk on.

Misha. Where are you? What are you seeing behind those eyes that are closed?

If God—the Jewish God—*Misha's* God—is the blowing of the wind, then why is it picking up the dust from the path and sending it into my eyes?

My bed is strewn with birthday presents. A pair of jeans. A stack of dollars. A lacquered jewelry box Babushka had sent me. Papa crushes me in his big arms, like I'm a cloth doll. Mama whispers, "Don't let yourself drown in sadness. We Jews must always be happy. No matter what. Smile through your tears. I have been praying. You should, too."

When they tiptoe out of my room and close the door gently, I place two candlesticks on the windowsill. I think of Rosa Aizerman saying that words are sacred, magical. It isn't even Shabbat, but I light the candles. *"Baruch Ata Adonai,"* I whisper into the sky. *"Wake up, Misha."*

"Blessed are you, my God," I say. A magical incantation, like in a fairytale.

I place my birthday cash into the small lacquered box Babushka sent me. I put it on the windowsill, right beside the flickering candles. I stare at the exquisite hand-painted design on its top—a traditional Russian beauty brushing her long blond hair in front of a mirror. "How do you like my *Tzedakkah* box, Misha?" I whisper.

Three days later, I go over to Rosa Aizerman's apartment. Her little daughter opens the door, then slams it into my nose.

I catch only a glimpse of a pale, pale face blotchy and wet from too many tears.

"Please . . . go away. . . . My parents aren't here." Her voice, cold and formal, as if I am a stranger, is muffled through the thick padding of the closed door.

"Excuse me."

I turn around. A heavyset woman is breathing hard as she makes her way up the stairs. She is carrying a big bowl wrapped up in newspapers and towels. She gives me a solemn nod, and then presses the door buzzer button.

"Go away—please!"

The woman frowns, confused. "It's me, Anechka—your neighbor," she says, glancing at me suspiciously. "I brought a macaroni and ground chicken casserole."

"Thank you," Anya Aizerman says through the door.

After a moment, she pulls it open again.

But I am gone. I don't want to see them. Those little cheeks stained with tears.

I leave slowly. One stair at a time. Down, down, down.

50

Freedom

The red flag with the hammer and the sickle is gone from the top of Regional School Number Eight. Instead, the tricolor of the Russian Republic waves gently in the light September wind. But underneath the flag, the concrete is as chipped as a year ago, and the walls of the pale pink building just as scraped as they were then.

I take it all in: the cheerful *vaam* of voices, the grins of my classmates as they try to wave to me or call my name, the unfair blueness of the sky, the warmth of September outside the window.

It all feels so unbelievable. That a week has passed. That all these people are here, exchanging easy laughter, that dandelions are blooming modestly under my feet.

This morning I shoved the breakfast down my throat, my slippery fingers barely able to hold the fork.

"I'll drop in at the first-day-of-school assembly," Mama said, her one hand holding the red telephone receiver, her other hand squeezing my shoulder.

I wanted to stay under the woolen blanket on my bed and lose myself to sleep. But I don't deserve that, I know it.

As I walk across the sun-burnt lawn, I hold on to the tiniest of possibilities. The craziest of hopes. That I will see him here. Now. That at the sight of me, he'll snap shut the next book he is reading and grin that sarcastic grin at me.

"*Son-ya!*" Olya, Kira, and Diana are running toward me, arms spread, like they've known me for centuries.

What they don't know is, if I don't find Misha right now, I will never be just another girl, not with this hole inside my heart, where every happy feeling will travel.

"Oh God of mine," Diana whispers.

"Luba told us," Tanya says.

But the others coming up to us, they don't know anything—they don't know.

"How was your summer?"

"Did you and Valentinov make peace at last?" Their voices pour out, jubilant, so full of life, competing with each other.

Baruch Ata Adonai, I pray.

Wake up, sleepyhead. You can't miss the first day of eleventh grade—not you, the school's biggest botanik.

"Have you seen him?" I whisper.

They stare at me, suddenly frowning in confusion.

"God, you still look horrid." Luba grabs my hand. "You're ice-cold."

"*Nu*, don't worry so," Bozhena says, clueless. "Look, here he is."

I whirl around, my heart leaping, only to see Ruslan Valentinov standing before us.

He stares straight into my eyes. "*Privet*," he mouths. *Hi*. Like he still has the right to say it, or to walk across this courtyard in these new black and brown sneakers with stripes. *Hi?* How dare he!

"Sonya, can I have a word?" he asks.

A word with me?

"Words are precious. Words have power." I have to believe that. He had used a word too, that night—*Jid*. An awful word, and not for the first time. "What about *him*?" My own words come out all distorted. "What about *his* words? Where is *he*? Can you tell me that?"

"*Nu*." He swallows. "That's what I wanted to talk to you—"

"Whoa, Solovay, which fly bit you this morning?" Someone else is speaking: Marina, Bozhena, Dimon, or another classmate who came up, I neither know, nor care. I am on top of him, my fists on his face, my fingers in his hair.

"Stop it! Stop it!"

I blink.

He is lying on the grass, hands up, shielding his face, while I am straddling him, pummeling him, my *yetzer ha-ra* pumping unworldly strength into my fists.

Misha's words come back to me. *It isn't a question of us having it: we all have it. It's how far we allow it to expand within us, how much power we grant it.*

I release my fists.

I can't let hate and pain determine the kind of person I want to be.

"Sonya," Luba says, "I was there. It was so crazy, with all the sticks and stones and bottles raining down on us from everywhere. People fighting. Are you sure you didn't make a mistake?"

I stare at her. I've had a lot of time to think back to what I saw that night. The cold fury in Ruslan's eyes, the knuckles on his one fist standing out sharply like barbed wire while his hand reached for something in his pocket. The white piece of concrete gleaming in his hand.

"I know it was crazy," I tell Luba. "But my eyes were open, finally. I saw enough."

Around us the crowd has swelled. Vitaly Semenovich, the physical culture teacher, is running up along with an old woman with a messy bun, stumbling in her heels.

I blink. Electrification.

"What's going on?" Her voice rings.

Vitaly stares at her. "Elektra Ivanovna? I thought . . . I didn't expect to see you today?"

She draws herself up to her full height. But something still seems to be broken about her. "I may have retired from teaching," she says, "but I still have the right to be here for my grandson." She reaches down to Ruslan, extends her hand to help him up.

He groans, his face covered with his hands still.

Gasps and whispers fly around us.

At last Ruslan takes his hands away from his face. His skin is ashen and blotchy. His eyes dull in the sunlight.

"Are you hurt?" Vitaly asks him.

"No." He doesn't get up. He stretches his hands out toward my face, but they freeze just before they reach me, like he is afraid to touch me. And he should be.

"I barely know myself what happened under that overpass," he whispers.

I get up. I don't have to listen to this. "I don't care," I say. "Not anymore."

All through the principal's speech in the large, second-floor hallway as he welcomes us all to the new school year and explains the traditions of the back-to-school concert dating back to 1982, I am trying to think—I am making myself do it. Maybe he is awake, but away, at some other hospital. After all, his parents are doctors: maybe they are taking good care of him. Or maybe they want to keep him out of school for a while. I don't blame them.

When I was here a year ago, Misha was in this crowd, likely, and I didn't even know it. Now, I make sure to look over every upperclassman boy coming in. *He could just be running late,* I keep thinking, though it's not like him. Misha Aizerman is never late.

Still. It could happen. He's only a person, he told me that himself once. Any second, he'll be here.

"*Baruch Ata Adonai.*" I say the magic words over and over and over.

"You young people have witnessed much in these ever-changing, complicated times," the principal, Anatoly Vladimirovich, says. I make myself pay attention, listen to his words, see the so-called stage with its elderly piano.

"Remember, you are the ones who will lead us into the future! I say, lead us on, with hearts strong, honest, and pure! And no matter how hard things get, don't forget to sing and dance and celebrate! Who would like the honor of opening our school concert this year?"

I look around, the weight of sadness, emptiness crushing me. And then I see a tall boy figure before me, in his hands a guitar. For the first time in days, something moist forms on the inside of my throat. Ruthlessly, not caring, I push, step, elbow my way toward the boy.

The crowd murmurs around me, the voice of the principal pleads for a volunteer. With one hand I touch the boy's guitar, with the other, I tug on his arm.

"What do you want?" The boy asks. His hair is dark. Chestnut-dark. Just a shade darker than mine. It's overgrown. But not curly. Not curly. He has freckles on his face.

I want to shake him. Misha didn't have freckles.

The boy pulls back on his guitar. But my fingers still won't release it.

Misha's fingers, they were long and soft over mine when he taught me the first chord, when we sat together on the floor of his room all these months ago. When I moaned how much the skin hurt on my fingers, he told me that one day it would hurt less. He told me to be patient, to let the soreness turn into the music. Now, water comes rushing to my eyes, my nose, from every corner of my being. I wish I hadn't let him go off with me. I wish I had shoved him off the bus. I wish I had never met him. Then he would be alive. He wanted to repair the world. But the only thing he got to do was fix up a part of me maybe. I must have closed my eyes, because when I open them, I discover tears everywhere—blessed, cleansing tears.

"What do you want?" the boy says again.

"Your guitar," I say, surprised at my own words, surprised to hear my voice still here. "Please . . . can I just . . . borrow it?"

When I make my way toward the stage, I don't know if Anatoly Vladimirovich can even see my eyes under those tears.

"My name is Sonya Solovay," I announce hoarsely, to the audience.

"Are you sure, Sonya?" Anatoly Vladimirovich asks, staring at my tear-stained cheeks.

I face the crowd, holding the strange guitar in my arms. I place my fingers over the strings, tough and unfamiliar. I look across the faces of people, mundane, indifferent, naïve, cynical, beautiful, haughty—most of them the same faces I saw a year ago. Except, this time I see my mama's face, in the back. The sight of her brings both pain and comfort.

"What's it going to be, then?" the principal asks me, and right away my hands start sweating, and I think, *What am I doing, standing here in Mama's thin magenta blouse, barely able to play guitar and trying to sniff back tears?* But then I think of Misha, on the barricades, fist in the air, soaking in fearlessness and friendship. "Who are you?" Misha asked me at the end of that night, when it turned wrong and awful, when he was in my arms, bleeding.

I don't have to look for the answer in the crowd. My fingers already know it. My voice reaches through other voices, pushing its way into the audience, pushing out the *kh-h-h*'s. *Hava, nagila hava, nagila hava, nagila ve ni sme ha . . .*

Words have power, didn't Rosa Aizerman tell me?

These words are for you, Misha.

The words run with my tears. I look at Mama's face as I sing. On a winter day in my room, when she first told me about an arts and singing school in New York City, I said I didn't have much of a voice. Even with moisture now loosening my vocal chords, somehow I know I was wrong; I know Misha would have told me so.

More people arrive in the back: an out-of-breath upperclassman, a too-young-for-school *devochka* pressing in between pupils and teachers. My mama turns around to look at the new arrivals. Her lips fly apart, her eyes widen.

"*Hava nerah-ne nah, kh-kh-havam ne r-r-rah-ne-nah,*" I sing, watching Mama shake hands with a softly blond middle-aged woman dressed so neat and looking almost slender in a navy skirt and suit.

I don't recognize her at first; I don't immediately recognize the little girl with bold dark eyes on a shy pale face. But I know that tall boy standing by their side in the front row. His curls are hidden in a messy bunch of white bandages wrapped around his head, the not-quite-white of the gauze stained with something green and yellow. Still, how can I miss the familiar dark eyes twinkling, those usually sarcastic lips moving now in tandem with mine?

I want to stop midword, I want to run out to him, touch his bandaged head, squeeze him hard in my arms, whisper, *Good morning, sleepyhead. Welcome back to the world. I am glad you made it.* Except, I have a song to complete.

He looks a little on the pale side. He leans a little on his mother as he smiles at mine. But, together, our two voices fill the hushed corridor. Curious faces lift up to catch the Jewish words of our ancestors. Higher and higher our voices soar, through the open small-hinged windowpane behind a musty lace curtain, across the dusty road where cars shove each other for space in traffic, over an empty bread store and the still unfinished apartment building, up and away, over the Mediterranean Sea, across the Atlantic Ocean, his a soft tenor, mine a surprising alto, announcing, low like a growl, *This is who I am, world.*

And it's only the beginning.

Dear Misha,

I am seventeen years old today, and I should know better. Still, when I peer through the small oval of the airplane window, I imagine a shape in the dark deep waters beneath, a giant many-headed monster waiting to swallow me up. As if on command the plane shakes, and I fall into the too-familiar feeling I thought I was leaving behind—I am scared.

A question steals my breath. What will happen if I never make it across?

And what will happen if I do?

I try to imagine where you can possibly be right now, what you can be doing in your new homeland. Remember: your beloved land has yetzer hara of its own. Under the bright Israeli sun, be true among the shadows. Remember your dream: tikkun olam. Make sure you live it, truly.

I promise I will do the same.

This past year has been unreal, hasn't it? The preparations, the language courses, the building of hopes—yours and mine. Now, Mama and Babushka both are telling me to get some rest, reminding me that my entrance test, and the auditions to that special school, is only a week away.

I am staring at these uneven letters scribbled in the scant light of the lamp above my seat, trying to picture how your forehead will crease when you read them.

Will you, Mr. Know-It-All, have the answers to my questions?

What will life be like in America?

Do you think the Americans will let me attend their prestigious high school for artists? If they do, I'll be what they call a "junior," attending classes with kids one year younger than me. Will I still make friends— good friends? Will my voice hold up at the auditions a week from now, a week from now!—or break into dust particles and blow away, back toward the sea?

The apartment Mama has rented for us is in a section of New York City called "Queens." Mama warned me not too expect too much luxury. "Not at first," she told me, winking. But it's hard to keep my expectations low with such a regal, "queenly" name for a neighborhood.

The plane keeps its brave journey westward, over the darkness, under the darkness, into the darkness, as if there is nothing much to it, puffing and breathing, and purring, rrrrrrr-hummmmmmmm. Babushka is frowning at me right now, and Mama is giggling, but I don't care. I open my arms, because it feels as though the plane's wings are my own, carrying me high above the monsters underneath.

Acknowledgments

My best reader and friend, my daughter Sev. Thank you for being there through this long journey. Thank you for asking for more chapters.

My son Zach, thank you for your astute comments and for your steadfast belief in me.

Bo, thank you for the book cemetery, for your beautiful songs, and for being my father. (And for giving me my other grandmother, Bella.)

The lovely Raina clan, thank you for waiting—I know it took a while!

Paul Olchváry of New Europe Books and Young Europe Books, thank you for falling in love with this story. Thank you for making it happen. Kurt Stengel, thank you for the cover of my heart; and Yogesh Kukshal and your team, for your meticulous work with New Europe Books through the proofreading process.

The early champions:

Teachers Kristi Holl and Alicia Rasley, your guidance and belief made a difference in the very beginning. First draft readers Keri Mikulski, Linda Lavin, Stephanie Natale-Boianelli: thank you for seeing so early that this book was meant to be. Adrienne Friedberg, your fierce belief and dedication helped bring out the truth of this story. Jess Regel, ours was one of the friendliest and most understanding splits in author-agent history, and I will always appreciate the love and time you have put into this book. Patti Brown, thank you for keeping me on my toes with your comments, again and again—and for still being there for me after all these years. Ilene Wong, your feedback was on point! Debbie Clarke, the MFA idea was a good one. Fran Alexander, thank you for believing, this whole time. Nan Marino, thank you for your love. I can feel your good wishes even from across state lines. Joyce Moyer Hostetter, thank you for cheering me on. Lyn Miller-Lachmann, you're a wonderful friend to have in one's writing corner. Anna Lidster, thank you for crying.

Master John Holland, though you are no longer with us, I will never forget how much you believed in me and waited for this book. Your inspiration pushed me forward in ways you probably never knew.

Barbara Krasner, you made all the difference by putting Young Europe Books on my radar.

Heather Demetrios, thank you for being the most amazing cheerleader! Your delight multiplies my own!

My mentors, friends, and tribe at the Vermont College of Fine Arts: your lessons and your love were the fuel I needed.

My Camden colleagues, I will never forget you. Nyque Brown, your friendship and your joy for my writing has always meant so much. I am on the lookout for your successes, keep going! Nware Burge, fellow artist and adventurer, I am honored to be your friend.

My Camden students and DC students, you inspire me and always will. I love you.

My new DC-area friends and neighbors, you are the coolest! Natalia Guerrido, thank you for all your efforts for this book. I am honored to know you, too. My friends and colleagues at DC International School: Mary Thomas, the most incredible school librarian I've ever met; Henry Dotson, the tech magician and wonderful human I can always count on; Marcus Johnson, the most supportive boss in the history of bosses; and, finally and most especially, my DCI BFFs, the stellar 6th grade English team, Toni Rose Deanon, Emily Culp, Livia Matteucci, and Brittany Todd, thank you for your love and excitement. I can't wait to share this story with you!

Topics & Questions for Discussion

1. The novel is titled *Castle of Concrete*. Why? What does the "castle" symbolize? What happens there? How does this image tie to Sonya's journey? What other symbols have you spotted throughout the story and what is their significance?

2. Describe Sonya's feelings for her mother and how they evolve. How does Sonya's relationship with her mother mirror her changing understanding of her "Jewishness"?

3. To Sonya, what does it mean to be Jewish? What makes being a Jew a challenge? What are the rewards?

4. If you were Sonya's friend in the story's beginning, what would you tell her? How do you think she would respond?

5. "What's the matter?" Ruslan asks Sonya, when he first meets her. "Scared?" Throughout the novel, Sonya strives to be brave. In your opinion, is she?

6. In the beginning of the story, Sonya thinks of Ruslan as her "Russian hero." "No traditional Russian beard on this rescuer, just a thin line of hair emerging above the lip, the eyebrows thin and golden, barely brown, like his hair. A

real-life *hero*, better than in any fairytale." When Ruslan is away at a demonstration, Sonya finds herself needing another "rescuer," and Misha comes through. How does Ruslan "save" Sonya? How does Misha? Does he, actually? In what ways does Sonya try to rescue both Ruslan and Misha? Does it work? Finally, how does Sonya save herself?

7. How would you describe Sonya and Ruslan's relationship? What attracts them to each other? What are the differences in how Sonya relates to each of the boys? Do you think Sonya has romantic feelings for Misha? What kinds of feelings does he have for her?

8. Consider these words Sonya says to Ruslan as they dine together in a newly opened McDonald's in Moscow: "'Don't you ever wish you were an American? I mean,' I add, trying to think, blushing harder, 'They have *all kinds* of people over there, and they all seem to belong.' He squeezes his eyebrows together like my words don't make sense. 'I mean,' I rush on, before he interrupts me again, 'Wouldn't it be cool to be like them? Loud? Brave? Not caring what other people think of you? *Smiling?*'" As seen through the eyes of Sonya, Ruslan, and Sonya's mother, what are some ways Russians seem to view America? How much of their perception is accurate?

9. One other thread the story explores is the idea of appearances vs. reality. "Under the sun the snow shines, a soft rug sewn with diamonds. But in those patches covered with shadows the snow is not quite black in its dullness.

I now notice pieces of ice underneath it, dotted with soot from someone's cigarette. *Why do I have to—notice?"* How does this relate to the journeys of the story's most important characters?

10. The novel is realistic historical fiction, but if you look closely you will find lots of threads of magic underneath. What are the many ways magic is infused into and portrayed in *Castle of Concrete*?

11. The story starts with Sonya's hopeful arrival in Moscow and ends with another Moscow trip—to the barricades. How do these two episodes mirror each other? What do the Moscow scenes in the novel's beginning and at the novel's end have in common, and what's different? What do these "bookends" suggest about the arc of Sonya's story?

12. The singing at the school assembly scenes serve as yet another set of "bookends." What are the similarities between Sonya's performance at the beginning and at the end of the novel? What do the differences tell us about the change in Sonya, her country, and her relationship with the world?

13. Ruslan is clearly the main antagonist of the story. But is he purely evil? Where does racial, national, and religious intolerance come from? Why do people hate "the other?" Can these distances ever be bridged? Is there hope for someone like him? For all of us?

Also from Young Europe Books

978-0-9850623-8-5

"A breathless . . . adventure
pits a poor, fatherless girl
against all sides in a battle
for a dragon's heart and
a city's freedom. . . . [A]
remarkable and distinctive
offering for devoted fantasy
fans." —**Kirkus Reviews**

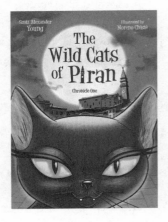

978-0-9900043-0-1

"Action aplenty . . . The
avuncular narrator can be
quite funny. . . . Chistè's full-
color illustrations add grace
notes, recalling animated
films." —**Kirkus Reviews**

Williamstown, Massachusetts

Available from New Europe Books

The Upright Heart: A Novel
Julia Ain-Krupa
978-0-9900043-8-7

Set in the ruins of the Holocaust, this page-turning novel follows a Jewish man, Wolf, as he navigates post–World War II Poland, his past sins, and the depths of his own mind and visions.

"Stylistic virtuosity, penetrating emotional power, and a postapocalyptic vision . . . a brilliant literary achievement. . . . Julia Ain-Krupa gives us something luminous." —*Philip K. Jason, Jewish Book Council*

Ballpoint: A Tale of Genius and Grit, Perilous Times, and the Invention that Changed the Way We Write. 978-0-9825781-1-7

The Devil Is a Black Dog: Stories from the Middle East and Beyond. 978-0-9900043-2-5

The Essential Guide to Being Hungarian: 50 Facts & Facets of Nationhood. 978-0-9825781-0-0

The Essential Guide to Being Polish: 50 Facts & Facets of Nationhood. 978-0-9850623-0-9

Illegal Liaisons. 978-0-9850623-6-1

Keeping Bedlam at Bay in the Prague Café. 978-0-9825781-8-6

The Most Beautiful Night of the Soul: More Stories from the Middle East and Beyond. 978-0-9973169-6-4

Notes from Cyberground: Trumpland and My Old Soviet Feeling. 978-0-9995416-0-9

Once Upon a Yugoslavia. 978-0-9000043-4-9

Voyage to Kazohinia. 978-0-9825781-2-4

New Europe Books
Williamstown, Massachusetts

Find our titles wherever books are sold,
or visit www.NewEuropeBooks.com for order information.